The Pirate Queen

The Paladin Princess Series Book 2

Also by Samaire Wynne

Mad World: EPIDEMIC

Mad World: SANCTUARY

Mad World: DESPERATION

ROMANOV

The Pirates of Moonlit Bay

The Pirate Queen

The Paladin Princess Series Book 2

Samaire Wynne

Black Raven Books

This is a work of fiction. All of the geography, characters, organizations, and events portrayed in this novel are either products of the author's imagination or are used fictitiously.

Black Raven Books

The Pirate Queen.
Copyright © 2019 by Samaire Wynne. All rights reserved.
Cover illustrations copyright © 2019 by Ravven
Printed in the United States of America.
For information, including permission to reproduce selections from this book, write to publisher@blackravenbooks.net or to
Black Raven Books, P.O. Box 3201, Martinsville VA 24115

The text was set in 12-point Californian FB

ISBN-13: 9781948594110

First Edition: July 2019

10 9 8 7 6 5 4 3 2 1

Dedicated to the hardest working woman I know, and to hard working women everywhere.

The Pirate Queen

Chapter One

Purple Mist

Djinns come in all forms, I'm told. Ours had come in the form of a man, but he preferred to fly in his natural state, which was the man but larger: about three meters tall, with a faint blue-purple-green tinge to his skin that defied any exact description. He flew above the main topmast of our ship, and kept up with us effortlessly. Everything seemed to come to him effortlessly. Everything physical, that is. Emotions were another matter. All these thoughts rolled around in my head as I watched him fly with us, his antics making me smile.

I leaned out over the railing on the fo'c'sle, my face bright with sunshine as a fine spray of sea water misted across it, making me laugh. The coast of Alkebulan was behind us, fast receding into the distance. We'd left Moonlit Bay, the port of call for the coastal Tambibo market, that morning. The winds were low, but the giant manta rays pulling our ship were strong and in fine shape after the breakfast of chopped-up black skipjacks and bluefin we'd fed them, and they streamed through the water, filtering out plankton and nibbling at small bits as they swam, pulling us along at a steady clip.

Our speed was faster than the wind, and our sails flipped over backward, slowing us enough so that we'd pulled in the main and foresails, leaving just the jibs up to flutter merrily against the deep blue sky. Our new friend, the djinn who we called Jim, was now perched on the fore topmast, sitting cross-legged, his wrists on his knees, in a classic yoga pose. His eyes were shut and his face serene, despite the fact that he was plunging forward at nearly 40 knots. The sun's rays on the djinn's form served to highlight the purples and greens, the light refracting into a dozen colorful rays as his hair, like a prism, sent it shining down on the decks below.

Down in the hold, our horses snorted and pawed in their stalls, happy to have the new grain we had traded for at Tambibo before we'd set sail. The barrel of black skipjacks and bluefin we'd offered in trade had gotten us a hold full of not only grain, but alfalfa bales: enough to tide us over for more than a few months. Khepri had arranged the deal, and was a wicked good negotiator who could barter a merchant down to his last-ditch hope.

That morning, I had brushed Shêtân until his ebony coat shone brilliantly. I'd been brushing his mane and tail out when Kym joined me. She'd picked out a soft brush and started on her pony Taimim's coat, working with such concentration that the tip of her tongue had peeked out between her lips. She'd soon had the pony's dark golden fur gleaming, and his blond tail silky and looking like a gold waterfall.

My mind had turned back to three days ago, when Kym, the second non-human member of our troupe, had discovered the scroll inside a hidden compartment in the bookcase in my quarters. The scroll was actually an old map leading to the fabled *Book of Mysteries*, said to hold all the knowledge of the ancients, who had come down from the stars and imparted it to mankind. The book was said to hold medical knowledge that would aid humanity in its quest for health and well-being, as well as the secrets to navigating the stars and heavens.

Kinah, the former captain of the ship we'd taken possession of, had been long on brawn but short on acuity, and we were sure she had not known of the scroll's existence. In fact, after examining the hidden compartment Kym had breached to find the scroll, I could not easily see how she'd managed to open it. I asked her to shut the scroll back into the small apse she'd retrieved it from, then tried to find the way in myself. It took me nearly a half hour, and I was only able to find it because I knew for a fact it was there. I was sure the space was not only invisible but irretrievable for anyone who didn't know where to look.

"Kym, how did you know it was there at all?" I asked. Kym had found a secret drawer in the hidden compartment of the bookcase, where she'd found a large bag. Inside the bag was an old brass tube, which, in turn, contained the scroll. But I wondered how she'd known the secret compartment was there at all, since it had become virtually invisible when she closed it again.

"You see the purple mist coming from the scroll?" Kym said.

I nodded. There was a very faint purple mist emanating from the surface of the parchment, a sign of its magical properties. But when we rolled it up, the mist all but disappeared, and with it inside the brass tube it was dark to the naked eye. That's how it had been when we'd discovered it: inside the bag, in the drawer, which had been shut and the compartment door closed.

How on earth...?

"The purple sprinkly misty color was spitting out the edge of the corner," Kym explained, pointing to where the hidden compartment edge supposedly was, though it was invisible to all of us.

I blinked.

"Oh, and you can smell it," Kym added.

I smelled a hint of elderberries when the scroll was unrolled; we surmised the parchment had been soaked in elderberry juice and other spell components to enchant its magical nature, but closed up in the bookcase, behind four different barriers, we smelled nothing. At least none of the humans could.

Kym was a different story. We had met her during our time in the fabled Aoudaghost oasis, a place of both riches and misery, or so Khepri told us. Her people had developed a huge mythology surrounding Aoudaghost, which she'd eventually shared with us – after we'd entered the oasis and had run into some pretty interesting magical effects. Kym had been in the form of a chimera, the creature we'd been searching for after Khepri had told us that finding it was the only way to escape the place. The chimera had played with us a bit before finally settling down for a real conversation. We'd discovered that she was actually young for her species, and in fact, was a very young child.

We'd made a deal: help the chimera (who had been apparently bored out of her skull) by taking her with us, and she'd help us with her talents. Kym had told us that her powers as a chimera were greatly reduced outside of the oasis, but then we'd seen her take the head off a slaver who'd attacked her, and we realized, she might not have as much magic outside the oasis, but she was still a massive chimera, with the head and forelegs of a lion. Ordinary lions can take a human's head off with one swipe. They are that strong. And Kym was even stronger.

So, she'd come with us, and we'd grown close. Kym was the little sister I'd wished I had. She turned into her human form whenever she thought 'human', but she could morph into any person she'd seen. Traveling, she remained in her own human form, which was to say, in the form of a six-year-old little girl. Kym had dark, dark skin, and her hair was currently arranged in braids. She wore a blue dress, and sandals. She looked like any other Alkebulan girl from the central regions. But we knew she wasn't ordinary at all. She was a chimera.

"You mean to tell me, you can see the purple mist leaking out of the edge of the secret compartment?" I asked.

"Of course," she said happily. "Can't you?"

I raised my eyes to the ceiling and breathed.

Wait a minute.

"Tupu, can you ask Jim to come in here. And Tam, too?"

Tam had been a member of the ship's crew from the beginning, back when Caroline and I had been kidnapped and sold into slavery. *Nearly a year ago.*

So much time had passed. So much had happened since that morning I was kidnapped last spring, I felt like so much more than a Swerighe Princess.

"Hey, Princess," Tam poked his head in the door a moment after I summoned him. "What's up?"

Tam, short for Tamerlane (a joke from his mother, he'd told me) enjoyed teasing me about my royal status and title.

"Tam, please come in."

Tam entered, an easy smile on his face. His light swagger made me grin. He was an able sailor and good with a sword, and had turned against Kinah to help us capture the ship. We considered him a friend.

Jim followed Tam into the room.

"Sit here, you two, please." I indicated the cushions lining the bench next to the door. "Face starboard."

They complied.

"Now, can you see anything odd over there?" I waved my hand in the general direction of the bookcase and waited.

Tam's brow furrowed, and he focused on the bookcase built into the wall on that side of the chamber. Standing up, he approached it slowly. He reached out and, long fingers extended, delicately ran his palm over the wall and bookcase, picking up a tome at random and bringing it out of the wooden shelf to sniff delicately, then returning to its place among the other books. He took a long time to scrutinize the entire wall before he finally sat back down next to Jim. Even then, he continued to stare at the area, trying to see anything odd.

Finally, he declared: "I don't see any irregular."

I looked at him for a long time. He seemed sincere.

Then I turned to Jim. The djinn was a very quiet person. He was in his human form now, that is to say, he looked like a normal man. He was maybe six-and-a-half feet tall, muscular, with brown hair and hazel eyes. A delicate jaw and thoughtful, merry eyes completed the picture. He was usually very reserved, offering his thoughts only when pressed, and sometimes not even then. I studied him for a minute. He sat easily, his billowing shirt and loose pants looking comfortable and worn. He, too, wore sandals, and his brown feet looked relaxed. He held his hands clasped together in front of his belly in a casual manner. His face was turned to the wall and bookcase, his expression pleasant and serene.

"Jim?" I said gently.

He turned to me, an eyebrow raised.

"Do you see anything abnormal there?" I indicated the bookcase in front of us.

He turned again to glance at the wall and bookcase, then back to me.

"Do you mean, besides the purple mist?" he asked.

Chapter Two
Preparations

That was how we figured out that the scroll was much easier for non-humans to detect. It stood to reason that it had likely been created by non-humans, as well.

"Magical items are notoriously hard to construct," Khepri had told us. "The court magicians take years to create such things, and even then, only the most skilled and learned of them can even manage it."

Hmmm, I'd thought.

"Kym," I called over to my young friend. Kym bounced over happily. *She really is like a six-year-old little girl,* I thought, not for the first time. Even though the chimera was over a thousand years old, she was still just a child.

I smiled as she approached and held out a clutch of kasaba berries. I plucked a few of the delicious fruit and munched on them as I spoke. Putting my arm around Kym's small waist, I pulled her close in a hug.

"Kym, can you make a flower for me?" I asked.

"Make?" she inquired.

"Yes, make one for me, in your hand," I said. "It's okay," I reassured her.

Kym cupped one of the kasaba berries in her hands, a look of concentration on her face. Within seconds there was a glow and the berry transformed into a small yellow-orange flower. She smiled and handed it to me.

"And what will this flower do?" I asked, seeing it glow faintly purple.

"This one will turn your hair white, and settle an upset stomach," Kym said.

"Did you pick those attributes yourself, then?" I asked.

Kym nodded and giggled.

I popped the flower into my mouth and chewed slowly, then swallowed it. I could feel a cool sensation traveling down my throat. Caroline reached out and brought one of my long curls around over my shoulder so I could see it. As the cool feeling of the magical flower traveled down to my belly, a pearly white color traveled down my lock of hair until it reached the end that Caroline held, smiling.

Khepri's eyebrows raised and threatened to disappear into her hair, and she remained speechless in surprise.

"I think Kym has some great abilities," said Caroline. "It's wise we kept her true form secret. The sheikhs would love to get hold of her." Caroline glanced over at Jim. "Of both of them," she said.

We were well aware of how obsessed the sheikhs of Alkebulan were, not only with money, but with power. Most of the magical creatures they'd captured had been exploited, at the expense of the creatures' dignity and freedom. Either that, or the creatures had been impossible to contain. Remembering the manticore that had attacked us out in the desert, it occurred to me that it had likely been extra aggressive because it was interacting with humans. I felt sad that I had been forced to kill it defending our party. At the time, I'd felt the thrill of victory, happiness and relief that it hadn't killed me, but I was quickly learning to see things from a non-human point of view.

I saw Kym studying my face then, an inscrutable look on her own, and I realized that most of the time I thought of her as human, even though I knew quite well that she was, in actuality, a massive mythical beast, an impressive, regal chimera. She was this creature, even when she appeared as a six-year-old human girl. She dealt with us as a chimera, but as a child – a curious, inquisitive child – exploring the world outside the Aoudaghost oasis, with our help.

I gathered Kym in my arms, pulling her into my lap, and held her close. She wrapped her small arms around me and nestled there, eventually falling asleep.

The next day found us discussing the scroll.

"*The Book of Mysteries*." I said the words over and over. "*The Book of Mysteries*."

"Two things come to mind, as I see them," said Tupu, sipping warm camel milk laced with honey as she did every morning. "*The Book of Mysteries* is an incredible object which can change much of our world. And," she said, taking another sip of her mug, "the quest to retrieve it will, without a doubt, be fraught with incredible danger and jeopardy."

She looked into my eyes. "We will be in great peril," she said, her eyebrows raised, indicating intense interest.

I agreed. "After the Tomb of Ancients and the treasure we pulled out ...," I began.

"Barely pulled out," Tupu amended.

I nodded. "Barely pulled out," I took a deep breath. "Even though the pocketfuls of gems were ridiculously small compared to the chests of loot we had hoped to bring out of the tomb,"

"Before we were so rudely accosted," said Tupu.

I smiled. "Before we were so rudely accosted, by a huge band of ghouls." I nodded. "They still have made each and every one of us ridiculously wealthy."

Caroline spoke up. "We could all retire to large estates and live the rest of our lives in comfort, that is certain."

"Hmmm," Khepri said quietly.

Christianne entered then and sat down with us. "What are we talking about?" she asked.

"Retiring with our Tomb of Ancients wealth," said Tupu.

"That sounds boring," said Christianne.

I sat up and pointed straight at her, not saying a word.

Kym laughed.

"Okay, so it's agreed," said Khepri.

"Yes," said Tupu.

"Yes," Caroline nodded her head with a grin.

"We will pursue *The Book of Mysteries*," I said. We were all thinking it.

"For the good of mankind," said Khepri.

"For the knowledge of the world," said Tupu.

"To benefit all magical learning," said Christianne, who'd begun to learn from Kym.

"So we can help more people," said Caroline.

Kym giggled. I smiled at her and nodded. "So we won't be retired and bored out of our skulls," said Kym.

"Bingo," I said, laughing.

A movement caught my eye.

Tupu was curling her hands around her belly, which had grown larger in the months since we'd escaped the Abü caliphate. Her baby would be here before the next solstice. I looked at her.

"It will be dangerous, for sure," I said quietly.

Tupu looked at me. "I know. I'm not scared at all."

Khepri leaned forward. "Anything that would hurt the growing babe would hurt you first. Your body protects the growing life within very well," she said.

I felt the need to press forward with cautious words one more time. "If common sense had a voice, it would say that caution is paramount." I looked around at my troupe. "There is no pressing reason to continue with this quest," I said quietly. "It is not necessary for life, for food, for shelter, for our subsistence, really, for anything we truly need in order to live." I sat back.

"Boredom can be deadly," Kym said very quietly from her position curled in my arms.

We thought and remembered Kym's beseeching words while in Aoudaghost. It was a somber memory.

I took a deep breath and sat up, placing Kym on the floor in front of me.

"Well," I stood up, "Safety and caution be damned. We all know what we want to do."

We all nodded.

Akim entered the cabin just then, with Tam and Jim. Curious, he came to sit with Kym. He had learned to listen quietly, as we came up with the most interesting conversations.

I smiled at him.

"Well," Tam asked. "What's the word, Captain Charlotte?"

"The word?" I smiled, thinking of caution and safety, and all the things a sensible person would object to, when faced with this adventure. "The word is no."

Tam just stared at me, his jaw dropping open slightly.

"We are therefore going anyway," I finished, smiling.

Tam's grin spread across his face from ear to ear.

Kym jumped up, "YAY!!!"

I shook my head and smiled.

"Now we get down to business," I said, spreading the scroll out on the large captain's table and securing the corners with several heavy objects. Caroline brought out a brass compass, sextant, curvimeter, and flat leg divider, and we set down to plot our course.

"We'll follow the coast about ten miles out, here," I indicated the northern coast of Alkebulan, and into the deeper Mare Internum. "It looks like we'll be dipping close to the Tyrrhenian Sea after a hundred miles, and these small islands here," I indicated, my finger tracing the treasure map's dotted line.

"These indicate passages along the coast of the larger island," Tupu said, pointing.

"They seem to go under the water," Caroline said.

"That may be a tunnel," Khepri suggested.

"It leads to the smaller island, there," pointed Christianne.

We were all gathered around the map and discussed the route well into the night, until we felt prepared.

We talked about centaurs.

"Who knows anything about these horsemen of the mountains?" I asked. "Anybody?"

No one knew a thing, except Kym.

"All I know is that they live in the mountains, in a faraway land, and they dislike strangers," she said.

"Dislike?" Christianne asked.

"Yes. Intense dislike," said Kym. "To the point of animosity. To the extreme of enmity."

"Enmity?" Christianne asked.

Khepri spoke then. "They will attack us if we go near them."

Oh.

"Okay, well, we'll be very cautious," I nodded to the others, "and we'll be ready for anything." I smiled. I felt so excited!

My head was buzzing, and I couldn't wait to get started on this adventure. Kym grinned at me then and laughed, and I smiled. She felt the same, I could tell.

This is going to be incredible, I thought.

Chapter Three

Whisper

Morning found the weather beautiful and the skies clear. I was up early and on the fo'c'sle, looking out to sea. We were headed northwest, and the spray from the bow cutting through the water hit me in the face. It felt exhilarating. I glanced back at Tam at the helm, his hands resting easily on the wheel of the ship, his eyes focused on the horizon. *He's a good first mate.* I'd found myself feeling uneasy when we'd first came on board, and he'd explained to me that I was now the captain, but he'd done most of the work, explaining everything that was happening, asking for my guidance in major decisions, and I felt at ease now, weeks later.

Jim was once again seated at the apex of the fore topmast, looking out to sea. I studied him from below the mast; something looked not quite right.

He glanced down at me then, and our eyes met. The look on his face said it all: My friend the djinn had something on his mind. I waved him down, and he descended slowly, his hands pulling him from mast to rope to rigging, looking reluctant.

He came to a stop next to me, and at nearly ten feet high, I had to crane my neck back to see his face.

"Oh, sorry," he mumbled, his blue-green-purple body shimmering down until he stood next to me as his human form, his broad chest clothed in the familiar blousy cotton shirt, his old trousers flapping in the wind. I noticed this time he had on comfy looking old brown boots, the leather so worn on them it looked fuzzy. He looked miserable.

"Jim," I put my hand on his arm, "What is it?"

We sat on a stack of sails, and I handed him some blackroot to chew on.

He looked as if he needed it.

I waited a few minutes for my quiet friend to gather his thoughts. Then I spoke.

"How are you doing, Jim?" I asked softly.

"Not so good," he answered.

"What's wrong?"

He took a deep breath. Then another.

I put my hand out again and rubbed him arm softly, the muscles feeling warm under his shirt.

"I feel rejected," Jim finally said.

"But why?"

"I feel aimless and unwanted," he explained. "Charlotte, I've always been a great boon to my masters. A wonderful tool they used to attain great happiness and fortune," he sighed.

"But you are a wonderful man, a wonderful djinn!" I tried to understand. I had thought I was doing the right thing by not using the djinn, by not taking advantage of his powers. By rejecting the ... *Oh.*

I looked down into my lap.

"I am sorry, Jim," I said softly. "I didn't understand."

He looked up.

"You feel like you have all these powers, and I'm refusing to use your help, right?" I asked.

He nodded.

"I could, if you wished it, retrieve this *Book of Mysteries* in an instant," he said plaintively. "You wouldn't have to go through any dangers or anything." He looked at me.

I smiled, "but what would be the fun in that?"

He looked troubled.

"It's the adventure, the experience, the exhilaration," I explained. "Like Kym said, being bored can be deadly."

"I guess I understand," Jim said quietly. "I've been a djinn for tens of thousands of years. It's all I know. I think I have to get used to a new paradigm."

He fell silent.

"I think you're going to have an exciting time, too, you know."

"I'm going with you?" He looked up.

"Well, of course you are going with us, you're part of our troupe, aren't you?" I smiled. "You're our friend. If you want to go with us, you will go with us." I thought for a moment. "Jim, if you don't want to go with us, you can stay here on the ship, or go anywhere you want."

"No, Charlotte. That's just it. I can't," Jim whispered.

Huh?

"What do you mean?" I asked.

"Charlotte, you rubbed the lamp. I know you don't want to be, but *you* are the master of the lamp," he said. "You *rubbed* it. You are my master."

"But, I don't ..."

"It doesn't matter whether you want it or not. You are the master of my lamp, and of me."

I took a deep breath.

"And, there's something else," Jim said.

"Oh?" I held my breath.

"I have grown fond of you and the others since I first emerged," he explained. "But the reason I followed you, even though you handed me back my lamp, is that I am tied to you."

"What do you mean?" I felt a foreboding.

"Because you are my master," Jim said, "it is physically painful when I am any distance from you. It hurts. It hurts to be ..." He swallowed, then continued. "Charlotte, it physically hurts when I'm far from my master, that's why I followed you," he finished miserably.

Oh my god.

"Oh, Jim," I turned and put my arms around him, tears in my eyes.

How could I be this insensitive?

He patted my shoulder awkwardly.

My shoulders shook with my sobs. I felt horrible. I hadn't realized, and I'd forcibly pulled this poor creature, in pain, along with me everywhere. Without caring how he felt, if he wanted to be pulled, not caring about his pain. *Oh, god...*

I remained like that for a while. I heard Kym bounce up to us, and then stop. A minute later she walked away without speaking, leaving Jim and me to our private moment.

I must be a sight. I sat up, wiping my eyes. My face felt hot and wet and splotchy.

Jim wordlessly handed me a handkerchief, and I saw it was the lace-edged one out of my quarters. I took it and blew my nose.

He really can summon anything to him, I thought.

I need to relate to Jim, I need to treat him how I would like to be treated.

I thought of my parents and how they'd always given me free rein to follow my heart, for the most part. I thought about Kym and how we'd all let her follow her heart, and explore and express herself how she wanted. I thought about Khepri: She'd told me she was desperate to get away from her uncle and the Abü caliphate, that he was holding her back and living in his compound was stifling. *That was why she wanted so much to come with us, that and our friendship.*

Jim and the rest of the troupe had friendship, but I realized we had something he did not. And that I had been callous not to notice his problems.

I sat up, wiping my eyes.

"May I have the lamp?" I asked.

He opened his hand, and it appeared. He handed it to me.

"Okay," I sniffed again. *Lord I hate being a big soppy crybaby. Let's solve this problem.* "Tell me exactly how the wishes work." I looked into his eyes, determined.

Jim smiled. "Well, you must state your wish, and then I must ask, 'Is this your wish' and you must answer, 'Yes, this is my wish,' and then I make it happen, I make it come true."

"Just like that?" I asked.

"Just like that, exactly like that," he answered.

We were starting to draw a crowd. Kym had returned, and she'd brought Caroline, Christianne and Tupu. Out of the corner of my eye I saw Akim sitting nearby, watching. Khepri was coming out of a cabin, wiping her hands, looking up to see what was going on. I could feel Tam's eyes on me, from his position at the wheel.

I thought for a long minute, formulating what I wanted to say. Then I took a deep breath and raised my eyes to Jim's. I held the lamp in my hands, gripping it tightly.

"Djinn of the magic lamp," I began.

Jim's back straightened. He began to grow.

"I wish ..." I continued.

Jim was now fully three meters tall, sitting next to me. His chest expanded and his arms grew thicker, as did his leg and torso also. His skin began to change into its true color.

The djinn's color was a blue, which was also green and also purple. It shaded in and out of each sub-color with where the skin was. The color near his armpits and shoulders was a darker purple, whereas the lighter coloring of his arms and chest was the fainter blue hue. His face was tinted green with purple and blueish purple near his temples and hairline.

He was holding his breath in anticipation.

I noticed he was floating an inch off the box I was sitting on.

I stared into his deep blue eyes, so full of hope and soul.

"Djinn of the lamp, I wish you were free," I said firmly.

Jim was so surprised he didn't say a word for a minute. Then, he cleared his throat and asked, "Princess Charlotte, master of the lamp, you have stated that you wish for the freedom of the djinn," Jim's voice remained steady, although I saw a tear roll down his cheek. He continued, "Is this indeed your wish?"

My voice was firm and steady and clear. "Yes, this is my wish. I wish for you to be free."

I suddenly felt the lamp I was grasping begin to disintegrate and I looked down. The old brass metal, cool and firm in my hands, came apart into a million pieces and was gone.

I looked back up into Jim's eyes and saw they were filled with tears. His mouth slowly formed into a wide grin.

I was astonished. I realized I had never seen him really happy before.

"Thank you," he whispered.

Chapter Four
We Have a Plan

"We've charted a course into the Mare Nostrum," I said. The Mare Nostrum was the inner sea inside the larger Mare Internum. The skies remained clear for three days, and the giant manta rays remained enthusiastic with the extra chopped black skipjacks and bluefin we gave them to supplement their diet of krill and the smaller fish they caught themselves.

Caroline and I plotted our path on the sea map, coordinated with the scroll's directions. The parchment plastered on the far wall of my cabin was a massive map of the entire Mare Internum. The sea map was detailed with warnings about whirlpools that led to sinkholes under the water, sea monsters of various sorts, from the giant sea snakes to the massive giant squids, and more. There were drawings of deadly sea-going denizens of the deep: a fifty-foot-long oarfish; sharks with frilled gills, and sharks with extending jaws; and a fish that looked like a rock until you stepped on it. Its toxins were reportedly strong enough to bring down a horse within a few minutes.

There were elaborate drawings of the colorful blueish-purple man-o-wars with floating tendrils reaching out hundreds of feet, ready to sting and kill anything that crossed its path. Then there were drawings of striped tiger sharks ready to attack anything that moved, or floated past them. These mindless killers had been known to attack rudders of ships. And speaking of ships, right near the middle of this elaborate, frightening, beautiful work of art, was painted a large sailing ship very similar to our own *Pride of the Sea* – with a massive monster engulfing it. Tentacled arms were reaching out of the sea and grabbing the ship to pull it down to the depths, and the ship itself appeared to be listing savagely, the pained crew silently screaming as they fought in vain to free themselves from the nightmare.

"The kraken," Tupu said, staring at the central focus of the wall map.

"Are these creatures all for real? Should we be worried about encountering them?" I asked. "Or are they imaginary?"

"Charlotte, your companions include a chimera and a djinn," Khepri pointed out. "I think it's safe to assume the depictions are of real creatures."

"True," I admitted. I put my arm around Kym, who lately had practically been my shadow, following me everywhere. She grinned up at me, then returned to studying the wall map.

I had put pins in the wall to mark our ship's course, and, following the scroll's map instructions to the Book of Mysteries, the small, black glass-headed pins led straight into the most dangerous regions depicted on the massive wall map.

I thought a minute, then turned to Caroline beside me.

"Carrie, will you please fetch Jim? I have some questions for him."

She departed, and I sat down, closing my eyes and rubbing my forehead.

Pride of the Sea was traveling fast, and was a day from entering the center of the Mare Nostrum, and into the thick of Sea-monster Central.

There was a knock at the door. Jim poked his head in.

"What's up?" he said. I noticed he was very carefree, as if a great weight had been lifted off him.

"Jim, come in, come in, my friend," I reached out with my hand and squeezed his fingers with fondness. "I was wondering a few things."

He sat down on the cushions and smiled at me expectantly.

"So," I smiled at him, "we are getting ready to advance into the Mare Nostrum, and will be skirting the southern region of the Tyrrhenian Sea." I stood and pointed out our pinned course on the wall map.

Jim leaned forward to study the huge design. His eyes widened as he followed my finger to the depiction of the kraken.

"We don't know if we'll encounter any of these creatures, but I wanted to show you what we're up against," I said.

Jim stood and approached the wall map, his eyes flitting all over its surface at the different depictions, taking in all the dangers we might be facing.

"I see," he said slowly. Then he reached his hand out to trace the outline on the wall map of the ship being attacked by the massive beast. "This," he turned to me for confirmation, "is the ...?"

"The kraken," I answered. "Maybe the biggest danger the sea has to offer."

I took a deep breath and sat back down again, studying my friend while he in turn studied the wall map.

Jim eventually turned to me, a grim look on his face.

"You want to know if I can help if the kraken attacks the ship?" he asked, bringing the obvious out into the open.

Straightforward, direct, and to the point. A valuable trait.

"Yes," I said. "We are all part of this troupe, we each use our gifts however we can. But not to the extent it would hurt us."

"I don't understand," said Jim, sitting back down.

"Well, Kym fights alongside us, but she does not transform to fight. If she exposed herself, she would be inviting every treasure seeker, every bounty hunter, every caliphate, to kidnap her. To steal her to use for their own greedy purposes. She would never be able to rest easy again." I fixed him with a grim look to punctuate the gravity of my words.

Jim took a deep breath and said nothing.

I waited.

"Charlotte," Jim began. "I have grown happy with my new friends." He reached out and squeezed my hand. "I am very, very grateful you freed me. I've been feeling so happy and free, and I'd like to stick around for a while with you all," he nodded to the others in the room. "The lamp was very confining," he said slowly, raising his eyebrows. "In more than one way."

He stopped and looked at me.

"Oh, Jim, of course you are welcome to stay with us, I assumed you would," I reached forward and hugged him.

"I will help as much as I can," Jim said quietly. "You should know that my powers are not as strong as they were when I was bound to the lamp. That enchantment seemed to contain much of the magic behind my strength."

I felt concerned.

"Have you tried to do things and been unable?" I asked.

"Well, it's not so much that as," he waved his hand and seemed to struggle to find the words. "Okay, early this morning, I was helping with the net draw."

Every morning and evening our sailors spread the net out and gathered in as many black skipjacks and bluefin as they could. Our crew had swollen to almost double its previous size since we'd come on board, and that was a lot of mouths to feed.

I nodded for him to continue.

"I reached my magic down into the sea and tried to gather more fish into the net." He stopped.

"It didn't work?" I asked.

"Oh, no, it worked," Jim answered. "But afterward I had to sit down for an hour. I felt exhausted. And I had a splitting headache," he finished and met my eyes, a helpless look on his face.

Ah.

"I understand," I said.

"Mind you, I'm still getting used to the new paradigm, I'm still feeling my way," he explained quickly.

I reached my hand out to stop him.

"Jim, you don't have to explain, I understand."

"I will help as much as I can, but I'm not sure how much help I will be," he said.

"I don't want you to harm yourself with any attempts at great magic," I said.

"Actually, weirdly enough, I think it was the great weight of the fish and the water I was reaching though, rather than the magic."

I raised my eyebrows. *Interesting.*

"The magic seems to be coming from me. The strength of the magic is what's been compromised." He reached out and flicked his hand, and a cascade of rose-colored sparks danced away from him in a long stream, in what looked like an effortless display.

I smiled. Kym clapped her hands in delight.

"This kraken looks huge," Jim pointed out, staring again at the wall map's depiction of the great sea monster. He turned back to me. "Perhaps it would be best if we tried very hard to avoid it?"

I laughed.

"Understood," I rose, and so did Jim, and we embraced. He smiled warmly close to my face.

"I will fight for the troupe, and defend you, Charlotte, with my life if need be. It just may not be enough." His smile turned grim, and his arm squeezed me around my waist.

I must remember this.

"Okay, people," I said louder to the room at large. "Important safety point."

I turned back to the wall map and stared at the depiction closer.

"What do we know of the kraken?" I turned to the others. "Is there just the one? Or are there many?"

Tupu spoke up. "I do think there are more than one, but I think they are very rare, much like Jim and Kym," she smiled at the two magical companions.

"And," I continued, staring back at the wall, "are they mostly found in the deep sea?" My hand traced the coloring of the map near the kraken, where the water was painted a much deeper blue than on the edges near land.

"I believe, from classic literature," Caroline said, "that the kraken is actually quite massive. So, it would follow that it should naturally prefer the deep sea."

"They say it lives at the bottom of the sea, in a huge cave deep under the surface, and that it is dark down there," Khepri said.

"That is why the legends say it attacks when the skies are stormy," said Christianne.

"I wonder why it's not known to attack during the night?" Khepri wondered aloud.

Jim spoke up. "I believe I might have a guess."

We turned to look at him.

"At night, it is generally very dark. But on stormy days, there is some light, which would highlight the silhouette of the ship against the surface of the water."

I looked at the wall map again, noticing the storm clouds depicted near the scene of the kraken attack.

"That makes sense," I said.

"Okay, plan, people," I stated firmly. "We will stay within five miles of the coastline, and venture around the deepest part of the Mare Nostrum, skirting around to the west, like this." I gestured in a wide arc down and around. "It may take a little longer, but it seems a wise course of action."

"Agreed," said Caroline.

The others nodded.

"Then," I indicated the islands to opposite the Tyrrhenian Sea, "we approach the islands cautiously. We land here." I indicated the southern island, where the scroll's map had recommended landfall should occur. I felt a surge of satisfaction.

We had a plan.

Chapter Five
Closer...

The next morning, we drew closer to the coast, staying where the water was a bright turquoise and leaving the darker blue waters to the north. Sea birds circled close to the nets the sailors were pulling in, and I saw Jim out with them, trying to help again. I walked out, buttoning my jacket as I walked.

We'd all acquired new outfits before we left Moonlit Bay, finding that pants instead of thawbs made for better movement climbing the rigging of *Pride of the Sea*. Most of the troupe still wore their keffiyeh headscarves against the warm sun, but I'd discarded mine, packing it away in my trunk belowdecks. My black pants and leather over-pant fitting along with my black blouse, made for a sensible captain's outfit that kept me warmer on the decks during the windy days. And it was always a windy day out on the high seas.

I reached the deck and stood next to Jim. He seemed happier.

"How's it going, my friend?" I asked.

"It's much the same as yesterday, although maybe a bit easier," Jim grimaced softly. "I'm determined to feel out how much strength I have, to better know how to handle myself, before we get into any tight spots."

I patted him on the back. "It's like working with an entirely new body, huh?"

"That's exactly it, actually," he smiled back.

"Let me know if you need any assistance."

"I will. I think I've got it handled. Tam's been helping me," he grinned as Tam walked up to us, peeling gloves off his rough hands.

"Hi Charlotte," Tam said. "I hear we might meet a kraken."

"Not if I can help it," I laughed and left them to their work.

The hold was full of fish, the giant manta rays were being fed extra chopped bluefin and black skipjacks, and they were thriving.

That afternoon, water dragons and dolphins played together off the starboard bow, entertaining us. The mood was lighthearted, the air filled with laughter and anticipation. The ship was practically buzzing with excitement at what lay ahead.

Our crew was well paid, thanks to the massive cache of gold coins I'd obtained in exchange for one of the smallest gems retrieved from the Tomb of Ancients.

Everyone was in high spirits.

Twilight came, and we all enjoyed a feast of fish, rum, and bread, with the blackroot flowing freely and the laughter ringing out loudly.

Night fell without incident.

I realized I was holding my breath at one point as I gazed out to sea. The stars appeared one by one, until the night sky was ablaze with them. I think I saw several shooting stars streak across the sky.

"They are said to portend auspicious events," Tupu stated, the dark beauty coming up beside me.

My hands rested easily on the railing of the ship, and I found myself unconsciously caressing the polished wood.

"I hope the event is a good one," I said, "If we are able to retrieve the book, it'll be extraordinary."

Tupu nodded sagely. Her hand drifted to her belly, now the size of a small melon.

"How is the growing child within doing?" I asked.

"He is still during my waking hours, especially as I walk about the ship," she smiled. "But when I eat or drink, he seems to awaken, and I can feel his body move within mine."

I nodded fondly. "And when you lay down to sleep?" I asked.

Tupu laughed. "Summersaults."

We reminisced and talked about our homes well into the night, and it was nearing midnight by the time I made my way to the captain's cabin. Yawning, I drew my boots off and settled in for a short nap, but soon found myself deeply asleep and dreaming of the sunny skies of Swerighe and a field of daisies and tulips.

"Charlotte!"

My eyes popped open. That was Caroline.

I sat up in bed as she entered and immediately came to the bed.

"The kraken's been sighted," she said breathlessly.

Christianne walked in, "Tam says it's about five nautical miles to the north, give or take."

I pulled on my boots. "How did Tam see it that far? Surely the crow's nest watch can't see nearly six miles out?" I grabbed my scimitar. Although I hoped I would not be that close to any enemy, I felt naked without it.

"Jim," said Caroline, her lips set. "He's been flying ahead of us all night, looking for it."

I stopped. "He didn't go looking for it?!"

"Bad choice of words," Caroline admitted. "Jim's been flying recon, going out a bit and then coming back, in circles. He said he wanted to know 'what was out there.'" She rolled her eyes.

Damned reckless, foolhardy, irresponsible....

"But he's okay?" I looked up at Caroline. "And it didn't see him?"

"He's okay. And I think he was pretty much invisible," said Caroline.

Huh?

"He transformed himself into a raincloud, Charlotte," said Christianne, smiling.

I whipped my head to look at her. "There's *nothing* funny about this, Chrissy. That thing could kill us all without a thought. It's a mindless beast. Jim was extremely careless to take it upon himself to scout." I scowled at the ground.

"Sorry, Charlotte," Christianne mumbled.

"Look," I said, putting my hands on her shoulders. "I'm just worried. I'm sorry I spoke harshly." I glanced at the wall map and the painting of the fierce kraken drowning a ship that was likely bigger than *Pride of the Sea.* "Let's go." I hugged them both and we ran out to the deck.

It was still black, dawn looked about ten minutes away. The northern horizon boasted a slim line of grey, I wouldn't have even called it light. It was more like 'not light' the hint of what's coming when night is ending.

I pulled my brass sight from my belt and tried to see past the dark horizon.

Nothing.

"Where's Jim?" I asked to no one in particular.

"He's up there," Tam gestured above us. I looked up and saw nothing.

"Keep looking," he advised.

I stared up, trying to discern anything other than the cloudy night sky.

Oh.

"Jim!?" I called, cupping my hands around my mouth, my face pointed to the sky.

A cloud separated itself from the others and descended. Jim's feet appeared first, slowly lowering himself to the mast, then down to the deck. He had fully materialized by the time he stood in front of me.

I tried to calm myself by breathing deeply, realizing that I'd been afraid for the djinn. I cleared my throat. "Are you okay?"

He nodded, then pointed to the northern deep seas of the Mare Nostrum. The blue waves looked black in the predawn light.

"The kraken is about five-and-a-half land miles that way," Jim said quietly, breathing hard. "And it's wrapped itself around another ship."

I looked at Jim's face sharply. " 'Another ship'?"

He nodded, still trying to catch his breath. He bent and put his hands on his knees, inhaling deeply, trying to slow his breathing. I put my hand around his shoulders and led him to a place to sit.

We sat on some boxes, and I rubbed his back slowly.

He tried to speak, but couldn't.

"Just take a minute, sweetie. Just breathe," I said quietly.

I nodded to Tam nearby, and mouthed the word 'water.'

I sat there for a while, while the djinn caught his breath. He must have pushed himself to the limit hurrying back to the ship with this news.

God almighty.

Tam arrived with a cup of water, and I took it from him and brought it to the djinn's lips. He took the cup in shaking hands and sipped its contents.

Jim was in human form, as he was most of the time. His skin was light tan, with a golden hue as if he was from some exotic land. But I looked closely at him now and saw he was pale, and his lips had a bluish tint.

He sipped more of the water and his color returned, and I breathed a silent sigh of relief.

Finally, he could speak.

"The kraken is to the north. I believe we can avoid it, mostly because it is busy sinking the other ship," he said, looking at me. "And listen, there's no way we can render aid to them."

"Why not?" I asked.

"Because," the djinn said. "That kraken is at least three times the size it is painted on that wall map of yours."

Chapter Six
Certain Death

Dawn was upon us as we plowed forward, steering our way around the kraken and its prey.

"Charlotte," Tam came up to me as I stood on the fo'c'sle, brass sight pressed firmly to my eye.

I lowered the sight and looked at him.

"We can see the kraken from the crow's nest. We're keeping it just out of sight."

I nodded.

"But there's a sou'wester pushing us toward the Tyrrhenian Sea. The mantas are fighting it, but it's slowly forcing us forward and north. Inch by inch, we are getting closer than we wanted to the beast." Tam's lips were pressed into a grimace.

"What do you suggest?" I asked.

"Well," he looked down, "I suggest we keep fighting it, keep steering away from it, and hope for the best. Generally speaking, the mantas cannot pull a ship against a strong wind; that's why they're used to aid the forward motion of the ship, rather than just steering it in whatever direction you wish to go."

"I will tell you that your idea of supplementing the manta's diet with the chopped fish likely not only aided their strength and fortitude, but endeared them to the crew. They are fighting like mad to go west," Tam said, nodding.

"Well," I said, "to be perfectly honest, they can probably sense the kraken this close to us, and want nothing to do with the monster."

Tam laughed. "You're probably closer to the mark than any of us." He walked off to check the ship again.

I turned to the troupe who'd gathered around us. "Okay, people. Let's be ready for this. Remember your drills. Check your stations. Make sure everything is perfect for this. Go! Go! Go!"

I turned back to Jim, who seemed to have almost fully recovered.

"Listen, I know you have your own mind about things, and want to be a useful part of this troupe, but," I leaned in, and Jim leaned his head forward to meet mine. "Please, do not ever go off half-cocked like that again. I'm the leader around here, not only on *Pride of the Sea*, but when we're off ship, too." I looked deeply into his eyes. "Do you understand me?"

Jim nodded solemnly.

"Now go belowdecks and get some breakfast, okay?" I slapped his shoulder affectionately as he grinned and walked off. Kym took his hand in hers, the djinn's huge palm dwarfing the small girl's tiny one. I winked at Kym over his shoulder, and she nodded. She would look after the djinn, who was still getting used to being in human form and running on less power altogether.

An hour later, the ship's bowsprit was dipping low and then bouncing back up high as the ship churned forward, the giant manta rays pulling with an exuberance I had never seen before.

"They are desperate to avoid the kraken," Tam said grimly.

"And are we – avoiding it, I mean? Have we moved any closer?"

"Slightly," he answered.

Crap.

I had to see this for myself.

I climbed the rigging to the crow's nest and settled myself, pulling the brass sight out from my waist and holding it to my eyes.

It couldn't be.

I looked again.

I could see the kraken clearly, and it was nearly below the water, the bow of the floundering ship poking high out of the sea, two of the kraken's tentacled arms wrapped firmly around the ship, one around the topmast and one against the hull.

I strained my ears but could not hear the screams of the drowned ship's sailors, but I could see them.

Dozens of heads bobbed in and around the sea surrounding the kraken. I could see their arms moving, trying to swim to safety. There were several lifeboats in the water, with sailors inside who were reaching over into the sea, trying to retrieve their shipmates.

"They struggle in vain," Tam said softly beside me. I looked at him.

"The kraken leaves no survivors. Not one body will be found." His grim expression matched his somber tone.

I looked back at the struggle. It appeared so close when viewed through the brass sight.

"Do you think it will come for us?" I whispered.

"It depends how fast we can move away."

I watched the kraken pulling the ship under. It seemed to take a long, long time. As if it were reading our minds, at one point I thought I saw the thing turn toward us, and shudder.

I jumped.

"I think it saw us," I whispered.

Tam slid back down to the deck, and began giving orders.

I kept watching through my brass sight. I could not look away.

The kraken seemed to rise out of the water, pushing the floundering ship down further, and stick its head high into the air. I could not make out where its eyes were, but I sensed it was looking over the water at us.

I brought the site down and looked with the naked eye, and I could not see anything. Well, maybe the tiniest speck.

"I guess that's how we look to it, like a tiny speck," I mumbled to myself.

"I wonder if it can sense us another way," Kym said quietly from beside me.

I jumped a foot.

"Sorry," Kym put her hand to her mouth and stifled a giggle.

I huffed.

"Anyway," she said, "like I was saying, I wonder if it can, for instance, smell us?"

I brought the brass sight back up to my eye to watch the monster. "I don't know, but I hope not," I whispered back.

I watched for a while, but the thing seemed to have its attention back on its prey.

"Let me have a look?" asked Kym.

I reluctantly handed over the brass sight, and squinted to look over the water with my naked eye. It was still just a speck.

"Charlotte," Kym said slowly, "it definitely sees us."

"Did it jump up out of the water again?"

"Yes, and it's now rocking back and forth."

"Lemme see." I put my hand out for the sight.

Kym handed it over.

I put it to me eye and looked. The kraken's body language, if it could be called that, looked like it saw our ship, but was unwilling to let go of the prey in hand.

"It doesn't want to let go of the ship it's got," I said, feeling a bit less worried.

"I don't think it does," Kym agreed.

"You know, I had no idea it took this long for the kraken to drown a ship. I mean, Jim was right, this beast looks like it's three times the size of the painting on the wall map in my cabin. At least, in comparison to the ship it's taking down." I lowered the brass sight and handed it back to Kym.

"So, that kraken? It's a big puppy. It's massive. But it is taking half the day to sink that ship, and it's not even done. I was worried we wouldn't have time to get away, but I think we're going to make it," I said.

"We've nearly passed it, and it's still got quite a way to go with that ship," Kym said.

"And Tam said it's going to clean up afterward, so it will go after every sailor in the water, and every lifeboat," I said. "He said it leaves nothing behind."

"Khepri was telling me last night," Kym said. "The legends say the kraken is so rarely seen because it leaves nothing behind. If a ship is attacked, that's it. No survivors. Probably no debris, no wood, no sails, nothing left behind."

"The only people who've seen the creature and lived to tell the tale must have seen it from another ship, like we're seeing it now," I said.

Kym lowered the sight and looked at me. "Exactly," she said. "It's spooky."

"What are the odds?" I wondered.

I took the sight from her and put it up to my eyes again. I could see Tam hanging off the foremast ahead of us, his own sight held up to his eyes, watching, too.

"I wonder how many ships frequent these waters," I mused aloud.

"It's autumn, Khepri said, and there's a lot of trading and shipping going on," Kym said quietly.

"I feel horrible saying this, but I guess it's our good luck that ship was out there first, and that the kraken took it down before we got here," I said. "Although, it seems foolhardy of them to have ventured that far north, into the deeper waters the kraken are known to frequent."

"Foolhardy," Kym repeated.

This was not the first time I had witnessed stupid actions leading to the downfall of a group of people. Not knowing your surroundings, not appreciating the predators that might be around you, not respecting nature. Nature was deadly; we were seeing it in action right before our eyes.

Kym and I watched the kraken break apart the lost ship for another hour, until it fell out of sight as we moved away from it. I gave silent thanks to the mantas for pulling the ship so strongly that the wind was flipping my hair back instead of forward, as I gazed forward across the water. I made a mental note to give them an extra helping of chopped black skipjacks and bluefin; they had saved us from certain death.

Or so we thought.

Chapter Seven
Pursued!

"Tam! TAM!" One of the sailors screamed for my first mate. I whipped my head around and saw the sailor was at the bow, and hanging by his feet. His boots were wrapped in a rope, and he was hanging over the side, gesticulating wildly.

I saw Tam run from the stern, where he'd been checking the wheel; it had been acting up earlier. He made it to the bow and leaned over the railing to reach the lowered sailor. In less than a minute he'd wrapped his boot on a rope and lowered himself past the point the first sailor had been.

A moment later, Tam was back up out of the water and calling to more sailors to help him.

Kym and I watched as more sailors went over the railing, dropping from ropes. I beckoned to a seasoned seafarer, and he climbed up to the crow's nest, hanging easily off the ropes as he explained.

"Manta's traces're tangled." The grizzled, whiskered old sailor chewed blackroot effortlessly as he held an old pipe firmly in his teeth. "One of 'em broke't 'n' whipped back 'n' tangled t'others up. T'ship cain't be pulled until t'traces're straight." He looked back down at the commotion.

The ship had drifted to a near stop while they tried to straighten out the mantas. The sou'wester buffeted against us, whipping our hair and clothing even fiercer than before.

"T' wind's kickin' up," the old sailor said. "Cain't be good. Bad omen." He wetted his finger and stuck it up in the air. "Goin't forty knots. Manta's are still. Cain't be good, no, Cap't. Y'better beware, I'm tellin' ya. Ship'll list, pull." He looked at me.

"The wind. Oh, my god." I pulled my brass sight from my waist holster once again and brought it to my eye. Searching for the kraken, I moved it around. We'd drifted quite a bit since sailing out of sight, and ...

"There'n 't'is," the old sailor touched my arm and pointed.

Oh, dear lord.

We'd drifted so close – or the beast had moved toward us, probably a combination of the two – and the kraken was now visible to the naked eye. With my brass sight it looked enormous. And it was focused on us.

"Christianne!" I called as I slid down the main mast ropes to the deck. My gloved hands burned with the heat of the rope but carried me down so fast I was on deck within seconds.

Christianne appeared in front of me. She'd regaled us with stories of how she'd grown up near an ocean inlet, and had spent most of her waking hours in the water. Early in our voyage, whenever there was a need to deal up close with the giant manta rays, she'd been the one to go in the water with me, for one very good reason: Christianne swam like a dolphin.

"We've got to get the traces cleared! The kraken has sighted us, abandoned the other ship, and is now moving in our direction!" I explained hurriedly.

"Oh, no!" Christianne raced to the bow where Tam was just coming up.

"Are they cleared?" I asked.

"I don't think so. We need more rope," he said.

I turned to Christianne. "We're running out of time," I said to her quietly. She glanced off the port bow and narrowed her eyes, squinting at the slowly advancing dot near the horizon – the monster. *Pride of the Sea* was probably irresistible to the kraken. And it would surely take her down given half the chance.

Christianne grabbed the loops of rope from Tam as he walked up. Tying a lead rope around her waist, she was over the railing before anyone could say anything.

I grabbed a sack of chopped fish another sailor handed me, and Tam and I swiftly followed her; in seconds, we were all in the water.

Must concentrate. Must put kraken out of my mind.

I felt a tap on my arm. Tam was pointing to the lead manta, it was idling in the water, its rope dangling uselessly, the end a frayed snap.

I swam to it, running my hand along its great fin to let it know I was there.

I'd grown fond of the giant rays, and had been down to swim with them nearly every day. They were used to me.

I drew a handful of chum out of the sack and reached over to its mouth, where it nibbled delicately from my hand. With my other hand, I grabbed the rope and ran my hand down near the frayed end. I brought a new length of rope out and began to tie the intricate double sheet bend sailor's knot I knew would be the best for this situation. Not only would it grow tighter with more tension, but it would become nearly impossible to untie once it had swollen in the water for a half-hour.

I pulled the double knot tight, and I felt Tam hold my waist to boost the tension. The knot was ready. Now I just had to swim across and attach the other end of the rope to one of the great iron rings embedded in the ship's massive oak planks.

The sea water was a mass of churning currents and bubbles. The giant manta rays were very nervous – they could sense the kraken's approach, it smelled of grave danger to the intelligent creatures.

I kicked hard and made it to one of the rings. Christianne was already at the next one over, mere yards away. I saw her looping her rope and tying the intricate sea knot, and I began to do the same.

I heard a rise in the panicked voice from the deck, *the crew must be getting louder*, I thought. The kraken was a slow swimmer, it took a long time to drown a ship, but once it reached a vessel, that ship was pretty much doomed.

I'd been reading everything I could on the beasts for the last two days. They were utterly deadly, and this one looked to be larger than normal.

I finished tying my knots. Tam was on my other side, finishing his. He motioned me up to the top, and we swam hard, our feet paddling quickly.

The sailors on deck hoisted us up out of the water and on board. The wind whipped at my face and buffeted my ears. My heart quickened at how much it had kicked up during the few minutes we'd been in the water.

Tam was calling orders to the rafters, and those in charge of the mantas barked out commands.

We surged forward.

I glanced over at the far port horizon.

The kraken had been but a dot in our field of vision before I'd dove into the sea; now, it was much bigger. Closer.

It's hunting us.

We had to get out of there. Now.

I turned to the aft mate. "Toss a barrel of chum over the aft port railing. Let's see if we can't attract something else for it to follow," I ordered. Nodding, she moved to carry out the order.

It was a race now.

Our bow was pointed to the island we'd aimed for. We'd come too far out to make for the mainland, and the shallow waters of the island's inlet were beckoning us.

"Charlotte!" Kym called from the crow's nest.

I looked up.

"It's still got the other ship! It's dragging it behind!" she called, pointing out to the northern waters.

The kraken was an animal, after all. Selfish and simple, it had apparently decided to hold on to its prize, while trying to capture us at the same time.

I took a deep breath.

Hopefully, dragging the other ship behind would slow it down.

Still, it would be close.

The mantas strained, surging forward. They could smell the kraken and wanted nothing to do with it. Fear was a powerful motivator. The new ropes went taut under the stress; we could see them less than ten feet below the water's surface. But they held. The massive, braided cables, made by the finest workmen in northern Alkebulan, held their forms, strong and sure.

The mantas swam faster and faster.

I climbed up halfway to Kym and wrapped the rope around my boot, freeing my hands and drawing the brass sight out once again. I sighted the beast; it was closer than ever.

I could see the arms, with their individual suckers, and they were fluctuating open and close, open and close, in excitement of a new kill. The kraken was in a frenzy.

Farther on still, just on its other side, I could distinguish the faint outline of the other ship. It was nearly underwater, but the main mast and mizzenmast were still visible above the waves. I dropped back to the deck.

"The beast's foolishness in not letting the first ship go will be its downfall," Tam said beside me.

"Surely," I said softly, hoping he was right.

The mantas pulled us closer to the island, which was now within sight, a tiny sliver low on the horizon. Clouds and mist obscured most of the land from our views, only parting enough for us to get a good look when it was within a few miles of our position.

Pride of the Sea drew closer to the island.

The kraken was swimming faster, shuddering with excitement. It was close enough that we could see it easily with the naked eye. Its many legs began to writhe about as it swam, trying to drive it faster through the water.

"Does it still have the first ship in its grip?" I called up to Kym.

"Yes, I think so," she cried back.

I paced back and forth.

"Miss, do you think we'll get away?" asked Caroline.

"I hope so, Carrie," I said grimly. "Although I feel like getting out and pulling the ship myself."

The beast was slowly gaining.

The wind had been against us from the start, pushing us northwest when we'd been trying to head straight west.

Now that the island got closer, the wind would finally aid us, as it loomed directly ahead and northwest.

"It's about time something went right for us," Tam mumbled beside us.

I stood, dripping, on the port bow, watching the kraken approach us. We'd done all we could; it was up to the giant manta rays pulling us, now.

We could see the break ahead, where the dark blue of the deep sea gave way to the lighter turquoise blue of the island's waters. We drew closer and closer, until we could see the island's atoll with the naked eye.

The kraken was within several hundred yards of us now. I imagined I could see its eyes, the twin darker spots on the upper squid-like body of the thing, the sucker-covered many legs writhing as it came.

"The thing seems very determined," Tam said beside me.

I glanced back at him.

I gripped my scimitar tightly on my belt.

"If that thing comes near my ship I will fight it with my dying breath. I will take its arms off one by one," I scowled.

"And I'll be right beside you, Charlotte," Tupu said beside me.

"Me, too, Miss," Caroline already had her sword out.

The thing gained. It was now maybe one hundred and fifty yards off our stern.

I turned and faced the head of the ship, I could see the bow dipping and rising as the mantas strained to pull us forward.

If they got us out of this, I will love them forever.

"Charlotte."

I glanced over at Tupu. The wind was flapping her blouse and creating a regal silhouette, and her belly, heavy with child, was outlined. She looked beautiful.

She turned to face me, holding her hair from her eyes.

"Charlotte, I want my baby born alive," she said softly. "Alive."

I nodded and swallowed. Striding to the bow railing, I leaned over.

"Pull, my beauties! PULL!" I knew the giant mantas couldn't hear me or understand what my words meant, but it felt good to cry out to them.

I knew if the kraken caught us, I would feel a massive blow to the ship, so I kept my eyes forward.

The island loomed larger and larger, and *Pride of the Sea* zipped and skimmed over the dark water like a bird. I had never known a ship could move this fast.

A loud cry filled the air. Deep and booming, and almost deafening. It was an ugly, threatening, aggressive cry, coming from a monster that should never have existed. It was the cry of the kraken.

It sounded quite close. I glanced back and saw the thing looming over us, less than a hundred yards away. It was lifted hundreds of feet out of the water, and I could see how massive the beast was.

It screamed thunderously again.

The ship surged forward.

"There!" Kym cried.

I glanced up. She was pointing frantically.

We were nearly to the shallows. We were closer to the turquoise waters than the kraken was to our ship.

The beast screamed out again, and there was a massive splashing sound.

I cringed involuntarily, looking behind us.

"It's let the other ship go!" cried one of the sailors who clung to the upper rigging.

Oh, no.

In its desperation to reach us, perhaps sensing it was about to lose us for good, it had abandoned its earlier prey, letting it go, so that it could travel even faster.

My heart beat so fast it threatened to leap out of my chest.

I looked back, and saw the beast was maybe 50 yards away. It seemed almost close enough to touch. I saw the kraken lifting its arms even higher into the air, then bring them crashing down. The resulting wave raced forward and smashed against the stern of the ship.

The giant wave lifted the back of the ship and tossed us into the air. We came down with a loud crash, and the kraken leaped over the wave top and was nearly upon us.

I heard another sound, one I hadn't heard for a while.

Seagulls.

We were that close.

A hundred feet.

A few dozen feet.

The kraken reached its near arms out, and the stinking smell of rotting fish filled our nostrils.

I raced back as I saw Khepri and Tam with their swords, swinging at the giant suckered cephalopod arms as they came close to the stern deck. I skidded to a halt next to them, extending my scimitar toward it.

The beast screamed again, it seemed to be in deep frustration.

I felt the ship shudder.

We were knocked off our feet as the keel scraped the bottom of the atoll.

The mantas continued pulling, and *Pride of the Sea* was lifted onto a sand bar and swayed there, then settled upright.

I let out a breath of relief as I got to my feet.

"Thank god it's low tide," mumbled Tam nearby.

The kraken screamed in fury and its arms thrashed, churning up the sea just a few dozen yards away.

I looked out at the beast, so close, yet unable to reach us. It made me extremely nervous.

My mind told me we were safe, but my gut was still churning.

Were we safe?

Chapter Eight
A New Danger

We watched as the massive kraken searched for a way into the lagoon. Perched at the edge of the atoll, we dropped anchor next to the sand bar and watched the beast from just thirty feet away.

It was agitated. It was crazy.

"What is going on with that thing?" I mused aloud.

"It's acting even crazier than it did a few minutes ago," said Tam.

"Charlotte! CHARLOTTE!!" Kym screamed. I looked over abruptly to see Kym leaning out of the crow's nest, her arm extended, her finger pointing.

Wait.

Kym was pointing to a spot between us and the island. To a spot *inside the lagoon.*

"THERE!" Kym cried.

Something hit the ship, and it shuddered; then a second impact rocked the whole vessel. I looked up and saw the masts were swaying.

Off shore, the kraken screamed angrily, the sound deafening. Spray shot over the stern, reeking of rotted fish and pelting us with, *what was that ...?*

"Oh, my gods, it's kraken snot! Charlotte!" Tupu nearly gagged in disgust as she wiped the gobs of mucous mixed with half-chewed briny fish guts out of her hair. I had never been so happy I was wearing a hat than in that moment.

"CHARLOTTE!" Kym screamed again.

The ship was struck and rocked yet again, listing to the side.

On the port side, which was now tilted five degrees, a massive ball of wriggling tentacles began to climb over the top rail.

Sailors ran to chop at the tentacles with their swords, and I hurried to join them.

My feet slid on the mucous-coated deck as I approached, and I fell before I could catch myself. I jumped back up, found firmer footing and ran to the edge.

The kraken screamed again.

"It's coming over the atoll!" someone yelled.

I glanced to the bow and saw the kraken rising out of the water and trying to climb the reef. It screamed over and over.

"It's a nest!" cried the sailor at the front of the melee, leaning over the railing ten feet from where the new threat was emerging.

He screamed as a new cluster of tentacled arms reached up and grabbed him, pulling him overboard. The water was churning with maybe two dozen miniature krakens – babies, but each the size of a cow! – and they were behaving exactly the same way the gigantic kraken had: attacking the ship.

Tam called out to him and jumped over the rail, trying to grab the sailor's leg before it disappeared.

"Tam!" Akim called. The boy raced to where his friend had last been seen.

I ran to the tentacles the men were fighting and swung my scimitar, slicing through an arm. Something screamed in the water, sounding more high-pitched than the huge kraken behind us. I swung my sword again. The things were slippery, and it was hard to get the edge of my sword to cut into the slimy bodies.

Over and over I swung, causing little damage.

I heard a cry and saw Tam climbing back over the railing, the other sailor in tow. He rushed up to me, his expression grim.

"It's a nest, all right. It's the kraken's nest."

"What?" I said.

"Aye, and we're sitting right on top of it."

"Can they do much damage?" I asked.

"Well, they can't break up the ship like their mother, no, but if they try, they can kill a man." He glanced over at the man he'd retrieved from the water. "They aren't really trying to kill. They're just panicked because we disturbed their nest, but the large one, she's halfway over the atoll already." He glanced off the stern, and we could see the massive adult kraken struggling to pass over the reef into the lagoon.

"AIEEE!" Another sailor was dragged overboard. Tam flew into action and jumped to drag the man back, only to disappear over the railing along with him.

I jumped to the railing to look, and my heart leaped into my throat.

The baby kraken nest was half under the bow of the ship; the smaller krakens had been disturbed and were a boiling mass coming up out of the water.

"TAM!" someone screamed.

Tam had made a grab for the lost sailor, who had fallen into the thickest part of the nest, where there was barely any water, just a mass of tentacles.

The creatures' beaks were snapping and blood was flying.

"AHHH!" The man screamed.

"OH GODS!" The young kraken had nearly torn off the man's arm, it barely hung on by the bone. The creatures seemed energized by the blood spurting out and covering their tentacles.

A scarlet bloom spread out across the lagoon. Blood was everywhere.

Tam lunged and made a grab for the man, and almost had him.

I clutched the railing and swung a leg over.

"Charlotte! THEY'LL EAT YOU!" I heard Kym's voice but did not hesitate. Over the side and into the water I jumped.

The creatures were more like eels down here than kraken. Slimmer bodies sported longer tentacled arms by proportion. I swung my sword back and forth, trying to get them off the sailor. He screamed again, this time weaker.

"GRAB MY HAND!" I heard Tam call.

The man floundered in the writhing mass of bloodthirsty creatures.

"OH GOD!" Tam screamed.

I swung harder, trying to reach him.

The mother kraken's scream filled the air, blasting out so loud it stunned us. It stunned the babies as well, interrupting their eating frenzy.

"Grab him!" I called.

A rope hit the water next to us, and Tam wrapped his arm around it, his other arm around the now-limp sailor.

The baby kraken mass began whipping around faster, probably realizing they were being robbed of their prey. When the two were lifted out of the water and safely out of reach, the bloodthirsty horde turned its attention to me.

Oh, no.

I realized the danger and turned to swim away from them, but my feet floundered on some rocks, slowing me down.

The first of the kraken young reached my leg and wrapped itself around me. The suckers were tearing into my skin, the pants did nothing to dull the pain.

"AAHHH!" I screamed. The creature pulled off my boot, and more of the tentacles reached higher to wrap around my thigh. Blood rose as the black fabric of my breeches tore, the tentacle wrapping itself so tightly that my leg went numb.

Pain flooded my brain, worse than any other I'd ever felt.

"AAAAAAAHH!" I screamed again.

My mind raced. These creatures were going to eat me alive if I didn't get out of there.

I reached out, scrabbling for any purchase they could find, but it was all water and slimy rock.

I blacked out.

I came to on the deck of *Pride of the Sea*, the concerned blue and green face of the djinn looking down at me.

My body was shuddering and seizing.

I heard Khepri's voice. "She's lost a lot of blood. Help me with this."

Something was tied around my leg up by my hip.

"Lift her legs up. The blood needs to drain out of them and into her head."

"Yes, good. Like this."

The djinn moved in close to me, until his cheek was pressed up against my shoulder.

What is he doing?

"Hey, Charlotte," he whispered as he worked to raise my hips and legs, "Don't leave just yet, okay? I heard Tam talking. I think he's sweet on you."

My head was so foggy I couldn't be sure of what the djinn had said.

"Wha...?" I said as I blacked out again.

"Okay, yeah, Tam get me a bowl, I think I can get her to eat."

That was Caroline's voice.

I opened my eyes.

I was in the captain's cabin, in bed. The cabin smelled weird.

"What's that smell?" I asked weakly.

"Hey! Look who's decided to join the world of the living," Caroline smiled down at me.

"Oh, Charlotte, I was so worried," said Christianne's voice behind me.

A knock sounded at the door, and it opened.

"Here you go," Tam handed Caroline a steaming crock with a spoon poking out of it.

"What happened?" I said, still sounding weak.

"What *didn't* happen. We lost a man, a sailor who bled to death on the deck just as we were trying to reach you. Those little monsters ripped most of his arm off," Caroline sounded bitter as she helped me sit up.

"You almost died, too, Charlotte," Christianne said. "The baby kraken horde hurt your leg and you lost a lot of blood."

Caroline spooned soup into my mouth. "Those things tore your boot off and then tore into your leg."

I felt a surge of alarm. I reached under the blanket for my legs. "Which one?" my voice was so quiet, even to my own ears.

"The right one, but Khepri fixed you all up." She fed me another spoonful of soup. "The wound is healed; the flesh is scarred but all there. You're just feeling weak because you lost so much blood."

"Khepri says you'll be better in a week. You have to get better fast, Charlotte, we grabbed the kraken baby that was wrapped around your leg and saved it."

Oh, gross.

"The others disappeared back into the water, and we saw them flipping over the atoll at high tide and disappearing with their mother." Christianne giggled.

What on earth is so funny about saving a dead tentacled squid creature that was almost the death of me?

I said as much to the room at large.

Caroline said nothing, just spooned more soup into my mouth, but I thought she pursed her lips tight. She seemed disgruntled.

"What? What is it?" I managed, weakly.

Caroline met my eyes, then nodded toward Christianne.

"Christianne, what is it?" I lifted my head to speak, then felt weaker and dropped back down.

Christianne began giggling so hard she almost fell over.

There was a knock at the door, and Kym's head appeared. She saw Christianne and stuck her arm into the room, motioning for the girl to follow her. Christianne got up and walked to the door. Just as she reached it, she turned to me and said, "The last kraken baby is alive. We've got it in a washtub. Kym wants to feed it and raise it, as a pet," her hand came up to her mouth and the giggles began again.

Huh?

I turned to Caroline, my eyebrows raised in question.

"Don't look at me for answers, I think it's a ridiculous thing," she said as she spooned more soup into my mouth.

Tam had moved the ship a hundred feet closer to the shore, and dropped anchor, safely away from the deep water.

The crew had rewarded our giant manta rays by feeding them massive quantities of chopped black skipjack and bluefin, along with flowers the first of them brought back after landing a small craft on the island's beach.

Kym told me she was among the sailors who explored that first hour, and how she'd collected armfuls of blue and yellow flowers, which she'd fed by hand to the tired but grateful mantas.

Caroline described how the giant rays, reaching more than fifty feet from wingtip to wingtip, had raised their faces out of the water to nibble the flowers from Kym's hand as delicately as Shêtân took sugar cubes from my palms.

Christianne told me she was so thankful for the sweet mantas that she'd spent hours in the water with them that first day, examining each one, making sure they had no lasting injuries, going back and forth between them, petting and cooing to them.

I was happy my crew had handled things so well in my absence.

I fell asleep with a smile on my face, relaxed for the first time in days.

It was good to be alive.

Chapter Nine
New Friends

The next day found us arguing amicably about who would go ashore to do more exploring. Kym was hopping from foot to foot in excitement, and kept telling me what she swore she had seen the afternoon before.

"I'm telling you, I saw them!" She laughed in delight.

I turned to her while I adjusted my belt. "Really?" I forced myself to sound skeptical. Inside, I was happy, happier than I'd been since we'd left Moonlit Bay.

"Yes! They were mermaids, Charlotte!" she insisted.

"Okay, okay," I said. "You say you saw mermaids, right?"

Kym nodded enthusiastically, happy to be believed.

I held up a hand. "Not so fast," I said, shaking my head. "I'm not saying I fully believe you."

Her face fell.

"I just have questions," I finished.

"Okay, go ahead and ask," she smiled.

"First of all, it was starting to get dark by the time you headed back, right?"

She nodded.

"And you said you saw them when you were already in the boat on your way back to the ship, isn't that so?"

She nodded again.

"The setting sun is famous for playing tricks on the eyes, you know, sweetheart."

She looked uncertain.

"And you said you saw them peeking out from behind the plants growing into the water, on the edge of the lagoon?" I looked at her.

She just looked up at me, her big, dark eyes opened wide, looking at me solemnly.

"Charlotte," she said.

"What?"

"I. Saw. Them." She stopped, looked at me for the beat of a minute, then continued. "There were three of them. Their hair was long and dark, their eyes were slitted sideways, and they were at the edge of the rocks."

"The edge of the rocks? Near the grotto?"

"Yes."

"Okay then, let's go and see," I smiled sweetly at her. She looked at me suspiciously, then broke into a laugh.

In the end, it was the original six – Caroline, Kym, Tupu, Khepri, Christianne, and I – plus Akim, who outfitted ourselves and stocked up on packs of food and water before heading out in the smaller boat. We brought so many supplies that we left half in the rowboat, and tied it to a tree before hiking down the beach to explore.

We hadn't gone fifty feet when we came upon the other end of the grotto, behind some huge trees. *It is so tropical here,* I thought. *Even though we're just a couple of hundred miles from the northern shore of Alkebulan, it's like an entirely different climate.*

We pushed through the low-hanging branches and came out on the sand, five feet from the water's edge. The small sound was protected by the curling isthmus that wrapped around from the inner corner of the atoll. The water was shallow here, maybe eight inches deep at the most, and it was cool, with small silver fish flitting here and there. The sunlight glinted off the rippling water, mesmerizing me. It was a gorgeous corner of the world, entirely cut off from the larger beach. I was charmed.

"Charlotte," Kym whispered, touching my elbow.

I looked up. She was nudging her head to the side, I followed her eyes, which were fixed on ...

Oh!

The mermaids sat in the water on the far end, partially hidden by the leaves, peering at us curiously from around the corner of the rock entrance to the grotto, before moving closer. They gathered about fifteen feet away, at the edge of a large boulder covered with ferns, and sat watching us.

Mermaids!

They were much smaller than we were. I'd seen many paintings of mermaids, and they'd always been depicted as human-size.

This pair looked no taller than four feet high. They were slim and tiny, their faces bright and curious.

The mermaids' dark green hair was draped with various types of sea grass and braided with pearls and corkscrew shells, and their pale moss-green skin seemed to glow from within. They looked to be entirely naked, from what we could see, and had broad, flexible tails, with smooth iridescent skin like a dolphin's running up past their belly buttons.

When one turned sideways to whisper to her companion, I could see her sparkling tail-skin covered nearly her entire back. A fin also ran from the tip of her tail, up along her back to her shoulder blades.

The mermaid's tail was flat, oriented in line with her shoulders like a dolphin's tail. The fin on her back started out small at the tip of her tail, grew to over a foot long, then tapered off again near her shoulders.

Their faces were otherworldly; there was no other way to put it. Large, unblinking eyes looked out at us, and sharp cheekbone ridges gave way to small fins that stretched back to become small ears.

Their mouths were the most human looking thing about them. They even sported lips that were a dark mossy green, matching the hue of their skin.

Their hands were webbed, and their fingers ended in sharp claws that looked deadly.

The thought came, unbidden: *I must remember to stay clear of those talons.* I shook my head.

The mermaids were watching us closely. They seemed just as curious about us as we seemed about them.

We decided to make camp then and there, and spend the day with the mermaids.

Tupu and Khepri sat and watched the mermaids, and made a small fire, while the rest of us searched the surrounding area, making sure there were no more surprises.

Khepri had bought a large black skipjack and a cutting board. She set up a food preparation station right there beside the fire, and had fileted and skewered over a dozen fish steaks by the time we returned. Akim had made a makeshift spit, and the sticks holding the fish were set against this, and were soon sizzling and dripping.

The mermaids watched us with deep fascination. There had initially been only two, but by the time the fish steaks were cooking, their delicious smells filling the air, five others had arrived to join them.

Khepri counted, and swiftly added another steak to cook, smiling over at the mermaids.

I laughed. "We are going to take the 'make friends' route that goes straight through their appetites, I see."

Kym giggled. She wanted so much to approach the mermaids, but I held her back, reminding her that these were wild creatures, and should be dealt with cautiously.

"Let's wait and let them approach first," I suggested.

The sun was high in the sky by the time the fish was cooked. We had all started a singalong, keeping our voices somewhat quiet at first, then slowly raising them, until the little beach was filled with happy song.

The mermaids kept watching us but did not approach closer.

Finally, Kym stood. "I can't wait any longer, Charlotte."

"I guess since you're the smallest, you should go first," I said. "Just be careful."

Kym held one of the skewered fish steaks, the aroma rising from it tantalizing, and walked slowly into the water and toward the mermaids.

They watched her intently as she approached.

"Careful, sweetie," I said under my breath.

"You are so cautious," Tupu said from beside me, laughing.

I raised my eyebrows.

"Look," she pointed her chin to indicate the mermaids.

I turned to look.

Kym was halfway to them. They looked eager. I looked closer. The mermaids weren't focused on Kym, they were concentrating on the skewered fish she held out.

"Ohhh, they are hungry."

Tupu nodded, smiling.

Kym held out the food when she reached the mermaids, who came forward through the shallow water eagerly and tried to take the fish off the stick. It was still hot, and the mermaid who had reached out to take it moved back in surprise. Kym giggled, and the mermaid came forward again. This time, Kym held out the other end of the stick.

It worked.

The mermaid held the stick and brought the fish steak to her nose to sniff. She must have liked what she smelled, because she was soon nibbling at the food, and making what could only be described as 'yummy sounds.'

Five minutes later, the mermaids were sitting next to us, their flexible tales curled under them like snakes, each holding a cooked fish steak on a skewer. They nibbled and smiled, and made appreciative sounds at us.

We spent several hours there, cutting off pieces of the black skipjack, and skewering them on the ends of the sticks, then holding them out over the fire to cook. The mermaids seemed eager to try it, and were soon roasting their own fish steaks over the fire, and laughing in delight.

The mermaids had their own language, and were animated as they spoke to us, using varied facial expressions and gesturing to the fish steaks. From what I gathered of their tones and hand gestures, they had never tried cooked fish before.

They loved it.

I had to admit, the succulent fresh fish *was* delicious. Khepri expertly filleted and scraped scales and presented us with perfectly carved fish meat for us to roast over the flames. We kept the campfire going even as dusk fell, until our bellies were overstuffed. Even our new friends looked full. They sat back, smiling and content, as they talking in their language to each other and to us.

The largest mermaid suddenly sat up, and spoke in a spirited tone to her fellow mermaids in their own language; she seemed to pose a suggestion, which the others greeted with enthusiasm. At this, she immediately left, slithering quickly off into the water of the grotto.

We passed around a waterskin, and I wiped the juice from my chin, then turned as I heard the mermaid returning.

She was carrying several large gourds that had been topped with a plug of seaweed, which she passed around to each of us, removing the stopper in her own.

Khepri followed the movements of the mermaid, undoing the seaweed plug and setting it aside. She brought the mouth of the gourd to her nose and inhaled deeply, then, a look of surprise on her face, she tipped it to her mouth and took a sip.

"Oh!" She exclaimed, then took another drink. "It's some kind of nectar, and it really packs a punch!" She passed the gourd to me.

I tipped the mouth of the gourd to my face and inhaled. *It smells like mead mixed with elderberry juice,* I thought. *With a hint of cherry.* I drank deeply from the gourd.

It was delicious.

We had soon passed the gourd around the fire several times, each of us drinking so much of the nectar that we were soon tipsy and laughing. Our mermaid friends looked very pleased with themselves, having found a contribution to the communal meal. We roasted black skipjack steaks and drank cherry elderberry nectar long into the night. As the fire died down, we all settled quite happily to sleep.

The next morning, I opened my eyes and found Khepri already awake. She smiled at me. "Sleep well?"

I burped. "Oh, god. That stuff was so good." I looked around. The mermaids were gone, but they had left the gourds, and each still had a small bit of nectar at the bottom. I found one and took a sip.

So good.

Khepri," I asked, suddenly realizing something odd. "Why don't I have a hangover? I've never drunk that much in my life."

She shrugged. "Not sure. It was actually pretty tame, as whiskies go, but it must have some qualities that make it easier on our systems."

Tupu yawned then, her eyes coming open. She groaned. "I have to pee," she mumbled, and stumbled into the bushes.

"That reminds me," I said, getting up and walking into the far bushes to relieve myself.

When I got back, the mermaids were there again. They were all smiles and looked very happy.

They indicated with sign language that we'd given them some wonderful new information on the culinary arts, and that they would be cooking their fish, when they could, every chance they got. Kym couldn't stop giggling at how they spoke using hand signals.

As we got ready to depart, we led them to the main beach, and indicated our ship anchored off shore. *Pride of the Sea* looked peaceful out in the bay, and there was no sign of the kraken, thank goodness.

The first mermaid Kym had approached touched Kym's arm and held out a seaweed-wrapped bundle, indicating it was a gift. Kym smiled and bowed, then reached forward to hug the mermaid.

When we unwrapped it, we saw it was filled with large, dark, charcoal grey pearls in varying hues. At least fifteen of them. They were beautiful.

"Oooh!" Kym exclaimed, touching them with her finger and examining them closely. They were quite spectacular. I grinned at Kym, very happy with the last twenty-four hours.

We had made some new friends.

Chapter Ten
Calling to the Babe

We returned to the ship and told the crew all about the mermaids, and everyone was amazed by our stories except for Jim; he looked troubled. The quiet man's brow was furrowed as he listened to the story of our encounter.

I pulled him aside as soon as I could.

"Jim, something troubles you?"

He remained silent.

"Is there some danger we should know about? Something concerning the mermaids?"

He spoke reluctantly. "The mermaids sound wonderful, and I'm glad you made a new alliance," he paused.

Alliance. I had not thought of it in those terms. Jim was right, though; with every alliance we made, our chances of success grew. *New friends; new help if needed. I must remember this.*

Jim took a deep breath. "It's probably nothing," he said.

I was still getting to know the djinn, and it was clear he had gathered plenty of wisdom through living so many millennia. I patted his shoulder. "Let me know if you want to talk." He nodded and moved away.

He seemed relieved to have avoided the conversation, and walked up the stairs to the higher poop deck, lost in thought.

We'd brought some of the nectar for the sailors to sample, and it was very popular; they finished it off, celebrating far into the evening.

And all was quiet.

Halfway through the night I woke up, restless from the prior day's event. My head was abuzz with excitement at what the next day would bring. I brewed myself some tea, and drank it, curled up on my chair with a good book, but even that did not make me sleepy again.

I decided to get a breath of fresh air, but I didn't want to disturb the night watch, so I bundled myself in my coat and quietly made my way to the rear of the ship. I found a quiet spot high on the poop deck, and settled down for some stargazing.

After a few minutes of gazing upward, I dropped my head to survey the decks of the ship below me. Everything looked quiet and serene. Sailors from the night watch were perched here and there. I saw Jim sitting in the crow's nest, looking out to sea. I wondered if he was expecting to see the kraken again.

Probably not, she likely headed out to deep water with her babies.

I remembered the kraken baby in the washtub down below. *I must remember to talk to Kym about it.* Even though it had been quiet and docile when I'd visited it, and it seemed to be a runt, since it looked smaller than I remembered the others were, I couldn't just let her have it as a pet in my hold.

For one thing, it would grow larger.

I smiled, remembering Kym's enthusiasm.

I must get that girl a real pet. Maybe a cat. Cats are so useful on board a sailing ship.

Movement caught my eye, and I turned and focused on the figure of Tupu emerging from belowdecks. She had both hands on her belly as she strolled.

Tupu walked to the side of the deck and bent over the railing and vomited.

Oh, dear.

She'd been telling us she felt nauseated. It was the pregnancy hormones, Khepri had told her. Being pregnant turned a woman's body chemistry haywire, apparently. Tupu must have had a bad bout of nausea. Khepri had told her cool air would help.

I saw her rinse out her mouth and spit overboard, then turn and stroll to the other side of the ship. The side facing the island.

Tupu sat on some canvas-covered ropes near the fo'c'sle, and leaned back to rest.

I watched her idly for a few minutes, then my eyes drifted back up to look at the millions of stars ablaze in the inky night sky.

It was silent, save for the gentle lapping of the water against the sides of the ship. Even the giant mantas slept.

Minutes passed.

I became aware of a faint song drifting over the water from the sea, very subtle at first, then growing in volume until it couldn't have been my imagination.

A song so alluring, it called to the senses.

I sat up, feeling pulled by the song.

Movement caught my eye for the second time that night. I looked down to see Tupu had risen from her spot and walked over to the port railing, the side of the ship facing the open sea.

The side the song seemed to come from.

I felt the lure of the song, but shook my head to clear my mind as I stared at Tupu. My heartbeat quickened in fear.

Tupu was leaning over the port railing, gazing into the moonlight shining on the water.

The light rippled on the dark sea, and the song deepened and grew louder.

Tupu was leaning over too far.

Did she not see the danger? I saw her arms and legs pinwheel as her weight tipped slowly over the railing.

My heart raced.

I jumped up, about to call out, then saw the djinn race through the air from the crow's nest.

Tupu tipped over and began to slide out of the ship.

The song was so alluring, part of me wanted to jump into the water with her.

Tupu disappeared over the side, the djinn a split second after her.

I heard water splashing.

I closed my eyes as a deep fear washed over me.

A tense few seconds later, the djinn reappeared, Tupu in his arms. Relief flooded my brain.

I heard another, louder splash, and my eyes darted out across the water just in time to see the flip of a large black tail, and the song ended.

What is that thing?

I felt a wave of fright, and jumped up, running down to the main deck to Tupu and the djinn.

Several sailors came then and escorted Tupu and the djinn belowdecks.

I motioned to them and we all headed for my cabin. It was the biggest room on the ship.

I closed the door after they entered, then turned to them both. The djinn was transforming into his human form, shimmering in the low light. I reached and turned up the wick on the main lantern, and a warm light filled the cabin, brighter than I had left it.

I turned to Tupu and looked her over. Her nightgown was wet in places. She was cradling her belly and the babe within, and crying softly.

"Let's get you warmed up." I helped Tupu out of her nightgown and into a soft shift I had, while Jim coaxed the kindling up in the small fireplace. I wrapped Tupu in my warmest quilt and settled her back into her chair. I brewed a hot chai and handed it to her, and sat down. I turned to Jim.

"What was that thing?"

He took a deep breath, and began to speak.

"It was a siren, calling to the babe," he whispered, and looked over at Tupu, who cringed. "This was why I was concerned, earlier."

A dawning realization hit me.

"A siren?" I repeated, louder. I had to be sure what I had heard.

A small gasp came from the other side of the cabin door, and I realized Kym had followed us and was listening from just outside.

"Yes. They often live near mermaids, and the two species have formed a symbiotic relationship. The mermaid cannot dive deep into the dark fathoms of the seas, but they require the stinger gland from the Tyrrhenian Deep Angler fish. The sirens can reach it, as they do not need to breathe air to survive." He shifted in his seat, seemingly in his element. "The mermaids are benign; they do not normally pose a threat to humans and other life."

"Wait. 'Normally'?" I asked.

"Well," he grimaced, "they can defend themselves as well as any other magical creature. What I meant was that they do not hunt humans."

I leaned forward.

He continued. "Sirens, on the other hand, are quite dangerous. I'm sure you've heard the legends of them luring sailors to their deaths?"

I nodded.

"If you remember the children's rhyme from long ago, the ancient poem's words that say, 'the sweet sound that calls the young sailors'?"

"Yes, my mother used to sing me that rhyme when I was very young," I said.

"Well, there's more truth to that particular poem than most people realize. The sirens are drawn to youth." He indicated Tupu's swollen belly. "A baby's essence would be nearly irresistible to them." He raised his eyebrows and sat back.

I put my arm around Tupu and held her close as Jim proceeded.

"The siren – and thank goodness there was only the one – was singing because she sensed Tupu's unborn babe. She was trying to lure her off the boat and into the sea." He pointed to Tupu's drying nightgown spread near the small fireplace.

"She actually did go overboard. It's a good fifteen feet from the railing to the water. I caught her by the leg as she reached the water, and pulled her out. Her arm and hair were already in when I reached for her."

"Look," Tupu showed me her arm. There were deep scratches along it, from wrist to elbow. I got up and poked my head out my cabin door, and whispered to Kym to fetch Khepri. Kym looked wide-eyed and sheepish at getting caught eavesdropping, but I just whispered *"hurry"* and shooed her down the short hall.

"The siren grabbed at her, but I yanked hard and pulled her back up," Jim said.

"You ... you s-saved my life," Tupu said, hiccupping. "Thank you, Jim."

She reached out her hand to the djinn and smiled gratefully. "I thought I was seeing my refection, but I ... I think it was ... something else." She shuddered.

"Tupu," Jim said quietly, "remember the song of the siren, and guard against it. The lure will grow stronger. Listen and learn, so you can protect your baby.

Tupu nodded, "I will."

I shifted in my seat. "Jim, are there other magical creatures that are drawn to steal babies?"

"To my knowledge, just the siren."

"And how did you come to know so much about this?" I was curious.

"Several thousand years ago, the lamp was in the possession of a sheikh who made a wish that ..." he stopped and looked down.

We waited for him to continue.

Finally, he looked up again and continued. "The sheikh wished for help in raising his son to be a noble prince. The boy was only three years old at the time. I spent a good twenty years educating and rearing the child." He raised his eyes to the ceiling.

"God, that sounds tedious," I said.

"You have no idea," Jim answered, half-rolling his eyes. "The sheikh was shrewd and made his other two wishes in a similar fashion. I was tied to that family for nearly a hundred years."

Regret, I thought. *Jim has regret.*

"You must be a treasure house of stories, Jim," I said quietly, squeezing his hand.

"You have no idea," he said again.

Khepri knocked on the door and poked her head in. "I'm needed?" she smiled.

"Come! Come! Tupu is hurt." I waved her in.

Khepri handed a small packet of herbs to Kym and sent her to boil them as tea, then sat down next to Tupu.

We quickly recounted the tale as Khepri examined Tupu's wounds. Her eyebrows rose as she listened, not saying a word. She cleaned the scratches and applied a salve that seemed to immediately soothe Tupu's pain. She wrapped the arm with soft cloth strips, tying them off and then speaking.

"There doesn't seem to be any infection, so I doubt the siren's claws were poisonous, which is a very good thing, because they have sharp spines on their backs that can kill, if I remember correctly."

"You do," said Jim.

"Young lady," Khepri scowled at Tupu, "Please be more careful from now on. Anything that threatens your baby threatens you and, by extension, all of us."

"I will be more careful," Tupu smoothed the bandage on her arm.

Kym brought the mug of tea and handed it to Tupu, who accepted it gratefully and took a sip.

She grimaced.

"Drink it all, every last drop," Khepri instructed. "And I think I will have you drink a mug morning and night, as a restorative, from now on."

Tupu mumbled something under her breath.

"What was that?" Khepri leaned forward. I tensed up.

"I said," Tupu raised her eyebrows and pressed her lips together, turning her head to the side to hide a smile, " 'Yes, mistress.' "

"Hmmph. That's better." Khepri patted the girl's slender hand.

Chapter Eleven
Isolated

"I think we should explore that grotto, Charlotte," Caroline said. Christianne stood next to her, nodding her head vigorously.

"Do you now?" I took another bite of fish. I was famished.

"Yes," said Khepri, coming up to us. "I'm curious, too." She smiled.

Not wanting to go against the general vote, I laughed.

"Okay, okay, but let's leave Tupu on the ship, I think she has to recuperate another day."

"Agreed."

An hour later, Caroline, Christianne, Khepri and I were making our way to shore. Kym had decided to stay with Tupu, once she'd been shown how to feel the baby move.

"Set this cup here," said Tupu, who was reclining in bed, favoring her sore arm. She'd had quite enough adventure for the day. She carefully set a small cup half filled with water atop her burgeoning belly, withdrew her hand, and waited.

Kym exclaimed and clapped her hands as the cup began to jiggle with the movements of the baby inside Tupu. And that's where we left them, both smiling at this new game.

We pulled our small craft up onto the beach and tied its rope on the tree we'd been using, then made our way through the leaves and to the grotto.

The mermaids were gone.

We called to them, holding up the fish and coconut candy we'd brought for them, but they were nowhere to be found.

"Guess they're off on some task," Khepri said, shrugging.

We waded out to the grotto and peered into the dark cave.

The walls glittered with bioluminescent moss, and small fish flitted about in water that glowed with an inner light. These fish lights reflected off the surface of the water and projected onto the grotto walls in such a merry brilliance we were rendered momentarily speechless. The effect was magical.

"I think it's empty, let's go farther in," I whispered.

The stone walls enlarged as we went further in, and there was a mild breeze flowing in from the outside.

We explored the entire grotto and found that way in the back the floor of rock under the water, fell away and there was a wide tunnel leading down so deep we couldn't see the bottom.

"Probably drops down a few dozen feet, then heads back out to the deeper water," Caroline guessed.

"So, this is how they get in and out?"

"That's my hunch."

"I'd call that an educated guess."

"Hey, look at this."

Christianne had moved down past the underwater tunnel leading down to the depths and was examining something in the water.

We moved to join her and found ...

"Pearls?"

"I guess so," said Christianne. She nudged her foot, and we saw that the floor of the creek was filled with what looked like pearls, of every shape, size, and color.

Khepri scooped a handful up out of the water and brought them to her face.

"Oooh, these are weird," she said.

"I wonder if these are valuable to the mermaids, or treated like water debris, like sand," I mused.

"The black pearls they brought us were much bigger, I'll bet these are just like the sand, common, and numerous, and look, there's so many of them," Christianne indicated.

After we drifted back to the grotto entrance, we saw more of the small, multicolored pearls, they were everywhere.

"I guess that confirms: There's so many of these smaller ones, I doubt they're valuable to them."

"Let's bring some back to the ship, okay?"

"Don't see why not. Haven't found any treasure to speak of in this grotto, but they're colorful. Kym would probably like them."

We filled a large sack with the baubles and returned to the ship.

That night, we consulted the scroll and discovered that, although we were quite close to the island on the map, it was not the one where we'd landed.

"Do you think the kraken's gone?" Tupu asked, feeling better after her long day of rest.

"Tam tells me it hasn't been sighted since it retreated," I said. "But to be safe, we should hug the coastline of these isles and skirt the deep waters if we can."

The others agreed.

That evening we gathered resources from the little island and loaded the hold with more fish.

"I cannot believe how many fish swim the Mare Nostrum," Jim said.

"Enough to feed us like kings," Tam laughed.

"We'll never starve, that's for sure," said Khepri.

I'd thought Kym would be the happiest to see the small, colorful pearls from the bottom of the grotto stream, but it was actually Tam who exclaimed in glee: "These can be used with the compass to plot our course in coordination with the stars!" Tam took the smallest of the pearly beads and set the compass on the table in the captain's quarters.

I had seen the old brass compass, with its mother-of-pearl face, in Tam's hands before, but he'd mentioned it was incomplete. I now saw why.

The sky was cloudy that night, and the stars were impossible to see, but Tam took a tray, put the open compass at its center, and placed delicate pearls into the middle. Then he waited.

"The pearls will line up with the star constellations and point the way north, even on cloudy days," he whispered.

"How is this possible?" I asked quietly.

"It's a magic compass."

"I see."

We waited.

Slowly, the small balls in pink, yellow, blue and purple, rolled to line up with the meridian, and the way was made clear.

"This is going to make navigation so much easier," smiled Tam.

The next morning found *Pride of the Sea* moving out of the atoll as the mantas pulled the ship round the curved southwestern shore of the little island.

We used the sails to aid in the ship's movement, so the giant manta rays weren't tired out too much; we didn't know if we'd need them to pull us to safety from the kraken again.

The kraken, for its part, was nowhere to be seen.

"Do you think it's gone?" I asked Tam as we stood on the fo'c'sle.

"I'm really not sure, but I hope so. It's very late in the year for the creature to be this far south, as I understand it." He inhaled the sea breeze, closing his eyes.

I laughed. "You love the sea, don't you?"

"Well, it's natural, I guess. I was born at sea." He smiled at me.

Born at sea? I wondered what that could mean. I guessed it meant born on a ship. But just as I was about to ask him what he meant, a sailor came up and drew Tam away with some questions about the ship.

I walked around the deck, watching how we stayed close to the island chain, moving almost directly west, the islands on our starboard side.

The dark waters of the Mare Nostrum, as the sea was called in this vicinity, were ominous and choppy with wind, off our port bow. I watched them uneasily, searching for any sign of the behemoth we had fled from just a few days before.

But there was no sign of the kraken, and it didn't bother us at all, as we sailed on around the island chain, skirting several isthmuses, and coming round near the Carthaga Nova. By the time the sun set, we had our bearings on the other side of the mermaid island. That night, the sailors brought the ship up between the two large islands, and it was after midnight when we came to the second one. Massive mountains on the island's coast came to the water's edge in cliffs that were dark and ominous. The map, however, led us to the other island farther south, thank goodness.

"I don't think there's a place to land even in a rowboat on that first island," Tam said, scratching his head. "In fact, I'm wondering if this mountain chain reaches all around the coast of it."

"Why don't we see?" I suggested. "It's not like we can land and explore here in the middle of the night."

The skies had cleared and the stars shone down on us, and with a nearly full moon, we could easily see the coastline of both islands.

So, we decided to take a few hours and continue up the coast of the mountain-ringed island, as I had come to think of it.

It turned out to be bigger than we had bargained for.

The sea charts were not that clear in this region of the Mare Internum, as the northern part of the Mare Nostrum was called. We continued around the western edge of the mountains until the sun had been in the sky several hours, and saw no end to the huge cliffs.

Tam was right: there was no place to land.

As we turned back to the southernmost island, I watched the mountains on the dark cliffs pass by, and wondered what the island might be hiding. If it was unreachable by ship, whatever was on the island, be it flora or fauna, or strange magical creature, would have lived under total remote concealment.

Isolated, perhaps for millennia.

Chapter Twelve
Lava Tube

As the noon hour approached, we sailed around the horn of the southern island and found landmarks that matched the map. An hour later, we were outfitting ourselves for the adventure ahead.

This outing was anticipated to be a long one. The map showed a clear, long path, on land, to the book.

"We'll likely be gone for a long, long time," I explained to Tam, whom I was leaving in charge. "Possibly weeks. Can you handle that?"

"Please," Tam had smirked and shook his head. "It's no problem. We'll spend the time exercising the horses. Don't worry. I can handle anything. You just take care of each other."

The only thing that worried me was that, the path on the map, that little dotted line that wound its way here and there in curves and curls? It went under the water.

"The path should be a dry one, if this map key is to be believed," Khepri said, studying the scroll.

Some of the markings were quite small, and the scroll was very old. I hoped it was accurate. We decided to bring it with us, but carry it in its brass tubing.

An hour later, we had landed on the beach and were consulting the scroll in the sunshine. It was the six of us, plus we'd brought Jim.

Tupu had insisted on coming.

"I'd like to see any of you try and stop me," she'd said defiantly.

Jim had felt protective of her ever since she'd escaped the siren, so he'd followed us onto the boat, albeit, floating alongside us, his legs crossed in a seated position.

"Jim?" I raised an eyebrow.

"Tupu," he said quietly, blushing.

Tupu patted the djinn's hand fondly. "I might need help with another siren. You never know." She winked at me.

Ah.

So there we were, walking in from the beach, seven adventurers. We'd waved to *Pride of the Sea* as our rowboat slowly approached the shore, and Tam and Akim and the other sailors had waved back.

"Don't get killed!" Tam called, laughing.

Ha ha ha. No chance of that, I thought as we walked into the jungle, my hand resting on the hilt of my scimitar.

We must have walked into the interior about a half mile, with Caroline holding the map and leading the way, when we came to a low cliff leading into a valley on the north side.

Caroline indicated the line on the map, and Khepri, holding the compass had nodded in agreement, so I shrugged and started down the slope, pushing aside tree branches as I came to them. In the large picture of things, this was a drop in the bucket, but I felt I was embarking on the biggest adventure I'd ever been on, and I said so out loud.

"Bigger than Aoudaghost?" asked Kym, her eyebrows raised. She was so proud of her oasis home.

"Maybe," I said.

"No way!" she laughed.

Tupu spoke up then, "Bigger than the Tomb of Ancients?"

"Well ..." I conceded the Tomb had been crazy.

"Wait, wait, wait," Kym put her arms out and stopped. "You cannot tell me that my oasis was not as big an adventure as that dumb Tomb!"

"Jim?" I turned to the djinn, who had been silent for most of the previous hour. "Do you want to defend the adventure into the Tomb of Ancients? That *is* where we found you."

He shrugged. "You only found me in that place because that is where the lamp had been dragged by the last owner. I believe he'd not wanted to share it and so had been buried with it. Which was why the lamp was in the Tomb. Which was very boring for me, at least the last several hundred years. Ghouls are *not* good company, I assure you," laughed Jim.

We hiked through the small valley, and then the map led us to the side of a large hill, where we found ...

"Another grotto?" said Kym. "You're kidding me, right?"

I studied the entrance to the cave, water lapping at the edge. It appeared to be flooded several inches, and there was a pond with a stream running out of it.

Christianne stuck her head in and called back over her shoulder, "It's a spring, just inside the entrance, maybe a dozen feet or less. Come on."

We hiked into the cavern, and the bottom rose up for several dozen feet, leaving the spring and stream behind. We were on dry land.

"This path here," said Kym, "This is where it goes under the sea." She traced the line on the map with her finger to show us, before we entered far into the cavern and the sunlight gave out. We lit the torches we'd brought and continued.

Walking in a few dozen feet, we found our path blocked by a solid wall of rock.

"Hmmm," I said, mostly to myself.

I found a flat, dry, clean part of the trail and spread the scroll out on it, holding my torch close to the section of the map that corresponded to our location.

"Hmmmmm," I said again. Then, "Aha."

I checked it three times before nodding to myself and standing up.

Stowing the scroll away in its brass case and back in my pack, I turned to the stone blocking our path. I walked to the left side, then back along the tunnel a dozen feet, searching low on the wall for the indentation.

Found it!

I held the torch up to the dark crease, and leaned my entire weight on it, and heard a slight '*thunk*' before lifting the inner block up a half inch. I then strode back to the wall of stone, and searched directly to the right of the end of the path.

There it was: a flat stone a bit taller than the rest. I stood on it.

Nothing happened.

I jumped up and down on it a few times.

Nothing.

"Let me try," said Jim, transforming into his djinn form. At nearly ten feet tall, he was a very large glass of water.

I stepped off the flat stone, and he placed both feet on it and waited.

Nothing.

He stretched his huge arms to the cave's ceiling and pushed.

There was a high-pitched creaking, then another low 'thunk,' and the stone pushed in about an inch. Jim stepped off it, changing back into his human form, and we watched the wall of stone blocking our path suddenly, seamlessly fall into the ground and become flush with the rest of the stone at our feet.

I smiled and thanked Jim, patting him on his now human-sized shoulder.

We walked on, our torches held high.

Within a hundred feet, the path turned steeply downward.

"Watch your footing, everyone," I called back over my shoulder.

The tunnel was shaped in an irregular circle, about eight feet in diameter. I was surprised how large it was.

Jim held Tupu's hand as she descended, and Khepri brought up the rear, her scimitar drawn and at the ready.

I led the way, and I found there was dry but slippery land for much of the decent. We took it slowly; it was easy to lose one's footing on the loose soil.

After maybe a hundred fifty feet the slope leveled off and proceeded forward into a huge underground cavern that took the form of a long tunnel.

"It's volcanic," Caroline said.

"What?"

"This tunnel was created when the volcano that made the island erupted," she said. "Tunnels like this are created when lava flows under the surface, where lava has already hardened. This huge, long tube was created when the molten lava was flowing fast; once it slowed, it left this tunnel behind. As the land cooled and began to erode, the tunnel itself was covered by the ocean." Her voice echoed off the stone walls around us.

The tunnel proceeded horizontally under the sea, and it was massive. From floor to ceiling, it was a good thirty or forty feet. I examined the side wall and tapped it with my scimitar. It was solid rock.

"It looks firm and permanent," said Christianne.

"I think it's been here for ages," Khepri said. "The scroll's map is extremely old, and it outlines this tunnel."

"It's probably been here for ten thousand years," said Tupu.

"Probably longer," I said.

I caught Jim's eye as he nodded and mouthed the words, *'longer than that.'*

We walked down the tunnel, awestruck at the size and age of the thing.

"Do you think we're under the water yet," I whispered to Caroline beside me.

"Most assuredly, Miss," said Caroline. She looked around, and put her hands on the walls.

It seemed solid enough.

Our torches were going fine, their flames flickering merrily, throwing all sorts of shapes on the walls, and we walked along at a good clip, wanting to get to the other side of the tunnel before our nerves gave out.

It took a while.

"How long has it been?" Kym asked no one in particular.

"Too long," Tupu answered drily.

We hiked at least an hour under the sea, the uneven floor of the tunnel making us pick our way carefully. But at last, the ground began to slope upwards. It wound around in a curve, then straightened out, and led to what we thought was sea level.

"We're still not out," said Khepri, stating the obvious.

We kept walking.

"We just passed under the beach back there, about ten minutes ago," said Jim. "We're now about a dozen feet above sea level."

"You can tell that?" asked Christianne.

"Well sure, it's a feeling I have. I just know where I am in relation to other landmarks," he said. "Can't you tell that too?"

"No," Christianne said.

"Neither can I," Caroline said.

I could not either, although I did not say so.

"Um," said Kym. We turned to her as we walked along. "I can tell," she said, giving Jim a high five.

I rolled my eyes.

The tunnel sloped up again, and turned in a different direction. Kym and Jim were happy to tell us we were now hiking parallel to the beach.

This went on for another hundred feet, then the path turned inland again.

"Kym, how do you keep your good mood all the time?" I asked, just to break up the monotony of the hike. Plus, my legs were sore and I wanted to get my mind off the pain.

"Charlotte, I was in the oasis for a Very Long Time. I'm just happy to be out and having a grand old adventure with you all," she giggled.

"Um, me too." Jim raised his hand tentatively. I looked back at him.

"I may not show it, but I have been in the best mood of my life ever since you made your wish, Charlotte." He grinned broadly.

I laughed.

I was growing really fond of our friend the djinn.

I glanced back again and caught Tupu smiling at Jim.

Well, perhaps not as fond as Tupu is of him.

I turned back to face front and continued the hike.

We took hours climbing out of the top of that tunnel, and I was sweating profusely by the time it leveled off. Thank goodness the ground had been smooth and the slope gentle as we hiking up toward the mouth of the cave, because we were getting very high up. Soon after the ground leveled off, we sighted the sun.

"Oh, my god, finally," I heard Caroline mumble. Grinning, I picked up the pace, and we were nearly running by the time we emerged out into the open.

We stopped at the cave entrance, to survey our surroundings and get our bearings.

"Huh," I said to no one in particular. "That is a sight."

Spread out before us was the mountain range that ringed the entire island, although I could not see the far ends, they disappeared into the distance.

"This island is huge," said Caroline.

"You're not kidding," I said. "If it wasn't marked as an island on the map, I'd've really wondered."

The cave we'd emerged from was very high up the inside slope of the mountain, and there was a natural plateau where we were standing.

The trees and ferns looked the same as on the other, southern island, but I spotter a few smaller animals in the trees, that I was pretty sure I had never seen before.

The sun shone down hot on our heads, and we were so exhausted that we decided to make camp then and there. We cleared a spot and set up our fire, and each of us laid out our bedding and plopped down. We soon had fish steaks sizzling on sticks propped over the fire, and were discussing our journey so far and what might lie ahead.

116

Chapter Thirteen

Unwelcomed

It was morning, and we were relaxing around our campfire. Kym and Khepri had found some wild carrots and the breakfast fish kebobs we'd cooked over the flames had been colorful and delicious.

"I think we are actually on the rim of the volcano that formed these islands," said Tupu. She indicated the mountain range on the map that matched the geography in front of us.

"The map leads down the eastern side of the inside," I ran my finger down the dotted line on the old parchment, then looked up at the surrounding forest. The area we had reached was represented on the map in a larger cutaway drawing on the side of the scroll. I studied it, committing it to memory, then remembered. "Listen, we need to be especially cautious for whatever we might meet. I heard a jaguar scream last night."

Christianne blinked. "What? I must've been sound asleep; I didn't hear anything."

"Well, it's probably more afraid of us than we are of it," I rolled the map up and reinserted it in its brass tube. "Point is, we should be extra cautious here."

I pulled my scimitar out of its sheath and examined the blade for nicks. Finding none, I nodded, and replaced it carefully back into the leather.

I patted my boot, feeling the dagger there. *The weapon of last resort.*

"Do you think humans have ever been on this island?" Christianne asked.

I smiled grimly at her and shook my head.

"Are you kidding me?" laughed Kym. "There's not a bit of whiff of human anywhere, not a trace."

Jim nodded, giving her a look.

I raised an eyebrow at them, and they both ducked their heads, smiling.

"Charlotte, you must've noticed that humans tend to shape the land to their whims." Kym grinned.

"But, ... so why is it funny, though?" I asked.

"Because we're about to go try and sneak up on some centaurs, that's why," Caroline said.

They were right.

Humans tended to barge in anywhere without caring how things were before they moved in, and immediately start changing everything to suit themselves.

I thought about how we could be more unobtrusive, and came up blank. Turning to Jim and Kym, I asked, "Well, do you have any suggestions?"

They both shrugged, saying nothing.

Christianne spoke then, "Yeah, I have a suggestion." I looked at her and waited. She laughed and said, "Not be here in the first place."

I rolled my eyes.

"Okay, well, that's not going to happen. We're already here. We've agreed to go for the book, a long time ago." I sighed, tired already.

"Kym put her hand up, "I thought of something."

I waited.

"We should try not to disturb the land too much. Try not to bother the animals that live here."

I nodded in agreement.

"And clean our campsites better. Bury the scraps of our meals, cover the cold fires completely," said Kym.

"Leave no trace," Jim said.

"I think those are all great ideas, and sure, we've grown a bit lax in things," I conceded. "Since we're likely the first humans here, let's leave a good impression, people."

Everyone nodded.

"One thing to understand, as well," Jim said. "It's a long way back. A very long way."

"If we have to retreat, we'll be running for hours," Tupu said. "And I don't really run too well these days," she rubbed her belly.

"You have nothing to worry about. I will protect you," Jim whispered as he squeezed her hand.

Christianne smiled.

"Okay, let's get on to the quest. The trail we must blaze is along the side of this mountain," I pointed. "Everyone, keep your eyes peeled for any hint of the centaurs, since we're now in the mountains, I expect we should come across them soon."

We started hiking again, cutting a path when we needed to with our scimitars. I made a mental note to sharpen the sword when we stopped for the night, noting that hacking vegetation would dull the blade. Still, we made some headway, maybe two miles at first. The land was pitched, and we were at a high altitude, so it was slow going.

An hour after we started hiking, we were coming around a copse of trees, and Tupu and I were discussing the animals we'd seen, when an arrow landed in the tree next to her arm, missing her by an inch.

TWANGGG!

The arrow was dark and long, with black fletching and a tiny, razor-sharp arrowhead.

"WHAT THE ...?" I grabbed Tupu and dove for the ground, and we crawled behind the tree to take cover.

Everyone was huddling behind the several large trees next to us.

We didn't make a sound.

I saw Christianne make a 'huh??' gesture with her shoulders. I had no answers.

Then it came to me: The centaurs! 'The horsemen of the mountains' indicated on the scroll.

We stayed behind the trees for several seconds; then I could wait no longer.

"Centaurs! We come in peace and mean you no harm!" I called out.

No reply.

Nothing.

I tried again. "We bring gifts for you, we come in peace!" I called out.

Silence.

I took a deep breath.

"Miss," Caroline whispered. "Perhaps if we tried ..."

She didn't have a chance to finish her sentence, leaving me to wonder what she was going to say, because at that moment she was interrupted quite abruptly by another arrow.

THWUMP!

This one landed less than an inch from my boot.

"Hey!" I said. I was getting angry at how close the arrows were, and how we were being treated.

"Why you try to shoot us?!" I hollered.

"Miss, shhhh," Caroline whispered.

"I will not shush, Carrie."

"Miss, please ..."

I tightened my lips in a thin line and scowled.

I waited a few minutes.

"Carrie," I whispered, "they could have killed us. Did you see how close those arrows came?"

"Exactly, Miss."

"What exactly?"

"I don't think they had to miss."

"Will you two shush?" came Khepri's whisper.

"Oh, come on, Carrie!"

TWANG   THWUMP   THWANG!!!!
Thutthutthutthutthut

Arrows flew all around us, sticking in trees and the dirt and the roots of the trees in the dirt, and ... just everywhere. The arrows all came within a few inches of us; in fact, there was an arrow outline of my head in the tree above me. I gulped, my eyes wide.

I held my breath.

Caroline made a 'See??!' gesture.

Jim and Tupu had had enough. They both rose to a crouch and ran back the way we'd come. Christianne and Kym followed closely behind.

Caroline and Khepri and I shrugged and followed them.

No more arrows came, thank goodness. I was almost waiting for one to be shot in my rear end as I ran, awkwardly, while in a crouch.

We ran over a mile down the way we'd come, and I had a stitch in my side by the time we stopped.

Jim and Tupu had taken cover behind a large boulder, a massive black rock that was half covered in soil and underbrush. They'd run across an open area before heading up a small rise and behind the boulder.

We all gathered there, breathing hard. I didn't remember ever running that fast.

I sat down, a little too hard, hurting my rump, and turned, my hands on the ground, to look back the way we'd come.

The open expanse was clear; nothing moved. I looked a ways farther and saw them.

Or rather, saw what they allowed us to see.

A lone centaur stood just before the next line of trees. He was huge, his well-muscled form, looking extremely intimidating; the bow he held cocked with an arrow pointed in our direction must have been six feet long.

"Oh, shit!" I ducked back around the boulder, worried he'd let the arrow fly.

The message was clear: Go away.

Chapter Fourteen

Hidden from Man

Lord almighty, what a start with the centaurs. We decided to back up all the way to our campsite the night before, so we hiked back to the entrance of the lava tube, and settled down to discuss what had happened.

"See?" Kym said, kicking at the fish bones half buried in the ashes from the fire last night.

"I think Kym might have a point," Caroline said, bending over to gather up the bones.

Khepri dug a hole in the ground, and we buried all the trash from the night before, then settled down for a second time in that spot.

"It's still hours before sunset," I said, squinting at the sky. I wondered if we shouldn't have tried harder with the centaurs.

As if reading my mind, Khepri came and sat beside me.

"They rained arrows down on us, Charlotte. I think we did the best thing by retreating. Let's try and figure this out."

"Let's make a plan," said Tupu, "instead of barreling right into their territory."

"Agreed," Kym said. "This is their home, after all."

"And they probably haven't ever seen a human before."

"We hiked in so fast, and they treated us as intruders. *Quelle surprise.*"

"Well, should we have snuck in?"

"If we had sent just one of us, they'd've come back full of arrows."

"We *all* nearly came back full of arrows!"

"I think if they'd wanted us to be stuck full of arrows, they'd've stuck us full of arrows."

"They knew exactly what they were doing."

"I think that was actually not such a bad outcome."

"What? Are you kidding me?"

"No, I'm not kidding you."

"Seriously, she's right. We have no lasting injuries."

"We could've been killed."

"No lasting injuries? What about my nerves?"

"You're fine, Miss."

"Charlotte is right, I feel lucky to still have my wits about me."

"You never had your wits about you to begin with."

"Yes, I did!"

"Girl, you barely made it through back to this campsite."

"Oh, shut up."

"Hey, hey, HEY!" we all looked at Kym. "I have a question," she said when she had our attention.

"What, sweetie?"

"Why are we even here?" asked Kym.

We all blinked at her in surprise. We'd discussed this weeks ago.

"What I mean is, are we trying to steal the book?"

My brow wrinkled in confusion.

"I mean, is it theirs? Maybe they're guarding it." She sat back.

Huh.

"Okay, well, first of all, Kym, we are on a quest to retrieve *The Book of Mysteries*, because," I held my finger up to stop her speaking. "BECAUSE, see, because we found this map ..."

"*I* found the scroll," she scowled.

I nodded. "Yes, you found the scroll, Kym. But we discussed this and we all agreed to go on this quest ..."

"I *know*," said Kym. "What I mean is, when we started out, we thought it was just some buried treasure. But now we have people shooting arrows at us. What if the book is *theirs?*"

I blinked.

"Okay, I understand what she's saying," said Caroline, "but Kym, *The Book of Mysteries* was written for humans. It said so right on the scroll."

"No, it said it was *hidden* from humans, so they didn't start a war over it."

We all started talking at once then, and I waited a few minutes before holding up my hand.

"Shush, everyone." I turned to Kym. "Sweetheart," I gently took hold of her hand, trying to keep her attention on my words. "There are a great many people in this world who are sick. Ill with some of the most devastating diseases known to man. Cancer, leprosy, ailments of the lungs, ailments of the skin, ailments of the womb, ailments of the brain, ailments of the eyes, Kym, so, so many sick people. And they're suffering. If we retrieve this book maybe we could help some of them."

"The book is also fabled to contain the secrets of navigating the stars and heavens," said Khepri. "It may contain the secrets of how people might be able to fly in the sky, like birds or butterflies."

"I guess I understand why you want to find it so bad," Kym said quietly.

I worried I had overwhelmed the chimera. "Kym, let's try and find a way to talk with the centaurs, shall we? I think that would be a good first step. We certainly don't mean to steal anyone's property."

"No, no we don't."

"Not at all."

"We are not thieves."

"Shush, remember us taking pocketfuls of loot from that Tomb."

"That was different."

Oh, god.

I rubbed my temples.

"Khepri, let's get another fire built, I'm hungry from all that running," I said softly.

"And from getting shot at."

"Shush, can't you see she's stressed out?"

"Yeah, so am I. Nearly getting an arrow shot up my ass did that."

"Shhhh!"

An hour later, a new fire was made, more fish and wild carrot kebobs were roasting, and I was feeling a tiny bit more relaxed. Caroline broke out the blackroot and passed it around. I wasn't sure how helpful it would be to be stoned if the centaurs decided to bring their bows and arrows and use us as target practice, but I took the proffered twig and began to chew on it.

I felt immediately better. We all did. That was good stuff.

Then Jim did something that helped some more. A lot more.

He produced a small flute and began to play it. The sweet lilting sound calmed everyone down and, with the blackroot, seemed to clear our minds and hearts of the panicked feeling that had flooded us earlier.

"Now, everyone, let's start at the beginning," I said softly, and withdrew the brass tube from my pack.

I spread the scroll out on the ground. It was rather large, so I was grateful when Tupu and Kym came and placed large rocks at the four corners. I bent down and began to examine the markings on the scroll again.

Caroline brought her torch close to the parchment so I could see better.

"Careful," Khepri cautioned.

Caroline nodded at her; she would be careful. Then she put her finger to her lips and turned to watch me.

I decided to start at the beginning again. *Maybe I missed something.* I cleared my throat and began to read.

" 'Be warned, traveler, for man,' " here I stopped, then continued. " 'for man was never meant to know all the knowledge of the ancients, which came to earth from beyond the stars'." I took a deep breath. *Be warned, traveler, for man was never meant to know all the knowledge of the ancients, which came to earth from beyond the stars.*

What could it mean?

I began to read more, " 'It is foretold that man will wage war to fight for possession of the Book, and that this war will devastate life on earth'." I swallowed. This sounded dangerous. " 'Therefore, *The Book of Mysteries* has been hidden from man, so that his life may be preserved; hidden away and guarded, by the horsemen of the mountains.' "

'Hidden from man.'

Hidden from man.

Oh, my god.

It slowly dawned on me, and I raised my head from the study of the scroll, and looked at my companions.

They were all focused on me, staring at me, and seemed to be holding their breath.

I said it out loud, unsure if it meant anything. *But I think it does,* I thought.

"Hidden from man," I said.

They all looked at me.

"Man," I repeated.

I looked pointedly at Caroline. "What does the word 'man' usually mean, Carrie?" I could always count on Caroline to remember a page out of a textbook, she'd learned from the palace scholars just as well as I did, heck, she sat next to me during every lesson.

" 'Human'," she promptly recited from memory. "The term 'man' usually designates any or all of the human race, regardless of gender or age. Traditionally, the word 'man' refers to the species, to mankind as a whole."

"To mankind as a species," I repeated, smiling.

They blinked at me, not understanding.

Then Caroline said, "Ohhh ..."

I shifted my stare to only Kym and Jim, who were seated next to each other, tilted my head to the side and raised my eyebrows.

Mankind. Humans.

"Kym, Jim; you are not human," I said, smiling at them.

"So," Kym said slowly, "the book is not hidden from nonhumans?"

"I'm not sure," I said, biting off another inch of the blackroot. "But I suspect that it is you two, our nonhuman friends, who will be able to approach the centaurs without getting shot at."

I smiled and raised my eyebrows, as they finally understood.

Chapter Fifteen

Centaurs from the Stars?

We stayed up making plans well into the night, and my heart raced with excitement. *This just had to work,* I thought. It was my only idea, my only plan. I fell asleep next to Caroline, our backs against each other, whispering back and forth, remembering our lessons on the different species, until we both fell to sleep, yawning.

The morning found us wide awake and preparing for the centaurs. We'd approach them again, but this time we'd hoped to be more successful.

"Khepri, Tupu, help me out here," said Caroline, covering the campfire with dirt and leaves from the forest floor.

We buried every last speck of our dinner scraps, leaving no trace. We were determined to do this properly, even if it had taken us a do-over to get things right.

Jim and Kym stood off to the side, whispering. When we were ready, our packs on our backs, they turned to us.

"Charlotte, please stay way back, and protect Tupu." Jim smiled, then corrected himself: "Protect *everyone*, okay?"

I nodded.

"We want you to stay here while we attempt this," stated Kym.

"But what if you need our help?" said Tupu and Christianne, at the same time.

I smiled.

In reply, Jim and Kym both started to transform.

In a shimmer of the air, like the space above a campfire, Kym's little-girl form blurred, and suddenly the chimera was standing before us in all her magnificence. Next to her, blue, purple and green, standing nearly ten feet tall, was the djinn.

"Okay, point taken," Tupu laughed.

They would not need help.

We watched as the two magnificent magical beings, our friends, walked down the hill and across the short valley, and up into the trees. We lost sight of them then, and I had to resist the urge to walk after them.

A few hours later, they returned.

We were sitting in a circle, playing a fist game Caroline had remembered from her childhood, called *Down Down the Breezy Way*. It consisted of waving the right fist, tapping it against the left, saying the words '*down down the breezy way*', and then at the last moment, covering the fist with the left hand, and opening a number of fingers out under the left palm. The other players had to guess how many fingers were held up. The trick was that you had to hold up just one more, or one less finger than you had the previous time, if no one had guessed correctly then. There was guesswork and also mathematics involved, and we were soon laughing at the way Christianne kept winning.

"Charlotte," came the voice of the djinn, deep and booming.

I whirled around and scrambled to my feet in surprise.

The djinn and the chimera had just walked into our campsite, and they weren't alone.

The centaurs with them were magnificent. There were four of them, all huge, all manifesting the strong, muscular bodies of massive steeds, bigger than Shêtân, bigger even than the enormous shire horses we had back in Swerighe to pull the heavy plows and the great wagons loaded down with grain.

The first centaur was black as night, and looked so shiny and beautiful, I blushed. He held his tail in a proud arch as he approached. His arms and chest were heavily tattooed in patterns of raised black swirls, and the dark skin showed the design off beautifully.

The second centaur was bronze in color, a rich and rosy chestnut-gold hue that shone like the sun. His hooves and mane were darker, almost red in color, and his long lashes shaded brilliant green eyes. He was smiling.

The third and fourth centaurs were white, their bodies polished to a shiny effulgence, and their manes and tails were an almost silvery white. These two stayed to the side of the other centaurs, almost like guards. Their demeanor was one of polite curiosity.

Out of the chests of the centaurs' horse bodies, grew powerful robust humanoid torsos, the muscled six packs standing out, and the broad shoulders with huge brawny arms crossed in front of them proudly. Their great bows and quivers full of deadly arrows were strapped on their backs. Their long hair was tied back in wide plaits, which continued down their back, and ended with tails that reached to the ground. Their handsome features were arranged in deadly serious expressions, although their glower did not frighten me. These were emissaries of a new kingdom, and they held the gravity of the occasion in every movement they made. It was plain to see this was a very proud people.

I brushed myself off and walked forward, then bowed deeply.

The djinn and the chimera came forward and stood between us and the centaurs, but to the side, and made introductions.

"Princess Charlotte, may I present Evys Iilcendorr, leader of the centaur tribe," The djinn bowed and indicated the jet-black centaur, who came forward then, and extended his right front hoof and bowed deeply, his torso bending forward far enough so that his forehead touched the knee of his extended leg.

I bowed as well, lifting my face back up to see the djinn smile approvingly.

"And this is the assistant to the Evys, Kiphaentren," the djinn indicated the chestnut centaur beside Iilcendorr, who bowed as well. I bowed in return.

"And these are the guards to Evys Iilcendorr, Rhalofetorr," the djinn indicated the white centaur on the left, "and Glynbelarr," he indicated the centaur on the right.

I bowed deeply to both centaurs.

"Prrincess Charrlotte," Evys Iilcendorr spoke with a very thick accent, rolling his R's and spiking his T's and it was charming. "Will you and yourr esteemed parrty please honorr us by joining us at ourr evening meal?" He bowed again, closing his eyes, his dark head and chest coming down, his arm folding in front of him.

"I would be our privilege, Evys Iilcendorr," I bowed again.

I glanced at the chimera, who had stayed silent throughout this formal conversation, and I would have sworn she winked at me, and smiled. I took a deep breath and smiled back, nodding. Then I turned to the others, my eyebrows raised.

I introduced everyone, and the centaurs seemed very happy to bow to each of us. We gathered up our packs and headed out.

Evys Iilcendorr led the way, followed by Kiphaentren, then Kym, still in her chimera form, then all of us in the troupe, then Jim, still in his djinn form. The two white centaurs, Rhalofetorr and Glynbelarr brought up the rear.

It was a Very Impressive Procession that hiked into the centaur village as the sun descended into the evening sky.

Dusk came early to this mountain-ringed island, and we were soon gathered around a huge fire in the center of town, seated on cushions, and provided with succulent meats and breads. Rabbit meat was roasted expressly for us. Kiphaentren had sent out his hunters, who had returned not long after with a half-dozen field dressed rabbit carcasses.

"They constantly invade our crops, stealing food," Glynbelarr had assured us. "Trust me, we are happy to thin the rabbit population to provide you with a hearty meal."

We sat and ate, making new friends in the centaur tribe, until we were full and laughing, exchanging stories with them all, and getting better acquainted. At last, everything settled down, and Iilcendorr rose from his center spot, and came to sit next to me.

He folded his legs under him delicately, and got comfortable. He seemed to look at me expectantly, and finally said, "Jim tells me you have many questions?" His eyebrow rose in query.

"Yes, thank you, Iilcendorr," I said. "Actually, we have come to your beautiful land on a quest, a quest for a very important item, and I wonder if you have ever heard of ..."

"*The Book of Mysteries*," he finished.

I nodded. "So, Jim already told you of this?"

"Yes, he did mention it. But we have already heard of this tome. It is part of our legends," said Iilcendorr. "In fact, it is our main legend. It is why we are here."

We talked long into the night. It turned out, *The Book of Mysteries* was the object of some major taboos in the centaurs' culture.

First and foremost was a strict prohibition against even going near it. Iilcendorr pointed to the far north of the island, to the largest of the mountains, and said they were cautioned against going anywhere near it.

"So, we have limited our crops to the southwestern part of the valley, you see. Actually very near where you first emerged from the Forbidden Caves."

"The Forbidden Caves?" asked Christianne.

Iilcendorr turned to her. "So named because we are forbidden to enter them."

"Iilcendorr, it sounds like your tribe is forbidden from doing quite a lot of things," Tupu said, looking sad. "Who made these taboos?"

"They have been in place for as long as we can remember. They are part of our culture. But they have limited us greatly."

"Can you explain more?" Caroline asked. "Was it your ancestors who made these taboos?"

"Oh, no, they were in place long before our ancestors walked the land. The Others made these rules, and we have always been warned to obey them," Iilcendorr said.

"Who are. Uh, were The Others?" I asked.

"The Others were like us," Iilcendorr placed his fingertips on his chest, "but they were from the stars." Here he pointed his other hand up to the night sky.

I looked up involuntarily. The sky was clear, and a million stars winked back at us as we watched. There were several lit arcs flaming across the sky. I had heard these shooting stars were magical portents of wondrous things to come.

Wondrous or terrible, I reminded myself.

I turned back to Iilcendorr. "Do you know why the book was brought here?"

He shook his head. "We do not know. We only know that we are to not only stay away from the place it is hidden, but we are also to guard it against any enemy who might visit the island to steal it."

"Oh, I assure you, we are not your enemy," Khepri said from my side.

"Oh, I know," said Iilcendorr. "You see, no one has ever come, not in a thousand generations. We realize now that our ancestors may have misread the warning. It was carried to us on flaming wood that has long since crumbled to dust." He looked at us kindly. "Princess Charlotte, we are trapped on this island. My people believe that if we leave the book unguarded, and leave the island, we will perish."

"Oh, my god," I mumbled.

"We have been here on the island for thousands of generations," said Iilcendorr. "It has gotten harder and harder to survive. We plant our crops, but the rabbits have multiplied until now there are so many that they eat much of the grain. Our stores this past winter were devastated, and this summer has produced only two-thirds of what we need to survive."

A small centaur child came up to us then, and handed me a sprig of green alfalfa grass, a long stalk of flowering buds reaching up two feet into the sky. I smiled gratefully and took it, put the end in my mouth and began chewing it. It was sweet and nutty and delicious. "Yum!" I smiled at Iilcendorr.

"Our population has been steadily decreasing in the past few decades, because of this problem. We hunt the rabbits and try to stamp them out, but we kill one and ten more pop up to take its place."

"Mmmm. Yes. We had a similar problem where I come from. Damn rabbits breed like crazy. For two years, our government encouraged the population to eat rabbit as our main source of meat, instead of beef. Not that I minded: Roast rabbit is delicious." I took another bite out of a new wild carrot and rabbit kebob Caroline handed me.

Iilcendorr got quiet then and leaned over toward us. "The truth is, I am tired of my tribe living in fear. We fear leaving the island, we fear retrieving the book, we fear running out of food, we fear what might happen if we stop guarding the book. It's exhausting and no way to live." He sighed, a sad and serious look on his handsome face.

I thought for a moment. "What do you mean, 'if we stop guarding the book'?"

"Our ancestors taught us that if we leave the book unguarded, we will die off as a people. We guard the entrance to its location. We have for a thousand years. We station five armed guards there, around the clock. We used to post only one, but about eighty years ago, the relief came for their shift and found the guard gone. We have no idea what happened to him. He was never found. Ever since, we post five guards, for their own safety."

My heart beat faster. "So, you know the location of *The Book of Mysteries*?"

Iilcendorr held up a finger. "We know the location of the entrance," he clarified.

"The entrance?" asked Caroline.

"Yes. There is only one way in," Iilcendorr explained. "Our legends say the way is filled with hardships and travails, and hidden dangers. It is said to be a long journey down, after one enters," He sat back.

Khepri turned to me and whispered in my ear, "I wonder what he means by 'a long journey down'?"

I shrugged but smiled at our hosts, and finished eating more rabbit kebobs than I had ever eaten in one sitting in my life.

"Iilcendorr," I said at one point, "Your legends are very messed up if they say you must guard the book or die off as a people. If follows from there that the only reason you exist is to guard the book."

The black centaur nodded sagely. "We have come to terms with the legends, and we know to value ourselves for our own art, knowledge, and storytelling, but there are some of us, mostly the elders, who cling to the old ways, and insist the reason we were put here on the island is to guard the book, and that we must continue to do this until the end of time."

"So, if the lore of your people says it was the Others who brought the book from the stars, but that they were like you, were the Others centaurs?" Christianne asked.

"Because it has been so long, we do not know for sure, but we believe so, yes," said the centaur.

Centaurs from the stars, I thought that night as I drifted off to sleep in the centaur village. I was unable to imagine centaurs from the stars, try as I might.

Chapter Sixteen

The Centaurs' Solution

The next morning found me up early and out by the fire. Caroline was already there, brewing some coffee, and I gratefully accepted a cup from her. We chatted for a while, until Iilcendorr approached us. I was happy to see him, because sleeping on our situation – and the situation facing the centaurs – had filled my mind with questions. There was one big one, in particular, and I knew Iilcendorr was the one to ask.

"How did you sleep, Princess?" The tall, ebony centaur stood magnificently against the dawn sky as he looked down at me.

"Oh, I was quite comfortable. Thank you and your village for the hospitality," I smiled. "I was wondering, sir, a question. After all that was revealed last night, and there was a significant amount of information exchanged, would you humor me?"

"Walk with me, Princess."

"Okay, but only if you call me Charlotte," I said.

He nodded and smiled.

We walked down the center of the village, where the people were just waking up and getting ready for their day. Children ran back and forth, bringing water, playing together, and, the older ones, gathering at the central elder's classroom.

They had explained last night that knowledge and wisdom was imparted from elders to children, and that every day, every event, held lessons.

Iilcendorr had further pointed out that yesterday's encounter with our troupe would provide lessons for at least a week, probably longer. And that was even before any more time and integration occurred. Today would likely add more things for the young centaurs to learn, to grow with.

I smiled and laughed as two young colts passed a ball made of leaves between themselves, and at one point, throwing it to Iilcendorr; he tossed it back playfully. *These people lead rich lives,* I thought. *They deserve to expand and spread out from this island.*

"Iilcendorr, you stated last night that there are many legends and taboos surrounding the book we seek. I am curious: Why did you allow contact between us and your village after speaking to the djinn and the chimera?"

"Charlotte! Charlotte!" Kym came running up to us. "Glynbelarr says he will take me to see the crop fields, and that you should come, too!" she stopped and put her hands on her knees and stood panting, waiting for my response.

I laughed. "Did you run a long way?"

"Sort of. Well, yes," she looked sheepish.

"Did you already go see the crops, Kym?

"Yes," she looked down, then back up at me. "Charlotte, you must come and see! Caroline and Christianne are already there, it's incredible!"

I turned to Iilcendorr. "It seems we are being diverted."

He laughed. "I'll come with you."

We turned and walked the other way. I was learning that the centaurs trotted nearly everywhere. I had to run to keep up. Or run and then walk and then jog. My pace varied so I could keep up with them. Kym was already running far ahead of me.

The sun was rising in the sky, and it looked like the day would be warm. I tied my hair in a ponytail as I walked, and felt instantly cooler. As we made our way, Khepri emerged from her door and joined us.

"I slept really well, how about you, Charlotte?"

"Sound as a baby," I laughed. I started trotting after Iilcendorr, as the centaur had pulled ahead of us. We jogged after him and got a good workout, and it felt wonderful to stretch my legs.

We finally emerged in a valley we hadn't seen before, and it was incredible. The huge expanse of land had been cultivated into separate patches of large gardens.

Several fields of alfalfa and oats grew alongside one another. They appeared as brilliant patches of soft gold that swayed back and forth in the breeze. The alfalfa was starting to turn a soft, pale green, with tiny purple buds flowering on the fragrant plants. The oats' small gold grains shivered in the gentle wind, creating a tinkling sound as we passed. It was a merry tone that reminded me of childhood.

There were fields of grapes, climbing up trellises more than ten feet high, with ripe bunches of the fruit growing on the thick vines. The whole effect was very colorful; the light green, almost the color of the inside of limes, contrasted beautifully with the multicolored grape, which varied from green and yellow, to different shades of pink, to red, then darker red, and all the way on to a light purple that reminded me of the flowering oats, to a darker purple that hinted of the plum trees back home. The grapes looked like multi-colored jewels in a field of peridot.

Iilcendorr was in good humor and allowed Kym to lead the way and show me all the things she had discovered. At our next stop, we saw carrots and strawberries. More brilliant green and darker green, they grew in alternate rows and made for a beautiful design across the acres. The centaurs working the fields handed us samples, and I closed my eyes in ecstasy at the glorious warm sweetness of the most delicious strawberries I had ever tasted. The carrots were varying hues of purple, black, and orange, and rivaled the grapes for their diversity of color.

In a field next to the strawberries, we saw massive blueberry bushes interspersed with raspberry and blackberry bushes. The entire plot of land was a mass of green leaves interspersed with different types of berries, changing row by row. I counted what seemed to be seven different types. A centaur tending the field handed us huge, plump blackberries that stained our hands as we gobbled them up. They were so ripe they nearly collapsed in our mouths, relieved to hand over copious amounts of the rich, dark sweet liquid that ran down our throats like nectar.

Among the vast fields of fruit trees, my favorite were the sweet cherry trees. The plump, bright red cherries with their firm, sweet meat were so good I ate a second helping. They were delicious! I realized the centaurs were masters of food cultivation, and especially fruit horticulture. I felt dazzled at all I'd seen.

"This farm is amazing," I marveled.

"Oh, there are many other farms across the island," said Iilcendorr, "this is simply the one closest to our village."

I turned to him; my eyebrow raised.

"And ours is not the only centaur village," he smiled.

We toured the farm for hours, until it was well past the high noon hour and our stomachs had begun to complain. Seeing all the food, taking small nibbles and samples here and there, was fascinating, but we were ready for a break.

"Let's just rest over here," Iilcendorr indicated an open-air amphitheater enclosed by a large trellis with dark full-leafed ivy growing over it. Several centaurs were already eating, and several others were preparing the meals.

There we were served the most magnificent fruit and leafy vegetable salads, adorned with pineapples and blueberries and cheese.

"What kind of cheese is this?" I asked, savoring another bite.

The centaurs pointed across the valley to a low-lying, open-walled building housing several dozen goats, and I laughed in delight.

"You have a very healthy diet. I am impressed, my friends."

The centaurs all grinned and seemed very happy with the compliment, then handed us cups full of fermented juice that tasted very much like mead.

It was very, very good.

As we ate, I tried to steer the conversation to its earlier topic.

Why had the centaurs welcomed us after Jim and Kym had presented our case?

We all indulged our appetites, and my own stomach felt utterly engorged, and I broached the subject again with Iilcendorr.

"Sir, I know your guards first shot at us because of the legends and taboos that charge your people with guarding the book."

He nodded, nibbling on a bright red plum.

I smiled and continued, "I was just wondering, what made you allow us to meet with you and your village, after speaking with our friends Kym and Jim?"

He leaned back on the cushions where we were seated and considered my question. Finally, he leaned his head forward and spoke. "Charlotte, so much time has passed since the Others charged us with guarding the book. We have had lifetimes to consider the implications of this task, and our elders realized long ago that it was harming our tribe by isolating us from those who might be friends or allies." He gestured toward our group. "While we understand the deep taboos surrounding the book and its legends, we grew to realize that, unless we became flexible with this guardianship, we as a people might very well perish here, without anyone knowing we ever existed."

I nodded, trying to understand his point of view.

"So," he continued, "After seeing your djinn and chimera friends, who we were extremely happy to see, by the way, and after consulting for over an hour with the elders of the village, we realized the good fortune of your arrival."

He smiled.

I waited.

He leaned forward, suddenly deadly serious.

"We want you to remove the book from our island."

Chapter Seventeen
Altered Legends

"Y ou want us to what?" *Had I drunk too much mead?*

I started again. "Iilcendorr, you just told us all about how you have all these customs about protecting the book, and now you want us to remove it? To do that, we'll have to go *get* the book, you realize?"

He nodded. "Charlotte, as long as the book is here, we're trapped. Eventually, we will die out, and the book will be unguarded and defenseless. We trust the djinn and the chimera; they alone are strong enough to ..."

A group of centaurs ran up in a gallop just then, and skidded to a halt, with Rhalofetorr at their head. He glanced at me, then hurried whispered to Iilcendorr, who immediately jumped up, looking shocked.

"Princess, er, I mean Charlotte, I must leave you now. We have an emergency."

"What is it? Maybe we can help." I motioned for the others to come with me as I followed alongside the large black centaur.

"Perhaps," he said, before galloping off.

We ran. Sprinting after a bunch of centaurs isn't a task for human legs. I ran like the wind, the others following me. Past all the groves and fields of crops, down the long path back to the village, I urged my body forward as fast as I could.

Still, we lost them.

As we ran back to the village, though, we could see other centaurs who'd just gotten word of whatever was the matter, and who were hastening down a new path we'd never been down. Figuring this was the way, we ran after them.

Within ten minutes the path led to some cliffs, and our ears were filled with the roaring of a massive waterfall. We ran around a corner and saw the huge cascade, and what looked like the whole village gathered there.

Adrenaline does interesting things to the body, including lending it extra energy for emergencies. I had just run several miles, and I was not the least winded.

We hurried up to the front to see what we could find out.

Spread out before us was quite a scene.

A young colt was lain out on the rocks under the side of the waterfall, approximately halfway down the high cliff.

He looked to be about fifty feet from the top rocks, and about a hundred feet from the bottom, where sharp, deadly boulders rested, sprayed dark wet by the water crashing down from above. The boy was bleeding from a bad gash on his foreleg, and he appeared unconscious. A centaur I assumed was his mother was kneeling by the cliff edge, crying into her hands. Several other centaurs stayed with her, trying to console her.

Nearby, a huge centaur lay on his side, breathing hard, bleeding from the head.

"He tried to reach the colt, but fell," someone said nearby.

I turned to Khepri. "Tend to the adult, I will try to reach the child," reaching in my pack for my leather gloves and a rope.

Always keep rope handy.

Khepri handed me a blanket, "This will come in handy."

Tupu touched my shoulder. "Charlotte, I'm the best climber you've got, I will go with you."

I gave her a quick nod and turned to the cliff edge, my thoughts on how I would reach the hurt child.

The waterfall dropped from over a hundred and fifty feet high and was deafening. Vegetation grew right up to the rock and trees overhung the edges of the cliff and waterfall.

The water was flowing very fast, and the rock looked rough and coarse, but it was a dark reddish-brown igneous rock that would provide plenty of footholds.

I just had to hold on, grip the rock tight, and not slip.

Easy as pie, Charlotte.

I eyed a good spot to start, and jumped.

"Don't fall, Charlotte!" Christianne and Kym laughed. I smiled. There was no way I was going to fall, and they knew it. I waved my hand at them, then looked at Tupu and smiled. She and I were very good at rock climbing. This rescue would be a piece of cake.

Tupu jumped behind me, and we both landed on the large outcropping a few feet from the edge. Grabbing the rock face, I eyed the next step.

"How about that one?" Tupu pointed at a small ledge farther up. I nodded and reached for the edge. I had to stand on tiptoe, but I was able to grab it and hoist myself up.

We had to grapple over the next several feet but made it fine to a long ledge where we had some space to work.

The colt was in sight, but we still had to get past a large overhang that stood between us and our objective. I ran and jumped, grabbing hold of the rough rock. My hands in the gloves gripped it well, and I said a silent *thank you* for the volcanic rock face. Igneous rock was one of the easiest surfaces to climb, but it was also one of the most treacherous if one were to fall. The rough surface both gripped your hand and footholds, but also readily ripped flesh from bone when one fell from it.

I was three feet from the ledge where the child lay. I hopped up and grabbed it, hoisting myself up. My leather chaps over my heavy woven pants protected my knees from getting torn up as I lifted my body up to the ledge.

I could see how it would be nearly impossible for the centaurs to mount a rescue; they were much larger than a human, plus their hooves would likely slip on the rock, and they had no clothing to protect themselves from the sharp and unforgiving surface.

I stood on the ledge and reached over, pulling Tupu up beside me. The injured centaur colt lay next to us; I bent down to examine him, and he groaned.

"Hi," I said softly.

He opened his eyes and saw us, then opened his eyes even wider.

"You ... you're ... you're the New Ones that came."

"We are."

"It hurts," he said weakly, dropped his head back down to the rock.

"We're going to get you out of here, little one. Just hold tight."

I unrolled the rope I'd slung over my back, tying one end securely to the rockface above us. Turning to look back over to the side of the cliff where Caroline and Christianne waited, I wondered if it might be too far to throw.

"The waterfall wind will make it harder to reach them with the rope, let me take it back over," Tupu said, close to my ear.

I nodded and handed her the end loop.

"Make sure you have enough play to make it across."

She nodded and estimated and unraveled maybe fifteen feet, then let out another five, before securing the loop to her back. Nodding to me, she started out back the way we'd come.

I knelt down next to the child and unfolded the blanket Khepri had handed me. I spread it out on the rock and carefully eased the injured colt onto it, gathered the corners around him and tied them tightly together. Then I waited.

Tupu was nearly there, and I watched her scamper across the rock with ease.

Boy, she wasn't kidding.

Then she was across and had the rope tied to a tree within minutes. The centaurs had seen what she was doing, and had come forward to help. Then they all waited on the bank of the waterfall ravine, watching me.

Tupu gave me a wave. The rope was secured; it was time to bring the injured centaur across.

Bending down to the blanket-bundled youth, I patted his shoulder, then lifted him up onto my lap. I tied a loop of rope around the secured blanket knot and then around the rope strung across to the other side. The rope bowed a bit, but Tupu had tied it tight enough, and it was taut, strong, and secure. The blanket bundle sway there as I held it.

I looked into the young centaur's face.

"Ready?"

He nodded nervously. I patted his shoulder and climbed up beside him, my legs crooked over the rope, my hands gripping it tight.

We eased out over the air. The waterfall sprayed a fine mist into our faces, and the boy closed his eyes and turned his head.

I pushed the bundle ahead of me. It was slick enough so that it slid when I pushed it, but not on its own.

Good. I crept along the rope, pushing the young centaur ahead of me, and inch by inch we made our way across. It took a while, but the sling finally came close to the place where the centaurs had gathered below, and arms reached out and grasped the sling. Seconds later, the child was in the arms of his mother.

I dropped my feet to the ground and brushed my hands off, and Tupu was there, patting me on the back and making me grin like an idiot from ear to ear.

Khepri had instructed the large centaur to be moved back to the village, and waved to the others that the colt should be taken there as well.

"I need an antiseptic room to work," she said, following the procession back down the path.

Back at the village, Khepri was led into a large room with covered tables, where her two patients were gently laid.

"I'll assist," said Kym, washing her hands alongside the healer.

We retreated outside to let them work in peace.

The villagers stayed huddled outside the hut, waiting with us.

"Most of the time when we have an injury like that, the centaur dies of the heat infection," Iilcendorr said, next to us.

"Please tell me you're kidding," said Caroline. "Sepsis is a horrible way to die."

Christianne stood up them. "Who would like to begin training as a healer?" She called to the crowd at large.

Four centaurs raised their hands and came forward. She beckoned them and nodded at me, then entered the medical tent, as I was mentally referring to it.

I turned to Iilcendorr. "She will teach them. And Kym and Khepri will show them too."

Iilcendorr seemed in awe.

"In the past, our traditions held that only the strong should survive. Those who were injured were seen as weak. It was a big problem."

I could not believe my ears. "I can see how that *would* be a *huge* problem." Turning to look into his eyes, I spoke solemnly. "You should know that a warrior can have a great injury, and be nursed back to health to fight another day, as strong as ever. I, myself, have been injured many times, and was once weak as a kitten and close to death." I turned and gestured to the medical tent. "Khepri healed me and nursed me back to full health and vigor."

He raised his eyebrows, and looked happy. "I am glad you did not die of your injuries, Charlotte. I think we would have been much poorer without your visit."

I nodded. I hoped Khepri could heal the two.

We retreated to a nearby area where full, rich, deep green grass was growing, shaded by a tall canopy. The sides of the canopy were left open, but a rough homespun fabric could be let down in inclement weather. We sat there in the cool grass to wait.

The injured centaur boy's mother came up to us then, and kneeled to hug me tightly, tears in her eyes.

"Princess Charlotte," she began, "The healer has asked we bring tubers for the mending, but I wanted to stop on my way out and thank you." She hugged me again. "Thank you for saving my son." She smiled and trotted off to find the plants Khepri had asked for.

I turned to Iilcendorr again. "Khepri prefers it if the loved ones of her patients help her heal their wounds. She says it imbues the treatment with an extra magic that helps them recuperate."

Iilcendorr smiled and shook his head in amazement. "I think we have much to learn from you." He looked into my eyes earnestly then, and asked, "Charlotte, would you consider spending some days helping us learn the ways of the healer?"

"Sure," I patted his hand. "We'd be happy to."

"I must say, our elders' decision to ask you to remove the book was fortuitous, but this day's actions have truly proven that you and your friends are trustworthy. Your visit, though short, has inspired the tribe to discuss things we haven't talked about in a hundred years. Our traditions will be revised to reflect the new information we have gathered, of that I am sure."

Chapter Eighteen
A Part of the Tribe

Khepri worked for hours, but finally emerged, a tired but triumphant look on her face. The four centaurs who had asked to learn at her side emerged from the medical tent and immediately came to Iilcendorr to confer and relay what had happened.

Kym, Khepri and Christianne came over and sat down, tired but happy. They washed up in the tub we had ready for them, and lay down on the soft, cool grass to relax. Khepri came and sat next to me.

"They're going to be okay," she said quietly. I glanced at her, and she continued. "These people have some weird ideas about medical care and inner strength."

"I heard. Iilcendorr has asked that we stay a few more days and teach them about healing. I think it's a good idea.

They have some very rough ideas and customs that I think they are now eager to change."

She nodded and lay back.

The four healers-in-training were speaking rapidly and enthusiastically to Iilcendorr, and I bent my head to listen discreetly.

"Iilcendorr, she made a paste of the tubers, and instead of eating it, she smeared it on their wounds, called it a *poultice*, said it would draw out the heat and infection ..."

"Iilcendorr, she used some kind of fibers and sewed the boy's leg gash up like a cloth! She called it *suturing* and said the hide would mend much faster and ..."

I smiled to myself.

That evening there was a grand celebration. The entire village was present in the center grassy square, and the large bonfire was lit and flamed high into the sky.

"Charlotte, you must taste some. It is a drink we bring out only on very special occasions." The white centaur named Rhalofetorr handed us all cups of raspberry nectar that was absolutely divine.

The centaurs were all dancing in a circle around the bonfire; their joy was palpable. The mother of the injured centaur colt draped flower wreaths around our necks, and foods were prepared for a feast: roasted rabbits and fruit and grass.

At one point in the festivities, we were approached by several of the centaur elders, along with Iilcendorr and Kiphaentren. They walked up to us and bowed deeply, their noses touching their outstretched forelegs.

"Newcomers no more," declared the oldest of the elders, "we welcome you into our tribe and declare you a part of our family! We now seal this pact with the mixing of the blood dewdrops."

The what?

Iilcendorr brought forward an ornate ceremonial dagger, carved out of volcanic glass and resplendent with what looked like deep blood-red rubies. The old centaur took the dagger from him and tested the point, which appeared to be razor sharp.

Iilcendorr came to my side then and began to explain. "The elder will pierce herself and produce a dewdrop of blood, and you are all asked to do the same."

Khepri sat up and whispered in my other ear: "I was expecting something like this, based on what I had already learned, but I did not know they meant a literal drop of blood."

Well, uh, I guess it's okay.

I eyed the massive dagger in the old centaur's grip.

I looked at the others, who'd been watching carefully. They nodded and extended their hands, palms up; everyone except Christianne.

"You have got to be kidding me," she said.

"It's some kind of honor, Christianne," I whispered.

She took a deep breath and looked sideways.

Khepri went to her and whispered in her ear, nodding as she talked. No one could hear anything, but Christianne seemed to relax a bit and, after a while, she finally shrugged and stuck out her hand to join the others.

The elders approached each of us in turn, beginning with me. I watched as she touched the dagger to my fingertip.

The knife was so sharp I could not perceive the cut, but when she withdrew it, I saw a small bead of blood well up. I felt no pain, and looked at my finger in mild amazement.

She moved to Caroline, Tupu, and Khepri, then Christianne and Kym, and finally Jim.

With each touch, a crimson red drop of blood was brought painlessly to the surface. Until she came to Kym.

Upon touching Kym's forefinger with the sharp ceremonial dagger, a bead of thick, purple liquid appeared, which slowly turned a different shade of red than our own human blood. Faint purple sparkles rose from it, and drifted lazily upward.

Then the elder came to Jim, and I leaned forward despite myself.

I did not know magical creatures had different colored blood.

I caught Khepri's eye, and she smiled, and something told me she had known this secret and was reveling in the fact that it was new to the rest of us.

I tried not to grin.

The dagger touched Jim's finger pad as the djinn watched, amazed. The elder withdrew the point and a bead of emerald green blood appeared, and welled up, growing larger, then settled onto his finger, and slowly began to turn to dark red, darker than our human blood. Green sparkles slowly appeared and rose into the air as the blood changed color.

Kym giggled, and I smiled.

We are an interesting bunch, of that I am sure.

The elder walked back to me, and drew the dagger's sharp blade across her palm, producing a cut several inches long. Her blood appeared a brilliant turquoise blue, which slowly turned to red. Ever so slowly, faint blue-green sparkles rose into the air from her palm and slowly gathered around her face. She did this with no hesitation, no flinching, and no facial expression whatsoever. She extended her bleeding hand outward, and as the centaurs approached her, I realized they all had pierced their fingers.

They came forward and touched their hands to their elder's palm, each giving one dewdrop of their blood to mix with hers.

Her palm slowly filled with the village's blood. By the end of this part of the ceremony, her palm was wet with the entire village's blood. This she slowly extended in my direction.

Without hesitating, I extended my finger to her palm, and watched as my blood blended into the large puddle there. She went down the line, and each of the others, my troupe, who I considered my family, touched their dewdrops of blood to the elder's red palm.

When she was done, she nodded and brought her palm to her face, uttering some magical-sounding words over it, and then held her palm up high. A beam of light suddenly appeared to emanate from the blood on her hand, and shot skyward with a loud *WHOOSH!* It was then that the whole village of centaurs cried out in triumph and began whooping and cheering as they fell into what I can only describe as an ecstatic euphoria.

I laughed, bringing my finger to my mouth to suck on. Just as it was about to reach my lips, Khepri spoke up.

"Hey, hold on, troupe," she said, pulling out a sterile cloth from her medical pouch. She withdrew a small bottle of antiseptic, unscrewed it with her mouth, and poured a dollop onto the fabric. "Here," she said, and held out the cloth so that we could wipe the blood off our fingers.

Iilcendorr came to us then and explained that the bright light and the loud *WHOOSH!* indicated that a formal bond had been created. We were now a part of their tribe.

"Each group," explained Iilcendorr, "both centaur and human," he nodded toward Kym and Jim, "and djinn and chimera, will be strengthened by this magical bond. We will now gain power from each other, from our tribe, from our family: We will last longer in battle, bleed less, and feel stronger of heart." He bowed and smiled.

I smiled as well and shook my head in amazement. This quest had certainly taken a turn for the better since we were shot at!

We spent the next several hours dancing and singing, in exuberance with our brand-new extended tribe. There was much drinking and celebrating, and it lasted long into the night.

At one point, Khepri disappeared and returned ten minutes later, and explained that both her patients were doing well and looked to be recuperating rapidly.

"No fevers, no warmth around the wounds, no dizziness, no incoherence, no extra bleeding. Everything looks good." She smiled. "I will keep checking on them several times a day. Infection is a funny thing, the quicker you catch it, the easier it is to eradicate. Of course, it helped that the water in the stream and waterfall was not polluted or infected. Clean is as clean does." She winked.

We finally retreated to our chambers and dropped off to sleep, but only after a wrinkled old centaur approached us, drunk from celebratory nectar, hiccupping and sweating profusely after dancing with every single girl in the village.

He grabbed our hands, pumping them vigorously, then sat down to regale us of all his exploits throughout his life. He explained that we had made it possible for him to start anew with a second career, that he planned to move to the other island through the volcanic lava tunnel, and try his hand at ship building.

Chapter Nineteen
We Wish You Success

We spent a week with the centaurs, teaching them all about healing and medicine, and making sure Khepri's patients were definitely on the mend. The centaurs healed quickly. By the time seven days had passed, they were both on their feet, and healthy.

"Iilcendorr, I think it's time we were on our way to retrieve *The Book of Mysteries*," I said one day at lunch. We were, once again, dining in the gardens, and a kaleidoscope of small iridescent blue butterflies that had recently emerged from their cocoons were fluttering everywhere. Kym was enchanted by them.

The gleaming black centaur smiled, "I was just thinking the same thing last night. This morning I consulted with the elders, and they have given me the order to show you the way."

That got our attention.

"Oh my god, I can't wait," Tupu exclaimed. She'd been chomping at the bit for days, eager to get on with the quest.

"Charlotte, can we bring a butterfly back to the ship?" Kym asked.

I just looked at her and stayed silent.

"Girl, you're crazy," said Christianne. "Any butterfly brought onto a ship would surely die. I mean, think about it; they eat the nectar of living flowers."

"Oh." Kym looked downcast. A small butterfly landed on her nose. She smiled and held very still, staring cross-eyed at the creature.

"You wouldn't want the butterfly to starve, would you?" I said, smiling.

She slowly shook her head '*no*,' trying not to dislodge the visitor on her face.

I turned back to Iilcendorr.

"We would greatly appreciate restocking our supplies before heading out."

"Of course. You are welcome to anything we have."

I inhaled deeply, smelling the honeysuckle and jasmine in the air. "I will miss this garden," I said wistfully.

I closed my eyes and sipped from my cup of juice.

I knew I was spoiling myself, indulging in all the delights the centaurs had to offer, but I wanted to take advantage of them while I could. Something told me the quest for the book was going to be not only austere, but dangerous. And when we returned to the ship, we knew fresh vegetables and fruits were a rare luxury.

I sat up, smiling. *Enough of this.* "I think we will leave tomorrow morning."

Christianne whooped and jumped out of her chair, hooked her elbow in Kym's, and they began to dance around in a circle, celebrating. Iilcendorr, Tupu, and I laughed.

That afternoon, everyone was abuzz, with the troupe running back and forth, filling lists of restocking supplies and visiting new acquaintances we'd made.

The four centaurs that had learned so much from Khepri were nervous about being left in charge of the entire village's medical needs.

"Don't worry, emergencies rarely come up," Khepri assured them. "In fact, it was just good luck that we happened to be visiting you when the waterfall mishap occurred."

"Do you realize neither of them would have lived had you not been here?" one of the centaurs said. "I almost wish you weren't going to leave," she finished with a nervous laugh.

"Listen; yes, it would be convenient if I were to stay and become your village healer," said Khepri, seriously. "But what would you do when I eventually passed away? You've got to be prepared yourselves. You've got to teach others how to do this, younger ones who can continue when you yourself are gone, and they, in turn, should teach others, who will in turn take their place."

They nodded in understanding.

"Do not let this knowledge die." I gave them each a serious look. They looked solemn and reflective. I caught Iilcendorr's eye then and saw him nodding in agreement.

"This is like the knowledge of growing crops," he said to them. "Guard this knowledge. Write it down."

"Make books," Khepri said. She carried her own book of healing with her at all times, I knew. The four centaur healers-in-training had been working day and night to copy it. They had just finished last night.

I was able to leaf through their copy, and it was beautiful. Whereas Khepri's book was older and the diagrams had faded, the centaurs' new book was colored with dyes they had made from various fruit, accented with gold detailing.

"Where did you get the gold paint?" I had asked. I was rewarded with Kym and Christianne bouncing up and showing me their nails, which had been painted with the same brilliant color. Then they showed me a small bowl of pigment accented with shaved gold flecks. I shook my head in amazement.

There were tearful goodbyes all around, and the four healers-in-training hugged Khepri hard, squeezing her until she squeaked out, "Honey, Khepri can't breathe."

They released her with a laugh.

The elders from the tribe came to bid us goodbye. They were very solemn and dignified, and their old, lined faces wished us well. The centaur children ran up to us giggling, and gave us small wreaths they had braided out of wildflowers, and the small centaur Khepri had nursed back to health came quietly up to her and held her waist for a long time, his mother behind him, smiling with grateful tears in her eyes.

Lastly, the centaur who'd tried to rescue the child from the fall at the waterfall came then and gave Khepri a kiss, making her blush.

We were all moist-eyed, we would dearly miss these people.

After we'd replenished our stores, Iilcendorr came forward with a small cloth illustrated with details about the path to *The Book of Mysteries*.

"This is a diagram of where I will take you tomorrow morning. Keep it with you, for when you emerge again, you may be disoriented." He handed me a cloth about seven inches square, and I held it flat, my two hands stretched out beneath it.

The rest of the troupe all gathered around to listen.

Iilcendorr indicated a winding path that curved along the side of the valley, around the crops and farms, passed the waterfall, and continued for miles. Then his finger pointed to a dark splotch.

"Here is where it is," he explained. "Sort of."

"Is it just there, then?" Caroline asked.

"Well," Iilcendorr flinched. "That is actually the beginning of the journey, not the end." He looked at us. "It is said the path takes many days, and our legend warns against starting down the path. I'm sorry to be cryptic, but no one has gone down that path in thousands of years."

"Why not?" Christianne asked. We looked at her pointedly. "Well, okay, I know you said your legends warn you all against going after the book, but" – she waved her hand in the air – "there's always someone, probably younger than an adult, who dares to try to find it. Someone who finds rule breaking to be a thrill. Someone who thinks rules are made to be broken. You know, someone who loves a challenge."

"Someone like you?" smiled Khepri.

"Well, yes," Christianne laughed, then looked at Iilcendorr with her eyebrows raised in question.

"I'm afraid you are right, Christianne. A few foolish young centaurs have gone in search of the book," Iilcendorr's expression was inscrutable. "The last one was about one hundred and thirty-five years ago."

We waited, although I had a sense of what he was going to say.

"The filly was never seen again. But we know she went there, because we found her hoofprints at the entrance."

Christianne's eyes widened, and she remained silent and thoughtful.

"Screw that! I can't wait to go looking for it," Kym cried. She could not sit still and began pacing. "If we remain afraid of this, what is the alternative?"

Iilcendorr grimaced. "We *do* want you to retrieve the book and remove it from our island, but there *is* an alternative. You could remain here with us, training more young centaurs with medical knowledge, engaging in new art and creativity, perhaps enjoying the fruit and vegetables we have growing here. You could feast on roasted rabbit for years and never run out!"

I laughed. We had seen for ourselves what he had meant by 'overrun with rabbits,' and he had not been exaggerating at all.

Caroline and Khepri spoke at the same time.

"That sounds nice but boring."

"I think this island is good for a visit but ..."

"Shush, don't be rude."

"I didn't mean to!"

"They're used to this life; we've got places to go."

"Tam and Akim are waiting on the ship."

"What about your parents, Miss?"

Oh, god ...

I rubbed my forehead slowly, trying to get rid of the headache that was threatening to pound its way out of my temples.

I held up my hand, and everyone fell silent.

"I think," I looked pointedly at Christianne, "that we will be cautious and we will be fine." Then I looked at Caroline and Khepri. "And although your island is gorgeous and perfect, we do have other obligations and people who are counting on us." I looked at Iilcendorr. "We are hoping to bring back the knowledge of *The Book of Mysteries* to help mankind. We understand the danger and the warnings inscribed on our own scroll, as well as the cautions from your tribe's legends. We will be okay. We work very well together, and I think," I paused and looked solemnly into his eyes, "I *know* that we will be fine."

"Very well then," said Iilcendorr, "We wish you success."

Chapter Twenty
Into the Mountain

We were up bright and early, munching on rabbit and berries as dawn pinked the mountaintops. There was a buzz of excitement I knew so well: my troupe was chomping at the bit to get started. Kym hopped back and forth from foot to foot, urging everyone to chew faster and swallow quicker. I worried she would have a stroke from the stress.

Finally, we were off.

The thing about our daylong journey across the huge valley is, well, I could tell you about the new wildlife we saw, and the poison ivy we fell in (thank goodness for Khepri), and how it was traveling with the centaur guard, and how we watched the centaurs hunt for food to feed us, then prepare it, and roast it that night, and how we laughed when we realize they were treating us like favorite pets, but I'd rather skip to the end.

Which is actually the beginning.

So, I will.

"Charlotte," Iilcendorr pointed, early the next morning. "There is where the book is."

I looked to where he was pointing. The tree and mountains were off to the side. There was a lot of vegetation. It was hard to see where he was pointing.

"Uh," I started.

"Charlotte," whispered Tupu in my ear.

I turned my head slightly, keeping my eyes on the area Iilcendorr had indicated.

"It's the mountain," she whispered.

"What? But that's ..."

A volcano. Iilcendorr had led us to a volcano. A big, rugged, mountainous, vegetation-going-up-partways-then-just-rock-and-an-ominous-smoke-drifting-lazily-up-from-inside, volcano.

A VOLCANO.

"Wait. What?" I turned to Iilcendorr. He had a grimace on his face.

"It is very dangerous," he said. "Be careful."

Wait just a damned minute, horseman.

The book was inside an active volcano?!

"Iilcendorr, wait. Wait just a minute, there, friend." I tried to gather my thoughts. The centaur waited.

I glanced at the mountain again. Birds flew across the side, and more smoke was drifting up from the center of the volcano. *Smoke. From the volcano. Where there was likely to be lava and fire and other terrible ways to die.* I glanced at Iilcendorr. His expression told me this was not a joke. He was dead serious.

Looked at the volcano again.

Looked at the centaur again.

Looked back at the volcano.

Tried to formulate a coherent thought.

Looked at my friends. They looked back at me blankly as if to say ...

"Please tell me you're kidding," said Christianne. "Charlotte? That there," she pointed to the volcano, "that is hell in a handbasket. Really."

"I ..." I tried to think of something to say, but found no words.

"Charlotte, you can't seriously expect us to just stroll into an active volcano?" Khepri whispered in my ear.

Tupu's jaw dropped as she stood staring at the scene before us. She was silent for several moments before she finally found her voice: "You gotta be out of your god damned mind."

"No, no. NO." this from Jim. Which made me extra nervous. *If the djinn doesn't want to go into the volcano, maybe we should listen to him.* I turned to him and raised an eyebrow. Jim had been mostly silent during our stay with the centaurs, absorbing everything about their culture and practices. He seemed startled to have the attention suddenly on him.

"I ... uh," he swallowed.

Iilcendorr raised his hand to gain our attention. We all turned to him and waited. *Maybe he has more cool, dangerous places for us to venture in.* I was feeling very skeptical.

"The volcano is indeed active, but it has not erupted in several hundred years. It smokes, that is all."

"Really??" said Christianne. I held up my hand to shush her, while keeping my eyes on the black centaur.

"Tell us more, please."

Iilcendorr nodded. "The path to the book is foretold,"

" 'Foretold'? You want us to get cooked in a volcano because something's been 'foretold'?"

"Christianne, please. Let him speak."

Iilcendorr took a deep breath and started again. "The way to *The Book of Mysteries* is *understood* by my people to be inside the volcano: There is a path down to the inside, where the book is fabled to be found." He paused, thinking, then continued. "Since the book was placed there many thousands of years ago, it is logical to assume that the volcano has not erupted in all that time."

"Look." He waved his hand at the smoking mountain. Our eyes followed his gesture. The amount of smoke rising from the caldera was minimal. The wisps drifted away quickly before they could even form clouds above the volcano.

"If it were about to erupt, there would be so much smoke that the sky would be blanketed," he said. "But it has been exactly how you see it, for as far back as the living memory of my tribe reaches. Thousands of years. So, it is an active, yet dormant, volcano. We were worried how you would react, but I assure you, it poses no threat. Yes, it is an imposing sight, but it is just a mountain."

"A mountain full of lava, you mean," Christianne mumbled.

I rolled my eyes and shushed her. Then I turned to Iilcendorr. "May we have a minute to discuss this, please?"

"Of course." He moved away maybe thirty feet.

I turned to the others. "Do you think he can hear us?" I whispered.

"Let's see," whispered Caroline. Then, in a normal speaking voice, she said, "I think Iilcendorr smells funny." She looked over her shoulder at Iilcendorr. He had not reacted.

"Don't be an idiot," Khepri punched her playfully in the arm.

"Okay, let's be serious a moment," I said. "This is a volcano. We see it smoking a little bit. We have been told by people we trust that it is safe." I shot a look over at Christianne, who'd been about to speak, and she shrugged. "We can see that there are old growth trees growing halfway up the volcanic mountain," I glanced over to the volcano, then back again, "and," I held up my finger, "*and*, it would be illogical to send us in if it were in any danger of erupting. I mean, they want us to retrieve the book and remove it from the island. If the volcano were about to erupt anyway, why wouldn't they just wait for that? Last time I checked, lava destroyed books."

"Magic books?" Kym asked.

"As far as I know," I answered.

"This is what I think," Jim said. "I think we should approach cautiously. Once we're closer, even at the edge of the top, we will surely be able to ascertain if it is near erupting, will we not?" He tilted his head to the side and raised his eyebrows.

"That's very true," said Khepri.

"Oh, all right." Christianne threw up her hands. "If the volcano is dormant, I guess I'm in."

"Me, too."

"And me."

"I guess I'm in, too."

"I hope you're right."

"She'd better be right, or we'll all be dead."

So that is how we found ourselves bidding goodbye to Iilcendorr and climbing up and over the large rocks on our hands and feet to maintain balance, finally attaining the top edge of the active-yet-dormant, scary-looking big fire mountain.

Jim held Tupu's hand and pulled her over the rocks, since she was getting a bit top-heavy. I glanced at her as she climbed and saw the morning sun behind her, creating a pretty silhouette. She looked like she had a small pack on the front of her stomach. Having known her since she was very early in her pregnancy, I know that she was actually very skinny, lithe and tall. That small bit of extra pooch was her baby.

And we are taking it down into a volcano. Well, at least it'll have stories to tell its grandchildren. I chuckled.

Kym was the first to reach the top. She disappeared from view. I waited a few minutes. Then I started climbing faster while calling, "Kym? Kyyyyymmm!"

"What?" she popped her head up over the rocks.

"Not funny," I grumbled.

A few minutes later, we were all at the top ridge overlooking the volcano.

"Huh. That doesn't look so bad," said Tupu.

"Are you kidding me?" Christianne said.

I shook my head at them.

There was a path leading down into the volcano, starting about ten feet down, and it was paved. In bricks. Black bricks.

"Well, that was awfully decent of someone," said Caroline.

I smiled, and shook my head again. *At least we're in good spirits.* I leaned over and saw the steps were shallow, made of what looked like slate, *apparently brought over from the other island,* and they looked to have been built into the volcano's side. They looked firm and permanent, as if they'd been there for a thousand years or more. They hugged the inside edge of the volcano, which seemed to have a hollow center. The smoke rose up from the center, which seemed to stretch several hundred feet across. *It's really quite big up close.*

The black steps were rough slate, but looked to have been smoothed in the middle by footsteps. They curled down and down, into the dark interior of the mountain.

"Seems legit," said Christianne beside me.

I chuckled.

"Okay everyone, looks like these steps have been here a very long time. They look pretty permanent and secure. Of course, we should still be very cautious and careful, and try not to slip."

On the left side of the spiraling staircase rose the sides of the mountain, covered with a growth of brush and bushes and wild grasses. I saw butterflies and dragonflies dipping into flowers here and there, which made me feel much better.

Always pay attention to how the wildlife is acting; they sense danger before anything else. Wilderness training 101.

On the right side of the curving stairs, the inner side of the volcano, grew more vegetation, this time on a gently pitched downward. It looked like if we were to fall, we'd likely not roll down very far. The bushes rose to waist level on both sides, higher in some cases.

We started down the steps, into the volcano. A fluttering feeling teased at the edges of my stomach, as well as my mind.

You don't even get seasick, Charlotte, don't get vertigo now.

The steps were shallow, which aided in our descent, and at the same time, created a dizzying sensation.

"Don't look into the volcano," Khepri suggested. "Look to the left, at the bushes and plants. Look down at your feet. That way you probably won't get too dizzy."

That was simple enough for a short distance. The problem was the steps seemed to go on forever, and there was no handrail. Jim held Tupu's hand, and she seemed to have the easiest time of it.

At one point, Caroline had to sit down.

"Sorry," she said. "Just a bit dizzy." She drank sips from her waterskin, and took deep breathes. It was ten minutes before she was able to continue.

Dizzy is as dizzy does, I thought, remembering an old nursery rhyme. The soles of my black leather boots gripped the rough slate steps well, and we took it nice and easy going down. I held Caroline's hand to steady her, and the others soon took my lead, and were holding hands as we walked down into the volcano together.

Chapter Twenty-One

Descent

The hike into the dormant volcano was taking a very long time; this was now the fifth time we had stopped for a rest. I peered up at the sun and saw it was at its apex. *Noon*, I thought. *So, we've been descending these stairs for hours.*

"Charlotte?" Kym whined. "When are we going to get there?"

Oh, lord.

I caught Khepri giving Kym the eye and holding her finger to her lips in a *shhhh* gesture and ducked to hide a smile. *Kym may be a few thousand years old, but she is an immature child, really.* We were reminded of this fact every few days.

We descended for more hours, stopping at one point to eat, and discuss our progress and what we might expect.

"What do you think we'll find down there, Charlotte?" asked Christianne, who I'd noticed had observed Kym's whining and was trying to act more mature than the little girl chimera. *Competition for who was going to be more adult. Huh. That's a good thing.*

"You know, Christianne, I am not sure," I thought for a second. "I don't think it's going to be at all like the Tomb of Ancients, though."

"Definitely not," nodded Khepri. "There's no treasure, for one thing."

"That we know of," said Christianne.

I nodded. "That we know of."

"Actually," Tupu said, "*The Book of Mysteries* sounds priceless. It could be thought of as a treasure."

"Very true," said Caroline, nodding. "A person could have all the priceless jewels in the world, but if they were sick with an incurable disease, those jewels wouldn't matter at all. 'You can't take it with you,' as my mother always said."

"Maybe we will find something else, something unknown, something we might never have thought of," Jim said slowly.

"Like what?"

"Like I have no idea," he laughed.

Okay, well ...

And on we continued. We were so deep in the caldera that the sky seemed distant, far above us now in a small blue circle. The light was so dim down there that we eventually lit our torches so we could see where we were going.

Very soon after that, the plants dwindled away and we just surrounded by rock, rubble and some dirt. But the stairs continued onward. I marveled that someone had gone to the trouble of carving the steps going down thousands of feet into the deep darkness of the earth.

"Caroline, how are you holding up?" I asked.

"I'm actually okay, Miss."

"Let me know if you need anything," Khepri said.

"I will."

"Let's stop for a break, I need a rest."

"Me, too."

We sat on the steps, handing waterskins back and forth and resting. I was chewing on some rabbit jerky Iilcendorr had given us, wondering if I liked it very much.

"You know, I heard some interesting philosophies back at the centaur village," Tupu said.

"Really? Like for instance?"

"Well, like their belief that we see things not as they are, but as we are."

"What do you mean? Can you explain?"

"I would be happy to, but I'm not sure I fully understand it."

I thought about this for a minute. "Maybe what it means is that we see something, and we make assumptions."

"Can you give an example?"

I pointed to an outcropping of rock on our left. "See that rocky bit?"

"Yes."

"Uh huh."

"I see the rock."

"So," I said, "you see a rock. Do you see anything else?"

We all looked at the large rock.

I saw it move a little.

My eyes went wide.

"Did you see ...?"

"What?"

"Nothing, I just thought ..."

"WHOA!"

The rock moved again. Something broke away from the large rock outcropping, making an audible *SNAP!* as the rock shifted a few inches.

We all leaned forward, and stared at the detached rock.

"Did it just break off from the other rock?"

"But all of a sudden?"

"Why would it break off with no warning?"

"Did you feel a tremor?"

"Is the volcano erupting? Is that what made it break away from the bigger one?"

"I have no idea."

We stared at the broken-off rock for several moments. Then Kym stood up and walked over, grabbing a torch along the way. She reached out and touched the rock.

Nothing happened.

She touched it again, this time a bit harder, tapping the top of it.

The thing rolled over slowly and came to a stop.

Then tiny legs and claws emerged from the rock, and eyes popped open and the thing started to crawl toward us. We stood up, amazed, and backed away a step.

But we were still staring at it. It moved very slowly, maybe an inch every ten seconds. It approached us gradually.

Tupu was out in front, and closest to it. She and Christianne.

The thing was almost cute. It was about the size of a large, curled-up cat. It slowly crawled forward, its eyes blinking every minute or so.

"Tupu," Jim quietly stepped close to Tupu and took her hand, drawing her away from the thing.

Now Christianne and Khepri were closest to it. Christianne shifted back a foot, unsure.

Khepri eyed the creature with a scientific gaze, trying to understand what we were seeing.

It seemed harmless except for the fact that we had never seen anything like it before.

"Do you think it's some kind of rat?"

"Maybe a racoon?"

"It looks like it's made of stone, though."

The thing inched closer, until it was about a foot from Khepri's boot. There, it stopped and opened its eyes wider, staring up at Khepri.

A wide mouth appeared on the round rock surface. It opened its large mouth, revealing dozens of sharp teeth, and growled.

It was the growl that got us. The deep, low growl was surprisingly loud for a small demonic living rock.

"AAAHHH!"

"OH, GOD!"

"HELL NO!"

"OH, FORGET IT!"

Tupu, Jim, Christianne, and Kym scrambled up the stairs in panic, screaming all the way.

Caroline, Khepri and I were farther down the steps when we'd stopped for a rest, and we jumped up and hurried in the opposite direction – down the steps – also screaming.

We did not look back, but jumped from step to step, heading downward at an increasingly dangerous pace.

We heard the others running up the steps, and heard their voices quickly recede in the distance.

We were running fast, down shallow stairs, with no handrail, although why on earth anyone would have a handrail on a shallow, outside stairway was beyond me, I quickly wished for a handrail, because I just knew this could not end well.

Khepri was the first to fall.

She tripped, her foot slipping on a step, and I saw her in front and to my left, pitch forward and fall, headlong. Her feet tried to catch her, but since she was going downhill, this just made her fall faster.

"Khepri!" I heard Caroline call, before her voice was cut short. I glanced back and saw she was tripping, too. With her attention on Khepri, her foot must've slipped: I saw her fall past me, her arms pinwheeling in panic, her face the picture of dread and shock, her eyes and mouth open wide in surprise.

Oh, no.

Yep.

I knew it was coming.

I felt myself fall forward as my own feet went out from under me. My momentum carried me forward and, as I tumbled down a few dozen steps, I felt a massive, bone-jarring CRACK as my head hit the slate rock. I finally came to a stop, flat on my belly.

Just before I blacked out I thought *something tripped me.*

Chapter Twenty-Two
Injured

I came to because my face and my hand hurt. Really hurt. I opened my eyes to a nearly full moon and groaned, disturbing the little rock demon who was gnawing on the side of my left hand.

"Hey!" I yelled, jerking my hand away. It looked at me. and I swore it looked reproachful, but it was hard to tell the expression on the face of a ... well ... a rock. I sat up, cradling my hand, which had teeth marks on it: little bloody bite marks all along the edge of the hand, below my pinky. The little monster had chewed on me as ferociously as a small kitten I'd had when I was ten.

I felt a wave of dizziness pass over me and put my hand to my head, feeling woozy. The hand came away bloody – far bloodier than the other hand. Blood was dripping down my forehead, and I winced as a drop slid into my eye. I blinked several times as I fumbled in my coat for a handkerchief.

I was dabbing at my head, hissing a warning at the rock demon not to come any closer, and trying to gather my wits, when I heard Caroline call.

Caroline!

I swung around, trying to locate her, but we had dropped our torches in our haste to flee. It was very dark: not exactly pitch black, but nearly there. I looked up and saw night was falling outside the volcano. All I had to see by was a small circle of light a thousand feet above me, and it wasn't much help at all.

"Carrie, I'm over here," I called.

She called out again, but I couldn't make out her words.

What was happening? Was she moving *away* from my location?

"Carrie, where are you?" I called louder. I was rewarded with a very faint cry, she sounded even farther away.

What the hell?

I shifted on the stair. The rock demon growled. I shrugged.

"Little rock demon, I am hurt. My head is bleeding, I feel dizzy, and I don't know why my friend's voice is growing farther away. If you want to gnaw on me again, I'm going to kick you into the volcano, I swear."

The rock demon stopped growling and looked at me quizzically. It turned its head to the side like a dog, and I laughed despite myself.

I shook my head. Never in a million years did I think I'd ever be talking to a living rock.

Okay, first things first, I thought. I had to get my head wound under control. Drop by drop, the blood was coming down. It had now begun to go down my chin. *Yuck.*

I looked around for my pack. *Oh, great.* I had nothing with me, not my pack, not my torch, not my friends.

I heard another cry from below: It was Caroline, calling out again.

"Here!" I called back.

I heard another voice calling, it was Khepri.

"Here, I'm up here," I called. It hurt to yell out like that, it made my head pound.

The rock demon whined.

Huh?

It sounded almost like a dog. A dog with razor sharp teeth, huge eyes and the body of a little boulder.

I stared at it. It stared back.

At least it was not baring its teeth anymore. I held my hand out, and made a clucking sound.

Silly. *Charlotte, it's not a horse.* I was so used to Shêtân. I missed his horsey nose so much. I hoped Tam and Akim were giving him some oats and carrots.

I saw movement out of the corner of my eye and turned to see the rock demon shuffle forward a few inches, then stop when it saw me looking at it.

Hmmm.

I clucked again, and wiggled my fingers. "Come on, come here, boy."

It shuffled forward a few more inches.

It was actually cute – if it kept its mouth shut. Those sharp little teeth made me nervous, *but if it keeps its mouth closed that should be okay, right?* I hoped so.

It shuffled a little closer.

I felt a wave of dizziness pass over me.

Oh, right. My head. I was going to look for something that would stop the bleeding.

I fell back to the ground.

I was shimmying in and out of consciousness and turned to look at the rock demon. It was closer still. I kept eye contact with it, to keep it in my sights but also to try and make a connection.

Do I sense intelligence in this creature?

I certainly hoped it was intelligent, instead of a blindly acting, bloodthirsty rock version of a piranha.

What could I use to stop the bleeding?

I put my hand on my head, feeling for wetness. I couldn't tell what was wet, and what was dry.

I heard another call from Caroline, this time a bit closer.

Oh, good, I thought, before passing out.

"Wake up, Charlotte."

I felt so dizzy ...

I felt a cool, wet cloth against my cheek.

"Oh, Miss ..." I heard a sad voice say.

Carrie ...

Then nothing.

"I think she's coming to."

"Good."

I felt a hand patting my shoulder, then I heard a trilling sound next to my arm, and something nudged me.

Huh?

I opened my eyes.

Khepri was looking into my face with a concerned look. "Well, hello. I'm glad you're awake."

Caroline came over then. "Miss, you're going to be okay," she said, smiling.

I felt a squirming next to my side.

"What ..." I tried to clear my throat. "Water," I said hoarsely.

Caroline put a cup to my lips and lifted my head, and I took a sip. The water was cool and delicious going down my throat. I swallowed some more.

Taking a deep breath, I tried to speak again. "Carrie ..."

"You're going to be okay," Caroline said, patting my arm. "You've been unconscious since we found you."

"You've sustained a bad gash to the head, Charlotte," said Khepri. "I've stopped the bleeding, and you've been unconscious for a day."

A day?

"What happened? Where're the others?"

I did not see anyone else there.

"We don't know where they are," Khepri said calmly. "After we all fell, Caroline and I ended up much farther down than you did. We've a got a few bruises, but nothing like that head injury of yours." She adjusted the bandage on my head.

"We came back up the steps and found you, Miss. Then Khepri tended to you while I went back up to get our packs and torches. I just got back last night," she said.

"Something interesting, Miss. When I went to retrieve our packs, the supplies belonging to Kym, Tupu, Christianne, and Jim were still there. I was able to retrieve all of it. I left a note saying we were taking everything down to the bottom of the stairs. I don't know where the others went. I climbing back up nearly a thousand steps passed the supplies searching and saw no sign of them."

I heard a low whine.

"Oh, and you have a new friend," Khepri smiled and gestured at my side.

I felt there and my finger came in contact with a bulging rock that shifted as I touched it; then, I felt a lick on my finger. I jumped about a foot, and my head went dizzy again.

"Ohh," I said, holding my head. I winced when my hand made contact with the bandage.

"Careful, there. It was quite a wound. I had to put in four stitches," said Khepri.

"Ugh," I looked to my side, then moved over a bit and turned to lie on my left arm.

"It won't leave your side, Miss," Caroline said of the rock creature. "When we found you, it was curled up against you. It even growled at us a bit, until we won it over."

I couldn't believe it. The rock demon was lying against me like a puppy.

"Please tell me it isn't violent," I said. "It chewed my hand."

I lifted my left hand up and saw it was bandaged and smelled of antiseptic.

"As far as I can tell, this creature is made of rock. But it's alive. I cannot explain why," said Khepri.

"And no one knows where Kym, Tupu, Jim and Christianne are?" I asked.

"I don't think they came down this way," Khepri looked around. "We fell the farthest, and we came up quite a bit to find you, and Caroline went all the way back up to where we'd dropped our supplies."

"I didn't see them, Miss. I just hope they can find us again," Caroline looked around us, at the outside wall, and then to the other side, which showed a steep decline. "I hope they didn't fall off the stairs."

An hour later it was dark and the only light came from our torches and a small fire. Night had fallen once again, and Caroline had brought some wood from higher up the staircase, and had made the little campfire. Khepri was trying to tempt the rock demon with a small bit of food. It refused all attempts to even coax it from my side.

I finished the last of the food from my bowl, and drank deeply from the waterskin Caroline handed me.

"I don't think it wants any," I chuckled, then groaned, holding my head.

"You're going to be sore for a while," said Khepri. She handed me a dark leaf from her pack. "Here, chew this, it should help a bit with the pain."

I took the offered leaf. It was about the size of my hand, dark green, and tasted bitter.

"Yuck," I said, forcing myself to chew and swallow it.
Khepri nodded.

"Now, we should go back up in the morning, to see if we can find the others," I said.

Caroline and Khepri looked at each other. "Miss, we talked about that while you were out, and we think it would be smarter to go down. I took a long time looking for them when I went up to get our packs. There was no sign of them. They could be anywhere."

"Charlotte, they can handle themselves. Jim and Kym are with them, and something tells me we'll meet up with them if we continue on the quest."

"But you said you didn't think they went down past you," I protested.

"But I am not one hundred percent sure," said Khepri. "They could be anywhere. They could be with the book by now, we don't know. You were unconscious for at least a day. Anything could've happened."

"We'll see them soon, Miss."

I stared off into space, absentmindedly cuddling the rock demon, my fingers rubbing what I assumed was its head. Its eyes were closed, and it was purring. I shook my head, a smile on my face, as Khepri looked on in amusement. I was worried about the others.

"I wish I knew where they were," I said.

"Me, too, Miss, but there's no use fretting. There's nothing we can do about it at the moment."

Khepri patted my hand. "Charlotte, I'd like to stay here another day or two, until you can walk without feeling dizzy. It would not be good if you fell down the stairs again."

"I can't wait that long, Khepri." I felt an urgency to find the others. "Is there anything I can do to hasten my recovery?"

She thought for a minute. "Chew the leaves three times a day, and lie down."

I reclined on my blanket.

"Stay down; try not to move too much." She thought some more. "Try not to talk too much, or worry too much. Stress is a killer. Relax. Try to sleep."

I nodded, then closed my eyes. I fell asleep with the rock demon in the curl of my arm. *I've got to think up a name*, was my last thought.

Chapter Twenty-Three

Key

It was a day and a half before my dizziness dissipated, and this was incredibly irritating to me. *I need to get going,* I kept thinking. Thank goodness I didn't take longer to feel better.

I still had to take it easy, and it was slow going at first. Caroline and Khepri walked on either side of me, ready to grab my arms if I so much as slipped. But I didn't. No slipping, no falling, no embuggerances.

Chowder, as we were now calling him, because we had to call him something, followed us. Well, he followed me, to be precise. In fact, I had to keep telling him to stay back a few feet, or he was going to trip me and make me fall head over arse again, probably break my head open completely this time.

We walked. It took us three more days to get to the bottom. If we'd been able to float or glide or fly, we'd've been there in an hour. It was a long way down.

A long way down to fall, too. We got to the bottom and were greeted by...

"Eww."

"Well I guess we know what happened to that filly Iilcendorr told us about."

"Oh dear."

The slate steps ended in a curve, and the land at the bottom of the volcano was relatively flat. In the center lay a centaur skeleton.

Khepri kneeled to examine the bones, while Caroline and I stood back a bit. I looked around the large area. It was covered in rocks, both large and small, and it was from some of these rocks that the smoke came from.

"Not as much coming out as I'd thought there would be," said Caroline, peering at the cracks the white smoke was drifting up from.

"I believe this is, indeed, the centaur who disappeared more than a hundred years ago after going to look for the book," Khepri said, rising to her feet. "Look at how the skeleton is smaller than Iilcendorr's body; he said she was just a teenager, so naturally her skeleton would be a bit smaller. Look here," she indicated the bones in several places. "The body landed so hard, from near the top, most likely, that the bones were shattered. Then, of course, scavengers have been at it for over a hundred years, which is why the skeleton is incomplete."

"Huh," I leaned over to have a closer look. "Yuck."

Khepri laughed. "I guess I'm more accustomed to these things than you are."

"You definitely are," I laughed.

I stood up and stretched my back. "I shouldn't feel this creaky, I'm only nineteen, for goodness sake."

"You put your body through a lot, Charlotte. Plus we've been through an intense workout just getting to this point." Khepri smiled grimly.

"And we're not even inside," I pouted, then laughed. "Eh, I'll bounce back. I'm in great shape." I did a few deep knee bends to show I was strong and promptly felt a twinge of pain. "Ow."

Khepri laughed. "Here," she rummaged around in her pack and withdrew a piece of blackroot. "This will help." I smiled and took the black twig, sticking it in the corner of my mouth and began to chew on it. I immediately began to feel the effect of the stimulant.

This is nice.

"Also, it doesn't help your aches and pains that it's so warm down here." She looked around. "We are in a dormant volcano, and that smoke coming up is warming things quite a bit."

We both turned as Caroline called from the far side of the expanse. "Hey, look at this."

We left the skeleton as it was and joined her.

It was a door. A locked, iron door, blackened by the ages.

"Someone forged an iron door to place here," I said. "They went to all that trouble."

"I wonder if that means there's a forge inside?" Caroline wondered.

"I don't know, but this door is locked, so unless we can find a key for it, we are out of luck," Khepri said.

"Let's spread out and search the rest of this wall," I walked off, examining the hard surface.

The wall around the bottom of the volcano had been made of strong oak, and appeared many thousands of years old. It had solidified into almost petrified wood, and was like stone to the touch. It was rough in places, and slightly curved. We examined every linear foot of it, finally settling on ...

"Found it," said Caroline.

We hurried over. She pointed at a chest half buried in the wall. There had been a recess built into the oak, so we knew it had been placed there on purpose.

"Huh," I said. "Now why would someone just put this here, where anyone could take it?" I reached for the lid.

"Stop," Khepri stilled my hand. She looked at me, "Really? You were just going to touch it?" She shook her head.

I stared at her, realizing she was right.

"There might be traps, hidden poison, anything, really. You don't know," she stared at the chest.

This chest was black, and it was hard to tell what it was made of, without touching it. It looked like oak with several iron bindings around it, but the material could've been anything. It was a few feet wide, and maybe a foot long and deep. There were dragons carved into the surface. Or cast into it, if it turned out to be iron. *Like Khepri said, we don't know.*

I did another quick search of the perimeter and saw nothing else, and returned to the small chest on the ground, where Khepri and Caroline were standing.

I looked down at the thing.

"How would I open, if I were a secret, spooky-looking chest with a possible key inside?" I thought aloud.

Khepri and Caroline chuckled.

Then I noticed Chowder rolling up. He bumped into my foot to get my attention.

I looked down. "What is it?" I asked, distracted.

Chowder crawled over to the chest and fumbled with it for a few seconds. The lid sprang open.

I was in shock.

Chowder looked up at me, his eyes wide.

"Miss, how did he know?" Caroline asked what we were all thinking.

I stared at that little rock demon, who had become like a puppy since I fell and nearly cracked my head open. I did not know what to make of him then, and I didn't know what to make of him now, but staring into his large eyes, I sensed an intelligence I hadn't noticed before.

Well, to be fair, it's hard to sense intelligence in a rock.

I bent down on one knee to get closer to Chowder.

"Chowder?"

He looked at me, he looked like he was waiting.

"Can you understand me?"

There was no mistaking it, Chowder was nodding.

Holy crap!

I stared at the little rock demon. Then I looked at the others, my eyes wide. "Have you ever heard of an animal made of rock?"

They shook their heads.

"...who can understand human speech?"

They shook their heads again, this time more vigorously.

I turned back to Chowder, who was still looking up at me, waiting.

"Chowder, are you our friend?" I asked in a small voice.

Because really, an animal is either your friend, or your enemy, at least where protection and attacks and that kind of thing come in to the equation.

Chowder was rolling around happily.

"Chowder?"

He stopped and looked up at me, and nodded. His mouth came open then, and all those teeth appeared, and a little rock tongue fell out of his mouth, and juggled there as he panted.

I shook my head slowly and smiled.

"Okay, important point: Chowder is intelligent, and he is our friend." *This might come in handy.* I looked down at the chest. Without touching it, I peered in. There was an old cloth at the bottom.

I turned back to Chowder. "Can I touch it?"

The little rock demon nodded.

This is so weird.

I slowly extended my hand and took the cloth. It was stuck to the bottom of the chest. I gave it a tug, then a stronger tug, and it tore away from the surface.

"Yuck." I pulled it all the way out and saw it was wrapped around...

A key.

I smiled and stood up, the key in my hand.

Glancing back at the box, its lid still wide open, I idly wondered if there *had* been any traps.

"Hold on a minute." I picked up a fist-sized rock.

I gently tossed it at the chest. Nothing happened. I grabbed another rock and threw it. This time I was rewarded with a *click* and a whirring sound. Then the space under the chest fell away, and the chest along with the dirt and rock it had been sitting on fell through the hole that had suddenly appeared beneath it.

I jumped back, as the space of ground that had fallen away reached halfway under one of my feet.

"Ohhh!" I almost fell backwards, and had to do a little hop of surprise to remain upright.

"Well, well, well," Khepri muttered, leaning over and peering down inside the hole. "Looks bottomless."

I turned to Chowder, picked up the little boulder and hugged him as he licked my face. His rough tongue felt so weird. "Thank you, Chowder," I smiled. "Good rock, good boy!"

Chapter Twenty-Four

Through the Looking Glass

We approached the door. Hot air blew up against us suddenly. *Weird.* I glanced back at the rocks strewn about behind us. White smoke still curled lazily up out of them. The gust had just been near us, the smoke hadn't been disturbed at all.

Very weird.

"I wish we knew where the others are, Miss."

"You never know, Carrie, we might very well find them inside."

"I have a feeling we will," Khepri said in a quiet voice. I stopped in my tracks and turned to her.

"You have a feeling we will?" I repeated.

Khepri looked at me. "Ever since we found this door I've had a foreboding. I'm not sure why or what exactly it is, but I just ... " she shrugged.

I had a thought.

"Chowder?" The little creature had been following me as I walked and was now resting against my foot, his large eyes staring up at me unblinkingly. *I will never get used to this.* "Chowder, do you know where our friends are?"

At first the little rock demon just stared at me, and I didn't think he was going to answer. Then, slowly, he nodded his head yes. A shiver went up my spine.

"And are they inside?" I indicated the iron door.

Chowder did not answer.

I knelt down and touched him with my hand in a gesture of friendship. "Sweetheart, this is really important."

The rock demon shivered almost imperceptibly.

I sat down beside him and picked him up, and held him in my lap, against my belly, petting him with my hand and murmuring to him. He closed his eyes and began to purr. We stayed that way for several minutes. Then I began to speak.

"Chowder, my sweet lil rock, you are so nice to help us. We are so thankful for all you are doing to help us. Thank you for helping us retrieve the key. Thank you for any help you can give with the return of our friends. We are so sad without them. We miss them so much." I cooed some more to the little creature, rocking back and forth.

I caught Caroline's and Khepri's eyes and nodded slightly toward the little rock in my arms. They both sat

216

down next to us and put their hands on him and murmured soothing whispers.

We stayed like that for a good ten minutes.

Finally, Chowder opened his eyes and looked at me. I asked him once more, "Our friends, are they inside?"

He nodded slowly, then shivered again.

"Should we be careful?"

He nodded.

"Is there danger beyond the door?"

He nodded.

"Are our friends hurt inside?"

He paused and seemed to think a moment, then his eyes went sideways and lost focus. After a while he shook his head. He seemed very sad.

It was creeping me out.

I got up, holding him still, and caressing him. Then I gently set him down and rubbed the side of his head. "Thank you for helping us, sweetie."

I glanced at Khepri and Caroline, who'd both gotten to their feet with me. I nodded and stepped toward the iron door, key extended. Slipping it into the lock, I was struck with how easily it went in, in contrast to how aged and rusted the lock itself looked. In fact, I was surprised I didn't feel any resistance. It was almost as if the key had slid into empty air.

I turned it and felt a *click* and the door swung inward a few inches. It was a wide doorway, it looked like it could fit the three of us side by side. I grabbed the edge and pushed and was rewarded with a rusty scraping sound. Chowder whined at my feet, and I stopped.

I glanced down at him. It was plain to see that little rock demon was afraid. But we needed to proceed. Chowder had said our friends were beyond the door. The map said the book was beyond the door. Everything important to us was beyond the damned door. *So, we are going through the door.* I glanced at Caroline and Khepri, nodded, and pushed the door open the rest of the way. It screeched metal on metal. *Huh, hinges must be rusty. Makes sense.*

I peered passed the doorway and saw a plain room, dust on the floor, nothing else. *Nothing else. Okay, then.* I shrugged and stepped across the threshold. One foot in and I heard Chowder whine. I stopped and looked back at him. He stayed behind the doorway and back a few inches. Khepri and Caroline looked at him, then at me, shrugged and stepped through with me.

One of the last things I heard before the blackness took over was Chowder's whine, and a dread sense of foreboding came over me then. As my head passed through the threshold his whine cut off abruptly, and it was like my eyes suddenly stopped working.

"Charlotte?" Caroline's whisper. I heard it right beside me, but when I reached my hand out, she was not there. I took another step into the room, and looked back. The doorway was gone, or closed, or something. The door was gone, too. I reached out and couldn't feel anything.

I inhaled deeply, my senses trying to take in some information, any information they could glean. I smelled cool, slightly damp air, much cooler than the outside air. With the difference in temperature, I realized that the outside air had been not only warm, but dry. The volcano had changed everything outside. The terrain had been rocks, dry air, and warmth, even at night. Inside this room it was the opposite. And I realized there was a slight breeze, it felt cool on my face. I took another deep breath.

"Hello?" I tried.

"*Hello?*" a voice sounded back. I could not tell if it was Caroline, Khepri, or my own voice echoing back at me.

My eyes should've begun to adjust to the darkness, but I saw nothing. There was only blackness.

I waited a minute, then another, then sighed. The feeling of foreboding was quickly getting replaced by impatience. I was eager to get things going.

Well, let's try ...

I crouched and tried to feel the surface I was standing on. As soon as my fingers touched the floor, it disintegrated.

"AHH!" I cried out as I pitched forward into the dark void.

I fell. And fell. I was overcome with a feeling of panic at first, but then realized that, even though I was still in total darkness, I seemed to be falling more slowly. I must have dropped a thousand feet or more, at first. But I was falling less quickly.

Slower, slower, slower, until I was basically floating to the ground. I glanced beneath me, trying to drop my feet so I'd land standing up, and saw a faint light. I couldn't make out exactly what it was, but as I got closer and closer, I discerned the vague shape of a square.

As I landed, I stumbled slightly but then regained my balance. I looked around. There was minimal light, but I'd been in the darkness long enough for my eyes to adjust and use what little illumination there was. The square of light I'd seen from above was several yards from me. The landscape was beyond sparse: There was basically nothing here. The ground was solid grey, it might have been stone but I could not tell. I walked over to the square of light in the ground and knelt by it.

"Huh, it's a ..." I said out loud. *It's a wooden trapdoor.* I looked down at the thing. It was a dark wood square about two feet on either side. There was a metal loop and opposite this, a heavy hinge. It did not fit flush with the grey ground, rather, there was a good half-inch all around it and this is where a bright light was shining through. I squinted at the illumination and wondered where it led, what was going on, and if I should look around or go through the trapdoor.

I looked around. This was getting very lonely very fast.

Where are the others?

I squinted in the dim light and saw nothing.

"Hello? HELLO?" I called out into the void around me.

Nothing.

Not even an echo.

I noticed a cold sensation emanating from the ground, I could feel it leaching up through the soles of my boots, and I shivered.

I'm inside the volcano; it should not be cold, it should be warm.

Kicking at the grey floor, I felt tempted to touch it to feel how cold it was.

"The last time I touched the ground, it disintegrated into nothing," I said aloud. It felt better to hear my own voice. "So, I won't touch the ground."

Turning away from the trapdoor, I decided to do some exploring. I walked a hundred paces in a direct line away from the wooden square in the ground. Then two hundred. Then a thousand.

I saw a light in the distance, and made for it.

It was another trapdoor lit from below.

"This looks exactly the same as the first one."

Hmmm.

I can't tell if it's a new one or the same one."

I spit onto the wooden trapdoor and turned to the right and jogged away.

I traveled nearly four hundred feet by my own estimation. But it was in a straight line. I stopped when I saw the faint light in the distance, then walked to it and looked down.

There was my spit, on the wood. It looked the same.

A shiver crawled up my back, and I felt a prickling on the back of my neck.

I swung around.

"HELLO?"

Nothing.

Okay, Charlotte, think.

I was in a void, alone, and the normal physical attributes of my own reality did not apply here. No matter how far I traveled from the backlit trapdoor, I always returned to it. There was no one else here. Sound was muffled.

I turned around a full circle, and then stared back down at my own spit on the wooden square.

"Well, there's not much to do around here," I said aloud.

No one answered back.

My stomach growled.

I felt the foreboding chill again. *It's like someone or something is trying to make me act. First the fall, then the trapdoor, then trying to get away from it only to be faced with it again. Now my stomach is growling? I just ate less than an hour ago.*

My stomach cramped viciously, as if I hadn't eaten in days.

Okay, okay, fine. Sheesh.

I bent and lifted the metal loop and pulled open the trapdoor. I could not see anything but light, could not make out any shape, any ladder, anything at all.

I got down on my hands and knees and looked closer. *I guess this floor isn't going to disintegrate.* My hands on the smooth, grey floor began to grow very cold. The floor was positively icy. I leaned over the trapdoor and tried to see what was in it, and could not see anything, even this close.

I sat down next to the square of light and dropped my leg into it. Then I turned and lowered myself up to my waist.

What is going on?

My mind felt the oddest sensation. Through the square of light, my legs did not fall straight down. They fell off to the side.

Gravity is changing.

I closed my eyes and lowered myself the rest of the way through the door and found myself pulled to the side. As I passed through the opening, gravity flipped, and I found myself lying on the ground; if I'd been able to push my arm through, it would have landed where I'd been sitting a minute before. In fact, it was such a weird sensation I put my hand back into the open trapdoor and around and felt the gravity change back.

I opened my eyes.

What the heck is going on?

I was lying on a grassy field, warm sunshine on my face, a breeze ruffling the grass. Except the grass was blue. I looked up and saw a red-hued cloudless sky. I blinked and looked again and realized why it was so bright: There were two suns in the sky.

Chapter Twenty-Five
Herded

"Miss! Oh Miss!" Caroline ran up to me and fell on top of me. I laughed and hugged her tight. Relief flooded my mind, and I felt euphoric at no longer being separated from my friend.

"Hey, HEY! You guys! There you are!" Tupu was trotting up to us from the opposite direction Caroline had come from.

"Ahhh! YAY!" Kym called from over in another direction.

Jim didn't say anything, he just rushed up to us all and began to cry. I laughed and hugged him.

Within a few minutes we were all together, all seven of us. I was flabbergasted.

A quick scan of the area revealed that we were the only people there. We didn't even see a butterfly. We decided to take a break and exchange stories of how we got there.

"Let's sit in a circle," Caroline said. She was nearly in tears from happiness at having been reunited with me, and she said as much, a big watery smile on her face.

I explained what had happened to me. Khepri then spoke.

"I had much the same thing happen to me, Charlotte. When I saw you go into the doorway, you were there, then you weren't. Caroline was right behind you, and I followed quickly. I think we thought you were just inside, that the darkness of the inside had just obscured you from our sight." She looked to Caroline for confirmation.

Caroline nodded. "Miss, I heard Chowder whine when you went in, then Khepri and I followed you. The last thing I remember before the black came, before my foot left the outside and before my hand let go of the edge of the door frame, I called out your name. I couldn't see you or Khepri anymore, I stuck my head in and I called your name out loud, quite noisily. I did not hear anything back, so I stepped through."

"I heard you call," I said. "I swear I heard you call out my name, but it sounded like ... like a far-away whisper." Fear surged in me at the memory, and I glanced around the meadow nervously, but I didn't see anything, and Christianne had begun to speak.

"After the rock creature rushed us, trying to bite us or something, I'm not sure but those teeth it had looked deadly," Christianne stopped to take a breath and Khepri chimed in.

"Chowder."

"What?" Christianne looked at her.

"His name is Chowder. He made friends with Charlotte and us after Charlotte fell and cracked her head."

"What?! The monster rock is your friend?"

"You've got to be kidding me!"

"The devil made of rock that tried to eat us?"

"It ... I ... " Jim was at a loss for words, and a look of foolishness began to spread across his face.

"So," said Christianne, "it's not a monster?"

"No," I replied, "although I understand how we all came to that conclusion. When Chowder rushed us, I was so startled I pitched forward down the stairs and hurt myself pretty badly." I touched the bandage still on my forehead.

"We got scared and ran up the stairs," Christianne said. "We ran pretty far up, I'm afraid."

"We weren't counting, we just ran," said Kym. "I was out in front and ran very fast." She grinned proudly.

"When we finally slowed down," Jim said, picking up the story, "we caught up to each other and saw the door in the wall, and rushed inside."

"Wait," I said. "What door? I don't remember seeing a door above our camp, only at the bottom."

"I don't think we saw it coming down the first time," said Tupu. "Only when we were rushing up away from the devil, er ... rock creature."

"Chowder," said Khepri.

"Chowder," repeated Tupu. "Funny name for a rock."

"That's why I picked it," I said, chuckling.

"Actually," said Christianne slowly, "I am pretty sure we *would* have seen it when we came down. We were going slowly, and looking at everything with new eyes. This is getting creepy."

"Creepier than falling into a black void?" I asked.

"Creepier than falling about a mile then floating the last bit?

"Maybe not quite, but pretty creepy," said Christianne. "I didn't see any door coming down, but it was there when we came back up. We ran up at least a couple hundred steps."

"The funny thing is, I think it appeared when we slowed down and stopped to catch our breath," said Jim. "I mean, I looked up and saw it there. Kym had already seen it, I think."

"Yes. I saw it first."

"But I was the first one who approached it and touched it," said Tupu.

"Anyway, it's been a weird day," said Christianne, taking a deep breath.

"What?" I asked, staring at her.

"I said, 'It's been a weird day'."

"Only a day?" Khepri's eyes opened wide.

"It's been a day," said Tupu. "Hasn't it?" She looked confused.

"I think so," said Jim.

I turned to Christianne. "When did you run up the stairs away from Chowder? When did you go through the door?"

"About two hours ago."

A chill ran up by back.

Khepri spoke in a whisper. "For us, it has been nearly a week."

We realized that magic was afoot when we noticed the plants moving on their own, in a way they should not have been. No, it was not because of the discrepancy on the amount of time that had passed, not because the sky was red or the grass was blue, and not because there were two suns in the sky, although that was certainly the oddest thing I'd ever seen; no, it was definitely when our exploration of the area brought us to the massive labyrinth of ten-foot-tall bushes, and when we went in.

"I knew we shouldn't have come in here."

"You did not. You were the first one in."

"Well, I just wanted a peek. I had no idea ..."

"I think we should just ..."

"Wait a minute ..."

"Okay, okay, everyone just calm down." I spread my arms out.

We had seen the hedge from maybe a quarter mile away – that's how huge it had been. We'd been exploring for much of the day and were drawn to the dark green maze. I had looked down on it from our vantage point on the crest of a small hill, and I won't lie: I was intrigued.

Kym had run down first, Christianne after her. Just a short time later, we had been at the entrance to the thing and seen how tall the thick bushes reached.

"That's ... " I'd felt awe.

Khepri had held back, but Kym had peered in and stepped forward, and I'd gone after her.

"Wait ... I think ... " I had said.

"Oh my god," Tupu whispered.

"The hedge, look."

"Hey, wait!"

The thick, dark green bushes had moved. They'd grown outward, reaching past Khepri and closing around her. Around all of us.

We were trapped.

"Okay, okay, everyone just calm down," I spread my arms out.

I looked around. "Let's explore the labyrinth!" said Kym.

"Let's not."

"Why not?"

"Because there might be ... "

"Because why did the hedge just close up on us? It moved. I mean, it MOVED!"

"Okay," I took a deep breath. *Think, Charlotte.* "Let's just take a break here, I don't feel comfortable going farther into the maze."

"Pffttt, neither do I," Tupu snorted.

Khepri sat down and unpacked her bag until she got to the flint and steel. "Well, it's getting late. I agree with Charlotte. Let's camp here. I'm making a fire." She pulled together some underbrush from the ground, and some kindling from the previous night's fire, and arranged them in a pyramid. Expertly flicking her wrists, she aimed the flying sparks at the dry tinder.

They refused to light.

I kneeled down to study the twigs and underbrush.

"They're not catching the sparks," she said, sounding frustrated.

"Is it damp?"

Khepri felt the tinder. "No, it's completely dry, even the underbrush." She tried again and again.

After ten minutes she stopped, sat back on her heels, and looked around.

The shadows were growing longer.

"The suns are setting; it's getting dark," Kym said.

"Well, there are two suns in the sky," I squinted upwards. "They seem somewhat close to each other, and I think they're both slowly setting."

"There's no way of telling how long we'll have daylight for," Tupu said.

"I'll bet this labyrinth will be darker than anything at night." Caroline shivered.

"Okay, well, since we can't start a fire, for some odd reason, maybe we should explore the maze before the suns set any farther," I suggested.

Khepri bent to pack up her bag, and Christianne bent to help her. "It'll be okay, Khepri."

I was worried, too. *What will we do when the darkness of night falls and it grows colder?*

There was no telling what would happen. There'd been no signs of any predators, in fact, there was no sign of any life here at all. *Not even birdsong.* I shivered.

Looking over at Tupu and Kym, who had their heads together and were whispering back and forth, and Caroline and Jim, who just stood silently and tried to look brave, I realized what was needed.

We can't help where we've found ourselves, but we can change our outlook.

I took a deep breath, then smiled. "Okay, well, we've got a maze to explore! Come on!" I grabbed Caroline's hand and bounced up and down a few times, laughing.

Kym grinned at me.

We started off down the maze, Tupu even broke into a happy song from her childhood. We walked two by two, and Jim brought up the rear.

The tall, dark green hedge bordered walkways of blue grass. I idly wondered how it grew so thick and lush when the light from the two suns likely did not reach all of it for very long during the day.

Tiny flowers hugged the edge of the bushes. Some were orange, some were yellow, and they looked like they had been planted deliberately. The hedge's straight, sharp lines made them look very manicured. The little flowers grew in a straight row alongside the bush's edge. The blue grass was mowed close to the ground, and upon closer examination, we could tell it had been cut recently.

We marched on, examining everything as we walked.

The sunlight gradually grew dimmer and dimmer.

After an hour or so, dusk fell. But the area did not grow much darker.

The grass was bioluminescent.

Kym giggled in delight.

"Well, that's actually very convenient," Tupu said, smiling.

The grass, which had been blue in the sunlight, glowed a soft bluey-purple in the dim illumination of dusk. It was bright enough to see by.

Shadows still lurked near the top of the hedges, but we soon rounded a corner and found a curved edge of bush that was rounded at the ground and arches overhead, creating a small cove fit for a group.

"It's almost as if it's made for us," whispered Christianne.

"I think it might have been," said Jim, settling down in the grass.

He put his fingers against the blades of glowing blue-purple.

"It's warm," he said.

"What?" Tupu asked.

He reached for her hand. "Come sit with me."

Tupu sat next to the djinn and ran her own fingers across the grass. "He's right. It is definitely warm."

We all sat down in the softly glowing grass. It *was* warm. I felt amazed.

We all settled down for the night and broke out the food from our packs, munching some dried fruit and rabbit jerky that Iilcendorr & Co. had supplied us with, and some dried fish from the ship's stores.

I was thoughtful. "You know, it's weird there are no animals or birds, not even any insects in this place." I looked around us.

"You know what's even weirder?" Khepri asked.

"What?"

"The way the hedge moved and closed around us?"

"Well," said Khepri. "Yes, but more. We aren't able to start a fire, which would provide us with warmth and light. Then the two suns set, night falls, and lo and behold, the grass glows and the ground is warm." She put her hand down to the thick, lush lawn. "The ground is even warmer than the sunlight was." She looked at us significantly.

"It's almost as if ..." I looked around. "Almost as if our needs were being met, on purpose, by someone or something."

"And, I don't know if anyone else realizes this, but we're being herded," said Kym.

I blinked.

"She's right," Jim said slowly. "The hedge closed around us, the way forward is encouraged. There is only one way to go."

"True. The many paths of the labyrinth do not go very far. They curve around and away, but end without giving passage. In each instance, there is only one way forward," I said.

"Isn't that how most mazes are?" Christianne asked.

"No. No, not at all," Caroline said. "There are labyrinths in many of the royal palaces in the north, including in the backyard of the royal palace where Charlotte grew up, back home in Swerighe. The maze back home stretches for dozens of acres, and each false path goes on for quite a distance before you discover whether it's a dead end or not."

"She's right, I've read about the others in books," I said. "And I've been down our own labyrinth many times."

"So," Jim looked around, "I just mentioned it because it's spooky."

"Herded." I thought for a minute. "By whom?"

Chapter Twenty-Six
Stay on Your Toes

The next morning, we decided to get out of the labyrinth.

"Okay," I said, munching on a piece of dried fish. "I'm going to try the obvious."

Shouldering my pack, I started back the way we'd come. And ten feet back encountered a brick wall. Well, a wall of hedge. But it might as well have been a brick wall. *Really?* I could not believe this.

"I'm starting to feel like we're a herd of cattle."

"Seriously."

"Let me try something else," I said. I drew my scimitar out of its scabbard and examined the hedge.

"Okay," I stuck the blade directly into the wall of bushes. It went in up to the hilt.

"Can you wiggle it around?" Tupu stuck her own sword in the hedge, alongside mine.

I wiggled my sword a bit. "Seems somewhat loose." I withdrew the sword. "Stand back, I'm going to try to cut through." I raised the sword and brought it down in a quick swing.

The scimitar cut into the bush, all right. But when I withdrew it for another slice, the bush seemed to repair itself. "Oh, man," I muttered. Tupu groaned.

I cleaned off my blade and resheathed it.

"I have an idea," Kym said. "Let's try to run through the maze, to get to the end as fast as we can."

"That's actually not a bad idea," said Caroline.

We all looked at each other, then turned and began to run through the labyrinth.

We jogged the path, our pounding feet making quick time. My pack bounced on my back as I ran, and felt happy, I felt we were making good time.

We switched it up a bit, I was in the front at first, then Kym, then Christianne, and then Tupu. It was when Caroline got out front that I stumbled.

The toe of my boot caught in the thick grass, and down I went on my face. As I tumbled to the blue ground, I thought, 'something tripped me.' And I was sure that the grass had reached up and grabbed my foot – either that or I'd stumbled over a depression in the smooth turf, which had been pretty much perfectly flat up to that point.

Either way, I went down hard.

"Oooff!"

"Charlotte!"

"Hey, you okay?"

The others all stopped to help me, which is always reassuring when you fall.

Except ...

"Grab her. GRAB HER!"

I felt something grip my leg. It squeezed my calf tightly and began to constrict it until it throbbed.

"AAH!" I screamed. It felt like a huge snake had wrapped itself around my leg and squeezed. I looked down and saw my leg had been swallowed up by the turf up to my knee. The sod was undulating and slowly making its way, inch by inch, up my leg.

"Help! HELP!!"

"Jim and Tupu grabbed my arms and pulled. Christianne had her scimitar out and was chopping at the grass.

"Get it in!" Khepri yelled as she slipped her scimitar beside my swallowed leg and then Caroline did the same on the other side.

"Be careful of her other leg!"

"PULL!"

"Gods, it's getting worse!"

I heard a roar, and suddenly the chimera was there. Kym had transformed.

"Hold on," she said grimly, then grabbed hold of my leg above the turf and wiggled a bit until her fangs had gone on either side of my thigh. I watched her, mesmerized. I trusted Kym with my life, and I wasn't afraid. I knew she would make sure not to hurt me. Still, it was harrowing.

The chimera pulled and drew my leg out of the turf that had swallowed it. We fell back. The chimera transformed and was Kym again.

I took a deep breath. Then another.

"OH NO!"

The thing that had wrapped itself around my leg, the thing living under the turf, was emerging. And it looked angry.

"RUN!"

It looked like a green snake, but had four heads, and it hissed as it came for us. Dark green fangs filled each mouth, in each of the four heads.

It struck again and again, nearly reaching us as we ran. The creature must've been huge. As I glanced over my shoulder, I could see that, even as it came for us, its many heads hissing angrily, the other end of the thing was still stuck in the ground. It just kept slithering out of the turf, like a never-ending nightmare.

The giant four-headed snake-monster whipped around the path after us, hissing angrily as it came. The hair on the back of my neck rose, and I felt a chill shiver through my body as I ran.

Everyone was deeply freaked out. We ran in a barely controlled panic.

Jim ran alongside Tupu, his hand at her back to hurry her along. He finally picked her up and ran with her, although she seemed to protest the help. Caroline and Khepri held me on either side as I hobbled along faster than I thought imaginable.

"Go! Go! Go!"

We raced on for a hundred yards, two hundred, and then three hundred. Whichever way we turned, the path went onward. There were no dead ends.

What are the odds?

I was soon able to race along on my own, and we all stepped it up and sprinted. Kym was in front, then Jim holding Tupu, then Caroline and I, side by side, then Christianne and Khepri.

"Let me down!"

"We can move faster this way, love."

"I am not an invalid!"

"No, but you are slower than I am, even carrying you."

Tupu let off a string of swear words, then went quiet. "Hey, I can't see it, I haven't seen it for a few minutes. I think we left it behind," she said.

"Better safe than sorry," Jim ran on.

"Dammit!"

We raced on for quite a while, then finally stopped.

Kym plopped down, gasping for air, then scrambled up and looked at the blue grass suspiciously. We all did, and then kicked at the turf for a few minutes, trying to see if there were any monsters under the sod.

It seemed monster free, so we sat and tried to catch our breath.

"Did ... did you see that thing?" Christianne said, still panting.

"It had ... four heads!" Caroline said.

"And three eyes on each head – did you see that?" Jim asked.

"What?"

"Three *eyes*?"

"Please tell me you're kidding."

"No, there were three eyes on each head. Two in the normal place, and the third on the top of each head, in between the other two."

"Are you sure those were *eyes*? They looked more like thorns."

"Well they were looking at us, so I'm going to call them 'eyes.' "

"Charlotte, let me check your leg where it had hold of you." Khepri bent to pull my trousers up.

The snake-monster had left a redness around my calf, but the skin was not broken.

"I think that's where it was squeezing," I said, touching the area gingerly. It smarted a bit, but I would be okay.

"Still," said Khepri, withdrawing her favorite ointment from her medical pouch. "It couldn't hurt." She looked in my eyes, and I nodded, and she bent to smooth it over the red skin, happy.

The tincture felt cool and healing, and as I watched it soak into the skin, I felt my whole body relax and begin to heal.

"That was a close call, Miss," Caroline, said smoothing my shoulder.

"Here, Charlotte," Kym held her waterskin to my lips and I drank deeply, feeling even better. Khepri glanced up from her ministrations and nodded.

"Everyone drink some water. I have a feeling we're going to need to be well hydrated and on our toes today." She paused and swallowed. "This last hour could have ended badly, really badly." She patted my shoulder, a worried look in her eyes.

And we slept.

Chapter Twenty-Seven

Reconnaissance

The next morning, I had a thought. "Jim, could you fly up and take a look? Maybe see where the exit is?"

"Did that this morning before you woke up, Charlotte. Saw the maze was pretty much endless. I think it's sentient, to be honest. But I'll go again if you'd like," said Jim.

"Yeah, okay, please check. See if it's the same or if anything changed."

Jim nodded and shimmered, transforming into his djinn form. He rose up into the air about fifty feet and hovered there, turning around and scanning the area. Then he sped off and was gone.

We sat, waiting.

"Charlotte, what do you think is going to happen next?" asked Christianne.

"I don't know. I have no idea," I answered.

"How are we going to get back home?" asked Tupu, looking up at the sky. I followed her gaze and studied the two suns, making sure not to look at them directly.

I don't think we are anywhere near home. I think we are very far away.

"Have we given up on finding the book, Charlotte?" Kym asked.

"No, we have not. I know we've found ourselves in an odd place, but I think that whoever drew the map and set those warnings, was the person who set the traps and made the stuff inside the volcano." I took a deep breath. "I am hoping we will be able to figure this out, obtain the book, and travel back home somehow. Remember: Akim, Tam and the others are still on the ship, waiting for us."

"And the centaurs are all waiting on the answer too, huh?" Kym smiled.

"Yes," I smiled back and nodded, "They are. And we can't let our friends down. Now, I think I see the djinn coming back; let's see what he has to say."

We all looked out over the hedge and across the sky. The djinn was racing back to us; he looked like he was moving very fast.

Indeed, he was.

He flew over the hedge and down to us, and plopped on the grass, panting as he changed from blue-green-purple-hued djinn back to cocoa-hued human.

We waited while he caught his breath.

"Charlotte, we must leave this maze immediately," he panted.

"Jim, catch your breath first and tell us what you found."

He shook his head.

Khepri came forward then. "He is not gaining his breath," she kneeled to check his heart. "He has some enchantment affecting him, I believe."

Jim nodded, waving at me.

He couldn't even speak now.

"Charlotte, bring forth your chalk and parchment," Khepri said, as Jim leaned forward and vomited.

"What is happening?" Christianne sounded panicked.

"He is ... "

"I don't think ... "

"Oh, there he goes."

Jim collapsed into the ground and lay still.

"We need to get him breathing again," Khepri said urgently. "Bring me a waterskin."

"Jim?" Tupu touched his arm, then his face. "Khepri he can't ... "

Khepri worked on the djinn for nearly an hour, and finally had him sitting up and feeling better as he sipped a special tincture she'd brewed for him.

"It's a stimulant. It's helping his heart to beat faster," she remarked, putting her herb pouches back int her medical bag.

I sat down in front of Jim, rubbed his forearms, and waited.

It was a few minutes before he began to speak, and then it was only in a whisper.

"Be very still and quiet," his voice was barely audible. He held the parchment in his hand, and began to draw.

Tupu held him from behind and watched as forms began to take shape at the end of the chalk.

I saw what he was drawing and looked up into Tupu's eyes, as Jim bent low over the parchment, concentrating.

Tupu's expression looked constricted.

The drawing Jim was making was a collection of runes that together formed a large sigil. I'd learned about sigils during my third year of studies at the academy back in Swerighe: They were an archaic form of magic and communication once used throughout the northlands, but one that had fallen out of use more than five hundred years before. I, however, was fluent in them thanks to my studies. I had been teaching the troupe the different forms every evening on board our ship as we made our way west, mainly so we could communicate silently if we had to.

I studied the sigil Jim was drawing. The entire parchment was filling with different marks, all forming a circle; this indicated Jim felt his message was all concerning the same issue.

The first rune was the mark for *watched*. Jim was telling us that we were being watched, most likely by a malicious entity. I concentrated on reading the form he was drawing. Jim's brow was furrowed in concentration as he worked.

The second rune was the mark for *draconian*. I took this to mean the land we were in was not all sunshine and flowers, but actually cruel and brutal. As if he could read my mind, he patted my hand. I raised my eyes to his, and I realized he'd been watching me read the sigils. He shook his head and gestured with his hand holding the chalk, in a wide swirling circle, encompassing the maze. The labyrinth was what he meant by the second sigil.

My heart raced faster.

The rest of the troupe had fallen silent, studying both of us and reading what Jim was trying to convey, by my facial expressions.

The third and fourth runes making up the sigil were the marks for *danger* and the mark for ... I concentrated, trying to remember.

What was that fourth rune?

I had it. *Weapon.* It was the rune for weapon. This could mean either that we were the focus of a weapon, or a collection of weapons, or Jim was suggesting that we draw our weapons. I looked up and studied Jim's face. He looked up at me and then down at the rune, then up again, his eyebrows raised. Then he very quickly glanced down at my belt, then up again. He lifted his chin and seemed to stretch his neck.

My belt. My belt. What was ... *Oh.*

I looked up at the others and met each face, widening my eyes for each one. Then I lazily dropped my hand to the pommel of my scimitar, which rested in its scabbard, which was threaded through my belt. Then I dropped my hand quickly down to rest against my leg. I didn't want to draw the attention of whoever or whatever was watching us.

My breath quickened as I watched the others do the same.

We all stood, Jim still a bit unsteady.

We were being watched by a malevolent entity or entities, the maze was a draconian labyrinth, we were in danger, and we would need our weapons.

Jim was sketching the final rune of the elaborate sigil.

The bottom rune in a sigil was always the base of the sigil. All the other runes pertained to this subject rune. Everything was better understood when you knew how it fit with the overall theme. And Jim had left the subject rune for last.

We all stood in a circle, shielding the djinn as he drew on the parchment. The chalk was almost down to a nub as he finished. I looked at what he'd drawn, and gulped, a cold chill crawling up my spine, and goosebumps rising all down my arms.

The last rune of the sigil was the mark for *plants*.

Jim was looking into my eyes, and his face looked both deadly serious and frightened. His eyes quickly swung around the outer edge of my face, almost faster than I could follow, then back to my eyes. Then he glanced down at the rune he's just drawn. The last rune.

Plants.

Oh, gods. Oh, dear gods.

I understood what Jim was trying to tell us. I understood why he hadn't been able to breathe for a while. I understood what he had seen from above.

It was the entire place. The reason we hadn't seen any animal or insect life was that the entities that inhabited this world, that ruled this world, were the very plants around us.

The labyrinth, the grass, the trees, the flowers. All of it.

That multiheaded snake that had come for me? It had been no snake, it had been a massive carnivorous vine.

I glanced around us and looked down. The blue grass had seemed so beautiful, so exotic. The little flowers so sweet and pretty. I looked at the hedge bushes surrounding us. We had thought them so fun and innocent, a maze to explore, as I had explored the labyrinth on the castle grounds, as a child.

But it was the plants that were the monsters here.

Chapter Twenty-Eight
A Rune of Healing

I held my breath.

Suddenly, Kym screamed, and I was instantly on alert.

I will never know if the hedge realized what Jim's message was, or if it had just decided that it had had enough of us, but as I swung around to face Kym, I saw why she had screamed.

The hedge was moving again, herding us. We rushed ahead, and I looked over my shoulder, worried that another carnivorous, man-eating vine might rise up out of the grass. But I needn't have worried, there was no giant vine.

It was the hedge.

I stopped.

Where was Kym?

She had been running right alongside me.

"Stop!" I screamed.

The others halted their headlong sprint.

I turned and looked back, just in time to see Kym being swallowed alive. The bushes were reaching out and surrounding her body, enveloping it, squeezing it, tightening their hold. The last thing I saw were Kym's eyes, wide in terror.

"Come on!" I called to the others. We raced back and, without pausing, I began slashing the hedge a foot to the side of where it had swallowed Kym.

"AARGH!" I yelled as I chopped. Pieces of hedge bush were flying everywhere. Caroline began swinging her scimitar on the other side of where Kym had been taken. We cut and we cut, and the others began chopping the labyrinth walls, too.

Together, we were making some headway. Pieces of hedge were falling all around us. The wall of bushes started to sway violently back and forth, as if buffeted by a strong wind. I began yelling at the monster bush, and my face grew red with the effort I was making.

Suddenly, the wall of bushes opened slightly and I could see Kym in there, deep in the foliage.

"Charlotte!" Kym cried out in a panic.

"Kymmy!" I yelled out, forgetting momentarily that she didn't like being called that nickname of a nickname. The bushes began to close up, and I reached out with my left arm, still swinging my sword with my right. But when I turned just a quarter of my attention from chopping the bush, and tried to grab Kym, and that was all it took.

A large piece of the hedge, bent down from above us, swung sideways and down, pounding me in the temple, momentarily stunning me. I swayed on my feet, seeing stars. My scimitar arm dropped.

"Charlotte!" I heard Khepri scream.

The bush was trying to swallow me.

I brought my sword up again and chopped from one side, while the others chopped at the hedge from the other.

It was repairing itself as fast as we could slice it.

We aren't going to win this.

My heart raced.

It's trying to kill us.

All of a sudden, I heard a loud roar, and the hedge around me practically exploded outward. Pieces of bush flew everywhere. It was the chimera. She roared again and swung wide, pounding the foliage with both massive lion's paws.

The hedge backed off from trying to swallow us.

We could see the walls of the labyrinth back off from the chimera. We all gathered around the beast, and the hedge backed away, until we were in a small clearing, with pieces of bush lying all around us. The chimera panted and swung around several times, eyeing the hedge and growling deep in her throat, but the plants did not attack again.

The chimera shimmered and transformed back into Kym.

"Kym, are you all right?" I asked, breathing hard. This situation was unreal.

"I think so," she looked at me, worried.

"Kym, maybe you should stay in chimera form until we get out of here?"

She nodded. Her body shimmered again, and the chimera was there once more. From the corner of my eye, I saw the bushes cringe and pull back another inch. It wasn't my imagination.

"We need to get out of here," Jim said.

"Agreed."

I looked around us and saw the maze led off ahead in only one direction. "I think this is the direction we were going."

"It won't matter," Jim said grimly. "The labyrinth changes almost continuously, when I was in the sky looking down I could see it shifting, transforming, undulating even. It was almost acting like a current in a large river."

This was not good news.

"All right," I said to the group at large. "I want everyone to stay together. Hook arms with your neighbor. Keep your weapon at the ready. Now, what does everyone think? Should we go forward? Back? Chop our way to the side?"

"I think Jim's correct, Miss. It won't matter. The maze will just move with us."

"Charlotte, I have an idea." Tupu gave me a significant look and nodded. I brought out the parchment and chalk again, and handed it to her.

She drew a picture of the chimera.

Just what I was thinking.

Kym peeked over our shoulders and saw what Tupu had drawn. Tupu kept drawing, and soon the scene on the parchment showed the hedge wall, the chimera and me. I understood. The chimera nodded in understanding.

We turned around, and I stepped forward.

"We demand to be released from this maze immediately. If you do not comply, we will destroy you," I gestured at the chimera to indicate our weapon.

The labyrinth did not react.

"This is your last warning," I added.

The chimera stalked forward a few feet and let out a massive roar that shook the air. The hedge leaned back a few inches.

Then, it enclosed us all in a large circle about fifteen feet in diameter, and slowly opened a pathway. It was a clear invitation.

We looked at one another.

"You think it's on the up-and-up?"

"Only one way to find out."

"Be on guard, everyone."

We walked forward; swords drawn. At the new archway into what we hoped was the exit, I paused, looking in. To the right was another hedge wall, to the left was another corner to turn.

Wait.

I felt a violent push from behind me, and stumbled forward, and the world went black.

"Hey!"

"What pushed me?"

"Oh, no."

"I can't see a thing.

"I think it's duped us again."

"I knew something like this might happen."

"Getting tired of this."

Gods this is getting tedious.

"Okay, back up, everyone. Just take a dozen steps backward," I said.

I began to step backward carefully, foot by foot. After maybe a half dozen steps, the sun suddenly switched on, and I blinked rapidly.

I swung around and quickly walked to the opposite edge of the large circle of hedge joining Khepri and Caroline who were already there. Jim, Tupu, and the chimera appeared a few seconds later.

"Where is Christianne?"

"Oh, gods, is she still in there?"

"CHRISTIANNE!"

"I'll go get her," I turned to Caroline. "Hold my waist?"

"I'll hold it, too."

"Me, too."

"I want to help."

In the end all six of us formed a human chain and, with Caroline holding onto my waist, I walked in to the utter, impenetrable darkness bullshit that the labyrinth was trying to envelope us with.

My eyes were useless in the blackness. I put out my arms and swung them slowly back and forth while calling out her name. "Christianne? Where are you?"

Nothing.

I wandered about the area, my arms reaching out, encountering only air or hedge bush. I stumbled a few times; it was hard to walk in an unfamiliar place when you couldn't see.

"Christianne?!" I called, but my voice seemed to get swallowed up in the darkness, as if it were a tangible, sound-deafening thing, as if it were alive.

I pushed back a shudder, drawing reassurance that my friends had me, the firm grip Caroline had on my waist my only tether to the world of the sane and living.

Get a grip. Find Christianne.

Finally, I found her on the floor, huddled against the far-right corner of the bushy side. When my hands found her, she jumped and then sobbed, leaping up into my arms.

"There, there, it's okay, shhhh. I've got you."

It had been less than ten minutes for her in that blackness, but she was shaking uncontrollably. I took a few minutes to calm and sooth her, and then I felt it.

The creeping cold, the mind-numbing uneasiness. The Fear.

"Okay, sweetie, let's get out of here." I held her tightly and backed out, the others practically pulling me in their eagerness to be out of the blackness. I got three steps back, and suddenly I could not move.

"It's got me," Christianne whispered.

"Press yourself against me, Chrissy." She flattened her torso and legs against mine, enfolding herself around me and tucking her head under my chin and her arms around my middle. I brought my scimitar up and cleaved down in a wide, blind arc. I felt it slice through a vine. I chopped at it a dozen times before it broke off its attack. I took a deep breath as I pulled Christianne away, the others pulling us firmly out.

Once we were back in the sunshine, we rushed to the back edge, away from the dark hedge hallway, and looked Christianne over carefully. Her leg looked like it took the brunt of the attack, the skin there was red and raised with bumps.

Khepri got to work on the wound right away as I held Christianne close. She was sobbing quietly, and I reminded myself that she was the youngest member of our little troupe. She was barely fourteen. Sure, Kym looked only six, but the chimera was thousands of years old. Christianne was just a child, really.

I held Christianne for a long time, rocking her back and forth, as her mild crying changed to gentle hiccoughs and then finally to silence.

Jim then sat down next to Christianne, and started quietly humming a lullaby. He held his hand out, palm up, and whispered a few words, and yellow and pink sparkles began to fly up a few inches from the palm of his hand. Christianne was mesmerized.

"May I color a bit of magic on your leg wrap?" he asked softly. She nodded, an intrigued look on her face. We all gathered close to see what he would do.

"My mother used to do this on my wounds when I was a child," he said softly as he worked. "Of course, that was a very long time ago, before the universe split into three." His eyes merry, a mischievous smile on his face, he finished and then held up his hands, cupped them together, blew gently into the middle and opened them again, and a small, brilliant blue butterfly emerged from inside. It crawled up Jim's finger and rested there, flexing its beautiful wings.

"This magic butterfly cannot live in such a place as this," Jim said. "He must be brought back home with us if he is to survive." He looked solemnly into Christianne's eyes. "Will you protect him and nurture him and keep him safe, all the way home?"

Christianne nodded earnestly.

Jim held up his other hand and blew into it and a small white cage appeared. He coaxed the butterfly inside. As he handed the little cage to Christianne, he said, "Give him a flower every day. Sing him to sleep. Keep him close to your heart, and he will thrive. When we get back home to the island, let him go in a field of flowers, and he will be happy."

Christianne took the butterfly solemnly, taking to heart all Jim had said.

Khepri's salve, bandage and final blessing, the butterfly, and the rune of healing drawn onto the dressing by Jim, made a cheerful sight that brought a smile to Christianne's face.

Chapter Twenty-Nine
Enough

We rested there for a bit, eyeing the hedge with deep suspicion.

"Make sure to stay right next to the group. In fact, let's stay in physical contact with each other," I said. "Keep your eyes peeled for anything, especially a bush or vine coming near us."

The labyrinth stayed quiet and away from us, perhaps wondering if we were okay or if we were compromised in any way. *It may be looking for a weakness. We must be constantly on alert.*

I hated to be on the defensive. Hated waiting for something to happen. If given the choice between fending off an attack and attacking first myself, I'd pick offense every time. I'd much rather be leading the action than being the victim.

Christianne seemed to recover her zazz after twenty minutes. She glanced at me with a sly smile on her face, and I saw that her resolve had returned. She hated being a sitting duck just as much as I did, and this situation was quickly becoming intolerable. We were the quarry here, and we were on the defensive. It was unacceptable.

We passed around some dried meat and berries we had from the centaur's gardens. The sky was calm, the hedge remained quiet, and it all gave me a sense of foreboding. Tupu and I exchanged much the same look that Christianne and I had. Then I caught Caroline's eye, and saw she felt much the same. It was all in a look, disgust married with resolve. We had had enough of this.

I looked at the labyrinth bush all around us; it seemed to be holding its breath, waiting for us to become vulnerable again. Almost waiting to make its next aggressive move against us.

Next aggressive move. Hmmm.

I threw down my dried rabbit meat and stood up.

"Kym," I said quietly, pulling the chimera aside; we communicated with the parchment and chalk. The others stood as well, surrounding us to shield us from the hedge. Jim kept Christianne close, holding her hand. He'd transformed into the strong looking djinn again, an impressive sight, to help guard Christianne. He and Tupu held her close.

Kym in chimera form was normally nearly ten feet tall, from her shoulder to the ground. But I'd remembered something she'd told me in passing, one night while we were aboard *Pride of the Sea* and gathered in my cabin after supper. Something Kym hadn't thought very important because she'd never been truly threatened by something as massive as the labyrinth.

"So, you can do this?" I whispered, gesturing to the drawing I had made on the thick parchment roll.

"Easily," the chimera smiled.

A large chimera smiling is a disconcerting sight, and, not for the first time, I whispered a *'thank you'* to her and felt grateful she was on our side. We nodded at one another and rose from where we'd been huddled.

"Jim, Tupu, stay close to Christianne. Everyone: weapons." I nodded at the chimera to begin.

Kym in chimera form let out a massive roar and began to grow. If she was impressive at ten feet tall, she was positively awe-inspiring at thirty feet tall. It took her less than thirty seconds to reach that height. Once she did, she spread her legs, smashing the hedge on either side in the process, and let out an absolutely deafening scream of fury.

The chimera rushed forward, swiping her massive paws right and left, sending bush and flower flying. She continued to roar and wreak devastation, at one point, leaping high and coming down heavily on a particularly threatening section of labyrinth that was trying to match her growth and overshadow her, attempting to enclose her even after she had attained her massive size.

We fought alongside the enormous chimera, our scimitars swiping wide arcs and cutting the hedge to bits.

"Khepri!" I heard Caroline call the healer and glanced back, and saw my friend launched into the air by the healer, and then Khepri followed her, and they both had jumped atop a particularly thick bit of hedge that had stayed back behind the chimera.

"Hey, what's that?" I called.

"They think it may be the brain of the thing," Christianne said, running up to my side.

"Good to see you fighting, my friend," I grinned at her. Christianne had always been a particularly fierce and cynical young lady, and she flashed a devilish grin at me as she jumped after Khepri. It gave me an extra surge of adrenalin.

"I'm going, too!" I laughed as I leaped up after them. I swayed a bit and then scrambled along the top of the thick, massive bush.

We stabbed through it, hacked at it like we were chopping firewood, and slashed away as if we were clearing an overgrowth, and it was a scene of enormous devastation.

The hedge was swaying back and forth, trying to enclose us. When that failed, it tried to smash us right and left, no longer hiding its intentions: It meant to kill us, and its ferocity was plain. Which was just fine with me, as we were trying very hard to kill it right back. I much preferred an open fight with honest combat to the sneaky subterfuge of earlier in the day.

I idly wonder if it meant to kill all forms of animal life on this world, or it there just hadn't been any at all.

I swung my scimitar wide, chopped branch after branch. The chimera fought beside us, paws on the ground, head high in the sky over the labyrinth, wreaking havoc everywhere. She was frightening; her deafening roar, her great paws and her teeth made the chimera invincible.

She had gone berserk, and moved faster than I could follow, swinging and smashing and slicing and visiting utter devastation upon the living labyrinth. The hedge tried to fight back, rose to nearly fifteen feet, but it was no match for the ravaging chimera. It was a massacre.

Caroline, Khepri, Christianne and I chopped and cut at the thick bush we had climbed atop until there was nothing much left of it, our four swords having hacked it to bits. I hopped down from the last three feet or so, and turned to cleave through another thick section of hedge. I had separated it from the main mass and hacked it to death, literally. There was nothing left but fragments, which quickly turned from green to black, withering before my eyes.

Within twenty-five minutes battling the labyrinth hedge, the scene was one of herbal devastation. Bits of blackened branches and bush lay everywhere. The hedge began to quickly fall back, leaving us standing on a meadow of blue grass. The labyrinth's decision to stop fighting, and escape with what life it still had, was abrupt. We watched as the maze shrank and withdrew from the meadow, roots undulating in and out of the soil as it retreated rapidly over the far-left hill.

We stood there, panting from the exertion, exhilarated from the battle. Tupu let out a happy cry and thrust her sword into the air in triumph, and we all followed suit, gleeful to have finally defeated the wretched labyrinth.

I grinned as I wiped my scimitar blade against my leg to clean off the sap and the remnants of battle.

Kym shimmered, and the giant chimera was gone, replaced by a small, grinning, six-year-old girl with dancing eyes.

"That was incredible," Christianne called into the meadow, and Caroline and Khepri made "*woop!*" noises of celebration that made me chuckle.

We scouted the area in a cursory check to make sure we were actually safe.

"I know the whole land is inhospitable and unfriendly, but I will say, I am so glad to be free of the stupid labyrinth."

"Very glad."

"I thought we'd never be free. Well, I mean, I *hoped* we'd be free. Soon."

"I never doubted us."

"Oh, please. You were just as worried as I was."

"No, I wasn't. Well, maybe I was, but I never had any doubt we'd eventually get free. No, honestly!

"Well, thanks to Jim, he really helped."

Jim blushed.

"Hey! I helped, too!"

"You certainly did, sweetheart. We couldn't have done it without you."

"Thank you."

"Haha, you were so badass, Kym!"

"HA! Hee hee! I guess I was. I'd just had enough of the thing."

"Ugh, me too."

"Soooo irritating."

The djinn shimmered and transformed back into Jim, shrinking in size and returning to his human color. He took a deep breath and smiled, and then turned to look around.

"Hey," said Jim, "Who is that?"

'Who'?

I looked up sharply and followed his pointing finger.

We all looked. My jaw dropped open.

Chapter Thirty
The City

We looked at the small hill to our right. At the top was what appeared to be a small boy. He was staring at us, unmoving.

I began walking toward him, not thinking about it, just wanting to ask him some questions. The boy turned and walked away, over the hill. He began to disappear as he walked down the far side of the slope.

"Hey," I called. "HEY!" I began to run, the others following me.

He'd been about seventy or eighty yards away when we'd spotted him, and he was disappearing from view fast, so I began to sprint. His head disappeared for good when I was still thirty yards away, and by the time I got to the apex of the hill and looked down, he was far down the other side. He was nearly to the bottom of the hill, maybe thirty yards away, and he was walking with purpose into the arms of a woman crouched at the bottom, arms outstretched. *His mother?*

The boy ran into his mother's embrace, and she picked him up, hugging him and then holding him on her hip and staring at us as we hurried down the hill. Before we could get to them, she set the child down and walked with him, hand in hand, off to the nearby rocky hillside to the left. They walked into a large cave and turned, watching us approach.

I hurried up to them, not wanting to lose them, and the others ran after me.

"Hello. Hello!" I said. "Listen, can you help us? We would like to find a safe place to rest. We battled the labyrinth ..." Here I gestured behind me, and turned to glance back. When I turned back to them, the pair had turned and begun to walk farther into the cave.

We followed them.

The cave floor was packed dirt, moist but not wet, and easy to walk on. The walls were some kind of natural rock, although they looked unfamiliar to me. As we got farther in, there were torches set in sconces on the walls, to light the path. The air was cool and crisp, as if a breeze blew through the cave regularly. The smell of moisture on rock was refreshing, and I smiled and breathed deeply as we walked after them.

The packed-earth path the pair led us on veered downward now, a gentle slope that was easy to walk. It extended nearly a half mile into the mountain before opening out into a huge, elaborate system of tunnels.

I gasped.

"Wow," I heard Caroline exclaim in awe beside me.

There were hundreds of people walking along more than a dozen paths under the rock. The mother walked with her little boy, off in a direction, and disappeared into the crowd. Just before they were swallowed by the mass of people, the boy let go of her hand and ran off, laughing.

Paths branched off in many different directions. Some led into natural rock formations that formed rooms, and in these rooms were wares for sale. We saw mushrooms, lichen, water bowls and other sundries on display, as well as what appeared to be colorful shoes, sandals and purses.

The people were adorned in bright clothing of different hues. The adults all wore some kind of foot covering, but the children, and there were plenty of them, were mostly barefoot.

The people did not appear human, but instead showed several markings and distinctive growths that appeared alien and beautiful. I saw several women with eyes that appeared almond-shaped and larger than normal for a human. The eyes were varying shades of blue and violet, and quite lovely. I saw a man with speckling on the side of his face, another with what appeared to be double ears on either side of his head. A third man and his companion both had fingers that were twice the length of ours.

We people-watched for a good ten minutes, not knowing what to do or where to go, content to just soak up this community. But all fun things come to an end, and after a while we saw a group of officials striding up to us with purpose.

"Greetings, visitors. Please follow us to the Deepening Hall," The man leading the group gestured to us and turned, leading us off one of the pathways. We dutifully followed; I think we were still tired from the fight with the hedge maze, plus we were very glad to see an actual mammal.

We entered a large room, where floor-to-ceiling banners of different hues and designs had been hung. Blues and greens were the most prominent colors, and the effect was bright and cheerful. We were led to the far end of the hall, to a large circle of cushions gathered on low benches.

"This looks very interesting."

"What do you think those banners are made of?"

"I think I'm going to like this place."

"I wonder if they have anything new to eat. I'm getting tired of dried meat and berries."

"I hope they do. That sounds good."

"Great, my stomach just grumbled."

"I hope they have a bathroom."

We settled down on the cushions, which were very soft and comfortable. The group of leaders sat with us, and then looked off toward a door in the corner, clapping their hands.

The sound of their clapping was almost musical, and together they sounded like varying sizes of bells. I felt charmed. The leaders smiled at us and began to speak.

"Welcome to the Deepening Hall. We greet you, kind visitors, in the name of the Three, and we wonder if you feel ready to answer our questions?" said the man who first spoke to us. "My name is Po, I greet you on behalf of the People of the City."

Po had just two ears, but the edges were rippled and reached out farther than ours. His eyes were slanted and a brilliant green, and almost seemed to glow from within. His arms and legs were very slender, and he looked almost too thin. His face was long, and his skin was dark tan with a pearly quality to it. His clothing was a billowing outfit of brilliant orange.

"Hello, I am Charlotte. My friends and I were transported here by some kind of magic. We would like a respite from the plants," I said.

"Yes, we are safe here in the city. The plants cannot follow." He gestured to the smooth rock ground.

"I guess the packed dirt floor outside is similarly blocked from the plants?" I asked.

"Yes. The dirt was brought in ages ago. The entire city system is surrounded by rock," he replied.

Several new people entered the room with cups and a jug of some kind of liquid.

"Are you thirsty?" The man took a cup and poured himself some of the beverage. It looked pearly white. "This is called tal."

"What is it made of?" Khepri asked.

"It is a drink brewed from the puffballs that grow near the outskirts of the city. It is both refreshing and enticing," he smiled and poured another cup and offered it to me.

I took it and smelled it. It had no odor, but the liquid swirled around in the cup, showing eddies of color, and appearing pearly white at the same time.

Khepri nodded and I took a sip. It was delicious. I smiled at the others, nodding.

Po seemed very pleased, and the server passed around cups, which were filled. We were all soon sipping the pearly liquid.

"We have just finished battling the labyrinth creature up above. It was most ferocious; it tried to kill us. Do you know of it?" I took another sip of tal.

Po seemed to expand with happiness. "We know. We saw the battle. There is a high-altitude vantage point where we can see the entire valley. We've actually been watching you for some time. When you entered the hedge maze, we were sure you wouldn't ever escape. The labyrinth is deadly."

Others of the People came forward to listen, sitting on the floor and seats near us, and watching us with rapt attention.

"You've been watching us?" Tupu asked.

Po nodded. "We saw you come down from the hills and were amazed. We haven't seen a visitor in hundreds of years."

"You and your people live underground to avoid the plants?" asked Khepri.

"That is correct. We moved into the tunnels and created this city several thousand years ago."

"What did you do before that?" asked Jim.

"We lived on the surface."

"So, the plants became carnivorous and you moved underground?" asked Christianne.

"No, the plants have always been carnivorous. It was when they evolved to be able to move and think that it became too dangerous to remain on the surface."

My eyebrows rose at this. *What an incredibly inhospitable place.*

"We were so happy to see you all triumph over the hedge maze. Word spread far and wide as it happened. We've been celebrating ever since." He beamed.

I smiled back. "We owe much of our victory to our friend Kym," I put my arm around Kym and brought her forward. She smiled shyly.

"We saw her transform into a massive animal. It was amazing," Po turned to Kym, "Young lady, what manner of creature are you, exactly?"

I nodded to Kym's questioning look, and she turned to Po. "I'm a chimera," she grinned proudly.

There was a murmur of excitement that moved through the people seated around us, they smiled and nodded, looking at each other and then at Kym.

"And there was a purple and green man as well?" Po asked.

"That was me," said Jim.

"What type of creature are you, may I ask? I apologize if we seem curious, it's just that none of us has ever seen such different creatures."

"I'm a djinn," Jim said. "I was freed from the lamp that had entrapped me, by Charlotte here," Jim turned and hugged me with one arm, then continued. "I am now free and part of the troupe."

"The troupe?" Po asked.

"We sailed here on our ship, *Pride of the Sea*, on a quest," said Jim.

"Yes, we are searching for *The Book of Mysteries*," I said, remembering our initial aim.

"The book of? Of mysteries?" Po asked.

"Yes, have you ever heard of it?" I answered.

"We have many books in our library, written by our artists and authors, and some from a very long time ago. We could search for this book, if you wish. But we only have books from our own people, nothing that was brought here."

"That would be nice." I smiled. "We have come along way looking for it."

"Where did you say you came from?" Po asked.

"We've come through the volcano, it seemed to magically transport us," Caroline said.

"You must be very strong and resourceful, because you defeated the maze, one of the most dangerous predators on the surface." Po gestured above his head. "I wish to hear more of this book you are seeking."

Another group of servants entered. One of them was carrying a brass chime hanging from a chain. He held it high and struck it gently with a small rod, and a high note rang out.

"Ah, it is our evening meal," Po smiled broadly. "Will you please join us for supper?"

"Certainly!" We all nodded enthusiastically. The battle with the labyrinth had been hard, and we'd worked up an appetite. Po had read my mind.

"Come. I will show where to wash up. I know it must've been sweaty work fighting that maze." Po walked off in a different direction from which we'd entered the room.

Down a long, cool hallway, then another. He then opened a door that led into a large dormitory type room, complete with many large cushions, pillows, and throws.

"There are water facilities through the far door. We hope you will be comfortable here while you stay with us?" Po gestured into the room.

"Thank you."

"Looks nice."

"Thanks a bunch."

"Oh, I need to wash my face."

"Me, too."

We entered the room, and dropped our bags on the side.

"When you are ready, please return to the Deepening Hall, where the meal will be laid out," Po smiled and bowed as he backed out of the room.

Chapter Thirty-One

Supper and Lullaby

Ten minutes later, we were walking back down the corridor to the Deepening Hall. I shouldered my bag and trotted after the others.

"I'm starving."

"It's weird, we ate this morning."

"That fight made me hungry."

I laughed, hugging Kym. "I'm not surprised, sweetheart, that was quite a workout you had."

"You stomped the hedge to smithereens." Caroline smiled at Kym, patting her on the back. "Excellent job, by the way."

Kym grinned broadly.

"I hope they have a lot of delicious food."

"It'll be all new things to eat, I expect."

We entered the Deepening Hall and saw that tables had been brought in, and they were laden with all kind of delicious smelling cuisine.

"Come, come, my friends," Po rushed forward and brought us to the tables of food. They were set in the center of the benches and cushions, and we sat and began to serve ourselves on thin white plates. Everything smelled like heaven.

There were several kinds of seafood, seaweed prepared in what looked like a salad, and there a wide variety of morels, mushrooms and puffballs. Some were in a sauce that tasted like beef, some were fried into a delicious golden crust, and others were baked into a hot pasty.

"Where does the pastry come from?" I asked Po after sitting down and settling in.

"They are created from dried lichen mixed with sealeafs, ground into a pounder and mixed with other ingredients. Do you like them?" He asked, smiling.

They were delicious, in fact, I'd taken a big bite out of one pastry and found myself unable to answer Po. I chuckled and gestured to my mouth, and he laughed in merriment.

We were silent for a several minutes as we all tucked in to our delicious meal. Servants came around with more tal and poured us all cups of the nectar, and we drank deeply. The food was so good I returned for seconds, after getting the nod from Po. *You never know what the customs are in a strange land. It pays to check.*

I finally sat back, completely stuffed from the main entrées and side dishes. A servant took my plate and returned with a smaller platter of sweets.

I groaned. I couldn't fit another bite.

Christianne eagerly accepted several and bit into one, closing her eyes in ecstasy. "Ohhhh, Charlotte, you need to try a bite."

She picked out the same one from the tray and held it out to me. It *did* look delicious. I shrugged and accepted the offered dessert, and took a small nibble from a corner of the delicacy.

She was right, it *was* wonderful. I nibbled further and ended up consuming the entire square.

"I really can't have another bite, now. Really." I laughed and set down the small plate.

I sat back and rested a few minutes, my stomach overfilled, and my eyes growing heavy.

Then I remembered, "Po," I said, sitting up, "I brought the map we followed; it has some information about *The Book of Mysteries*. I thought it might help in finding it."

"Perhaps, perhaps. Do you have it now?" said Po.

"Yes," I drew out the parchment from my bag and unrolled it on my lap.

Po leaned over and studied it for a few minutes, then asked, "May I hold it, please?"

"Sure, but be very careful with it, it's very old and brittle."

"I found it. It was hidden on our ship," Kym said proudly.

Po took a long time studying the map. He handed it back to me, a thoughtful look on his face.

"Do you see the warnings, just there," he pointed to the script in the corner.

"Yes, and we have vowed to guard the book with our lives. But we wish to find it and bring it back with us, to aid mankind. Many people are suffering and afflicted by illness; we hope the book can help them." I said.

Khepri leaned forward, "Po, I am a healer, and the promise of healing even one illness would bring untold benefits to our people. Do you have illness here in your city?"

Po nodded, looking thoughtful. "Yes, our healers work on a small number of illnesses every day. Our apothecaries and chemists devise new ways of making life healthier every year. Do you not also have these in your land?"

"Our healers have many ways to heal injuries, but we have been less successful in treating illness. We would benefit from the knowledge in this book," Khepri said.

Po nodded. "I wonder if our chief healer wouldn't have knowledge of this book you seek."

"I would love to consult with them," Khepri smiled. "Who knows, your culture might have healing secrets I could bring home with me, as well as knowledge of the book."

"Let us make the journey in the morning, shall we?" Po took a sip of his cup, draining the last of the tal in it. "Have you all filled your bellies?" He smiled at Kym, who was just finishing another sweet from the dessert tray.

"It was all so delicious," said Tupu. "We can't thank you enough."

Jim raised his hand to get Po's attention. "Do you have any water to drink, Po? The supper and dessert were so rich, I fear the tal might make me feel even more full."

Po clapped his hands and gestured to one of the servants, who exited and quickly returned with a new jug. Jim extended a cup, and the man filled it with freezing cold water. He took a sip, "Ooh! Cold and crisp and even a little sweet. Yum!" and we chuckled.

We soon retired to the room assigned to us, and everyone picked a bed, setting their bags in front and reclining to get comfortable.

"I ate too much." Jim burped lightly. "Excuse me," he said, laughing.

"Charlotte, do you think the book is here in this land?" Caroline asked, bent over the parchment and studying the map.

"I don't know. I think there's a very good chance. After all, we followed the map exactly."

"Do you think the magic that transported us from the volcano to this land was installed by the mapmakers themselves?" asked Khepri.

"I hope so."

"Why would two different advanced people make two different magic portals leading to two different places?"

"That's true."

I thought for a bit. *I wonder...*

"You know, I was not too surprised to see us in another world," I began, "But I *was* somewhat surprised *not* to find centaurs here."

"That is very true, Charlotte," said Tupu. "The map did say that *The Book of Mysteries* was brought to us from beyond the stars, and hidden from man by the horsemen of the mountains."

"I haven't seen anyone that could be called horsemen of the mountains.," said Jim.

"Hmmm, I think I will ask Po about this first thing in the morning," I said.

"But ... didn't Po look at the parchment map? Didn't he look at it for a long, long time?" asked Christianne.

A worried feeling began to invade my stomach.

"Charlotte? You okay?" Caroline gently put her hand on my arm.

"Yeah, I'm just a little worried." I sighed. I was still very full, and drowsy. The sleeping cushions beckoned.

"What if we can't find the book? What if Po saw the part about the horsemen of the mountains and knew what it meant but didn't tell us? What if ..." I groaned and put my hand to my head, rubbed my temple.

"Listen," Jim said, "it'll be okay. We won't stop looking for *The Book of Mysteries*. And even if Po knows more than what he's telling us, we'll still eventually find the book, because, like I said, we won't ever stop looking for it."

"Princess, I will soothe you," said Caroline, coming over to sit behind me, and gently rubbing my neck and shoulders. She used to rub my shoulders like this when I was a little girl. *Oh, how it felt sooo good.* I closed my eyes.

Caroline began to hum a Swerighe lullaby from home. My heart swelled up. Without opening my eyes, I whispered, "Carrie, do you think mother and father are okay?"

"Yes, I do, Princess, I think they are just fine."

"Do you think they got our letters back home by now?"

"Yes, I'm sure they have."

Caroline continued to hum the lullaby and I fell asleep sitting up. The last thing I remember is swaying to the side, and Carrie gently lowering me to the bed, while still humming the lullaby.

Chapter Thirty-Two
To the Healers

I woke refreshed and happy, pleasant dreams fading into the background. At first, I couldn't find my bag, but then discovered it under a nearby chair. Relieved, I swung it over my shoulder.

We were all dressed with faces washed and boots on, and out the door an hour after dawn.

"Let's do some exploring before breakfast."

"Sounds like a grand idea."

"A brisk walk will do us good."

"I'm so curious about some of the shops we saw yesterday."

"Po is probably still asleep."

"Yep."

We walked out the door and down the corridor, and into the Deepening Hall. Everything had been tidied, and the big room was clean and bright.

"Where is their light coming from, I wonder?"

"Look, there, in the corner."

"Ahh."

No one was about, so we walked out the other door and back where we'd first seen the city.

A few people were out walking early this morning, and we smiled at them as we explored, trying to blend in. The stores were not yet open, but it was fun to window shop.

"Look at this, Christianne," I exclaimed, patting her arm and gesturing at a store display. There was a selection of what looked like metal boxes, all decorated in different ways. "This looks similar to the wares we have in the northlands." I tapped the front glass window.

Christianne put her nose to the clear glass. "What is this?" She touched the glass pane covering the store window.

"I forgot, I don't think they have large glass windows in Alkebulan, do they?" I asked.

"Mmm, they do in a few private palaces," said Khepri.

Christianne was staring at a deep rose-colored decoration. "I'll bet that's for the hair," she murmured. I looked closer.

"See, how it has a comb in the back?" she said.

"Probably then, ... yes," I said softly. I'd spotted a necklace that looked made of pearls, but the pearls were a light moss green.

"Let's walk on ahead," said Tupu. "I think I see maps and globes at the end of the street."

"Oh?" I looked up. She pointed at a shop some distance away. I squinted and saw what she meant. "Oh wow! Let's go, troupe."

We trotted down the walkway toward the map shop.

"Charlotte, look at this," Jim pointed as we walked. "The pathway we're on, here, ends at this sort of curb, and then drops down to that other part, it looks like cobblestones."

"So?"

"So why do they have a sidewalk and a street?" he asked. "I haven't seen any horses or wagons, or anything like that, have you?"

"No," I looked thoughtfully at the street as I walked. It *was* weird. "Maybe we can ask about it later." I filed it away to wonder about at a later date. The map shop was next on our right. I smiled. We had arrived.

"These maps. They look ... different." Khepri said, unnecessarily.

The maps in the window were large and round, and carved into what looked like shale. *It's probably not shale.*

I peered closer. The carved areas had dye rubbed into them, very expertly, making them look three-dimensional.

"Ooh," Christianne whispered, "Look at the globe."

The round globe had been fashioned out of some substance – what, it was impossible to tell – but the awe-inspiring part was the carving. Continents and oceans were depicted, using some kind of clay and the same dyes that were used on the maps.

"If this is an accurate depiction of this land, then ..." Khepri's voice trailed off.

I pressed my face against the glass, trying to take in every aspect of the magnificent globe.

There weren't very many oceans, the seas took up maybe ten percent of the surface area. The rest was land, but while the land above was depicted, the cities under the rock, hills and mountains were shown, in a very detailed way. The carving somehow included both the surface and underground areas, although one had to view it from different angles to see each different view. It was utterly fascinating.

"Hello! There you are!"

We all jumped a foot and turned to see Po standing behind us, smiling.

"Aren't they beautiful?"

"What?" I said, feeling like I'd been caught doing something against the rules.

He gestured to the globes and maps in the window. "A local artist crafts them. I think they are exquisite."

We glanced back at the maps and the globe.

"Yes," I turned back to him, "They are actually amazing." I smiled.

He beamed. "Is anyone hungry for breakfast?" he asked.

"Oh, my gods," Kym said.

"Yes, please."

"I'm starving."

"You are not."

"Yes, I am, Christianne."

My stomach growled. My eyes widened at the sound.

Po laughed, "I guess so. Come with me, please." He led the way back to the Deepening Hall, where more food had been laid out.

We spent an hour eating. There were different egg dishes, and some of the same dishes we'd feasted on the night before.

"Po," Kym asked, "Those maps, how did the artist know what the outer planet looked like, to create the depictions?"

"Oh, that's easy. We have had expeditions to the outside, and we have air pillows that can go as far as two days away, then back again," Po answered.

"What are 'air pillows'?" I asked.

"Uhh, hmmm, let me see." Po looked around.

A servant came and whispered in his ear. Po looked up and nodded. The servant left the room and returned swiftly, carrying a painting.

It was about two feet by three feet, and it was an elaborate depiction of a bunch of ...

"Hot air balloons," I said. I glanced at Po and explained, "That is what we call these objects," I gestured at the colorful hot air balloons in the painting. "Except we have smaller woven baskets big enough to hold maybe five people hanging under them."

The painting had recognizable hot air balloons, about seven or eight of them, floating in midair about a green and blue landscape, and under a brilliant red sky. It was a depiction of a scene in this land we had found ourselves in. But under each balloon was a shallow, curved bowl. Each bowl held at least ten or twenty people, all seated, with pillows all around them.

"These hot air balloons look much bigger than the ones we have back home," Khepri said.

"Well, to answer your initial question, we have expeditions in these air pillows, these ... ," he looked at me, " 'hot air balloons' " I nodded. "We also have maps and paintings from the past, to document what our world looks like on all sides." Po smiled proudly as he looked at the painting the servant held. "In fact, the artist painted this more than a hundred years ago." He nodded to the servant, who retreated with the painting held carefully in his hands.

"Fascinating," I said. "I am deeply impressed with the art your people have created, Po."

He closed his eyes and grinned with pride.

"I do have one question," I said.

"I am happy to answer it," Po smiled.

"Well, yesterday you saw the parchment map showing the way to *The Book of Mysteries*, correct?"

He nodded.

"On the map, it says *The Book of Mysteries* was brought to my people's land from beyond the stars, and hidden from man by the horsemen of the mountains."

Po nodded; his brow furrowed in concentration.

"We met the descendants of the 'horsemen of the mountain' – they live in the villages not far from the volcano we entered, where we encountered the magic that transported us here to your land."

Po nodded again.

I took a deep breath. "Are there any horsemen, any centaurs, here in your world?"

"Centaurs?"

I dug around in my bag for the scrap of parchment Kym had originally drawn the centaur on.

"Here it is, Charlotte," Kym handed it to me. "It was in Khepri's bag."

I remembered I had given it to the healer for safe-keeping when we were packing to go ashore onto the southern island.

I handed the depiction to Po, who took it and studied it for a minute.

"Oh, this is a quamernat." He looked up, happy.

"You have these creatures here, on your world?" I held my breath, hoping against hope for a positive answer, a fresh lead in our quest for the book.

"Yes, they live on the other side of the sea, near the grand mountains."

I gulped. "And how would we get there?" I idly asked, trying not to seem too eager.

"You could take a large air pillow," he answered. "We have several extra-large ones." He grinned happily.

I could not believe our luck.

We finished breakfast and then washed up, and were ready to visit the healer. Po led the way again, and we found out what the streets were made to contain.

"Rafts? You're kidding!" I threw my head back and let out a belly laugh.

There was a large, flat-bottomed raft made of what appeared to be some kind of sealed spongey material.

Po smiled as he led the way, turning and waving his palm outward in a flourish, inviting us aboard. We stepped onto the structure, with help from a child already aboard whose apparent job it was to steady boarding passengers.

There were several benches in rows on the raft, and there was room for fifteen or twenty people. I saw a half dozen or so pedestrians get on after our party, and sit down along both edges of the craft.

"It is our custom to sit on either side of the barge so it is balanced," Po looked at us with a sparkle in his eye. "Do you like our transportation?"

"Oh, yes," Kym said.

"I am wondering," Tupu asked. "How do you go uphill once you've floated down?"

Po wiggled his eyebrows mysteriously, smiling broadly.

"I guess we'll find out," I laughed.

The raft was ready to go. Po gave a signal, and there was a bump as water was released and knocked the back of the craft. Slowly but surely, as the water flowed more steadily, and got deeper, the raft rose and began to move. I saw the water was nearly to the top of the curb on either edge.

The raft moved faster and faster, until we were moving as fast as a trotting horse. My eyes tried to follow all the sights on either side of the street; homes, shops, even a school, it was clear this was a large community.

"What if someone wishes to get off?" I asked Po.

"We stop the barge, of course," he answered easily.

I looked and noticed the men on either side of the rear edge, they held thick rods, and held them down to run into the water as we floated downhill. They seemed to drag the rods to slow down our speed, as needed, and I saw how controlled our flight was. It had seemed rather unchecked, but these People had it under more control than I'd first realized.

We were soon at our destination, the men behind us having slowed our progress to an eventual halt. Disembarking from the raft with the child's steadying hands helping us, we found ourselves in front of a larger building. It appeared to be a big building made of stone and brick.

Po stood at the door, "This is where our healers and chemists study their craft. We don't have much illness to cure, but there are a few injuries and such that they attend to. The rest of the time is used studying ancient documents. Just recently, we unearthed new artifacts from an area of the underground that we had previously thought was lost to us. They are currently deep in the study of these relics." He led us inside.

Chapter Thirty-Three

The Alchemist

The building was a maze of laboratory tables, once we got past the outer offices. There was no one waiting to be seen, proving Po's earlier assertion that the People rarely needed a healer. Once past those waiting areas and examination rooms, we were led to the back, and down a few stairs, to the area dedicated to scientific study. There were chemists, apothecaries and healers deeply engaged in the work of alchemy. There were flames and glass tubes and magnifying glasses, all concentrated in study by women and men bent over parchment papers and engaged in intensive discussion.

Po led us to the far corner, where one of the alchemists was holding an especially engrossing discussion with several of her peers. She looked very earnest, her brown hair streaked with silver, the lines in her face accentuating the intelligent look in her eyes.

Po came to a halt at the back of the group and turned to us, his finger at his lips, before turning back to listen to the discussion until it was our turn. We waited, and the best part of this waiting was the listening.

"Ra, let's try to expose it to the tincture Li just made last night; it might react and shed its secrets."

"Do you think the elixir will have any effect on the next patients we'll see?"

"No, to tell you the truth, I do not. I think we should concentrate our studies on the relic."

"I agree, but it is also important to attend to applying the new knowledge to all the extracts we need to."

"Very well," she nodded to the scientists. "Continue your work, we meet again this afternoon." They nodded and dispersed to their various stations, and the alchemist turned to us.

"Po, how good to see you again." She reached out to wrap forearms with Po and touch foreheads.

"Mistress Azaphon, how bright this day begins." Po bowed deeply, then gestured at us.

"These are newcomers to our lands, they come seeking a book. They are following a map that has led them here from a distant world." Po looked earnestly at Azaphon. "They battled the southern hedge maze and defeated it, sending it limping away, with much of it left behind on the battlefield." He bowed and retreated back a few steps.

The alchemist's eyebrows rose into her hair. "By the three! That is an amazing feat." She held out her arms and touch them to ours. "Welcome to our land. I am sorry you met with such an inhospitable greeting as the hedge maze, but I am heartened by its defeat at the hands of new friends." She smiled broadly and invited us into an adjoining room, her hand waving us in with a beckoning gesture.

We all filed into the room, Po coming last and shutting the door quietly.

"I am Azaphon, head chemist in this humble study. I welcome you to our laboratory in the name of the Three. Please call me Az," she smiled expectantly at us.

"We are a troupe of explorers on a quest for *The Book of Mysteries*," I began, bowing. "I am Charlotte, leader of this ragtag bunch."

"Greetings Charlotte, and welcome to our land."

"This is Kym, Tupu, Christianne, Caroline, Jim, and Khepri, our healer," I put a hand out and beckoned her forward. "Khepri is very skilled in the arts of healing and alchemy." I bowed.

"Khepri, how very wonderful to meet you. I am always eager to discuss methodology with another chemist!" Az dipped her head. "Please, everyone, make yourselves at home."

We all took seats at the conferring table presented to us.

Az donned a pair of glasses, setting them on the end her nose and adjusting them carefully. She then pulled a bottle containing a swirling gold liquid within, from the shelf. "This will help us see more clearly." She tipped the bottle over carefully, holding out her finger to catch a single drop of the pearly yellow liquid. She put the finger into her mouth, sucking on it, then carefully stoppered the bottle and returned it to the shelf. "There."

I wondered what the liquid was. How would it help her to see more clearly?

Az's eyes now held a spark, a tiny pinprick of light in the same shade as the golden liquid she had just tasted.

Po moved between Az and me, his back to me, effectively blocking my view.

"Az, they have brought a map they say leads to the book they are seeking. When I glimpsed it, I knew you would be interested in it," Po said. He gestured, and Az looked expectantly in my direction.

I pulled my bag up to my lap, reached in, and began to withdraw the parchment, then stopped. Looking up at the alchemist Az, I wondered if she had a personal interest in possessing the map for herself. So instead of handing over the parchment, I looked at her thoughtfully and began to speak.

"Az, have you ever heard of such a thing as *The Book of Mysteries*? We've come a very long way to find it. It is said to possess all the knowledge of antiquity. It is said to contain wisdom given to man, from cures to all cancers, to the secrets of navigating the stars and heavens. It is said to have come to earth from beyond the stars." I leaned forward intently.

"I believe we have been transported over a vast distance by the magic we encountered inside a dormant volcano. This is where the map led us. Your world must contain the book, else why would the map lead us here in our quest?"

Az was thoughtful for a minute. Then, "May I see the map, please?"

I hesitated. *But why?* I had readily let Po look at the map. I stared at this alchemist for a while. She was an enigma. I could not tell if she was friend or foe.

"I trust Az with my life, she will not harm the map," said Po.

But will she take it for herself, I wonder?

I sensed movement and turned to see Khepri, Tupu, and Jim rise and circle around us in this room. *Searching for traps, or secret doors, or anything that might be used against us, I'd wager.* Tupu circled round and came to stand beside me, her hand resting easily on the pommel of her scimitar.

I hesitated. Looking at Az, I slowly said, "I will hold the map. You may look at it over my shoulder."

Az nodded and rose. She had no weapon I could see, but she did possess the skills of alchemy, and I had a feeling of unease. But we had come this far, so I slowly withdrew the parchment, counting on Tupu and my friends to guard against any mischief that might occur.

I held both curling ends of the old parchment in my hands, gently pulling them apart to reveal the ancient map.

Az moved to stand right next to me, and bent over the intricate piece of history, studying it closely.

She moved her finger along the areas she was concentrating on, without touching the parchment. Her finger hovered an inch over some obscure markings in the lower corners, strange markings I had not been able to decipher before.

"You were right in being protective of this map, Charlotte. See here and here." She indicated not only the words in Arabic, but the markings on the bottom corners that I had thought were just designs. "These indicate the warnings to you, the people on earth, but the lower writing is a message to us, on our world, a planet far distance from your own. This is written in our own language, and the makers likely thought we were the only ones who could read it."

She bent and read the markings again, then remained silent.

Po looked at Az, and his eyebrows rose. Az straightened and gave him a significant look.

"Well, what does it say?" asked Khepri.

Az and Po remained silent.

My sense of unease grew.

I turned to Po, "Sir, can you read the bottom?"

Po looked at me uncertainly. Finally, he spoke: "Yes, of course I can. It's in my own language, the language I learned in my infancy." He sounded troubled. Looking down at his hands, which were fumbling with a cloth tie from his tunic, he sighed.

"Az, Po, what does it say?" asked Tupu.

"It gives instructions on how to help you find the book," Az said at last.

Po looked very troubled, then spoke: "Yes, that is what it says."

Charlotte, may I examine the map in my own hands? I wish to study it more thoroughly," asked Az.

"Why can't you look at it while she holds it?" Jim asked.

"Yes, it's right here, why can't you just stand next to Charlotte and look?" asked Khepri.

Az remained silent.

Po glanced up at us, then became flustered. "Would everybody like a meal? Lunchtime is nearly upon us. I think we can find a hall here in this building where we can all enjoy some delicious food."

We stayed where we were, not moving. We'd been together long enough that we could nearly read each other's minds. We knew something odd was happening.

I noticed Az's silence had become odd. Movement caught my eye, and I glanced down. The alchemist's fingers were nearly twitching with desire to touch the map.

"Do you want to tell me what the writing at the bottom really says?" I asked quietly.

"No, I do not," whispered Az. She gripped her hands tightly and fell silent.

"Then I think we are at an impasse.

Chapter Thirty-Four
Fleeing!

Christianne tapped my shoulder. "Charlotte, I think we should leave this place," she whispered in my ear. "Look at Kym."

I followed her eyes to the far corner where Kym was standing. Her eyes were tightly closed and her fists clenched. The hair on her arms was standing straight up, like raised hackles. I saw all this as if in slow motion. While I was taking in the sight of Kym, Az moved surreptitiously and made a grab for the parchment map.

Quicker than I could follow, Jim transformed, and shoved Az away before she could get a good hold on the parchment.

The djinn held Az easily, his arms wrapped firmly around the alchemist. "Not today," he said grimly.

Po shrieked, "Hey!"

"What?!" I whirled on him, rolling up the map and placing it back in its tube while I talked. "You have no problem with thievery Po?" I growled angrily at him. "She tried to grab the map. That's why you brought us here, isn't it?"

Po glowered.

Az struggled against the iron grip of the djinn.

"Now, something tells me neither one of you is going to tell us what the bottom writing on the map says, so I believe we'll be on our way, and thanks for nothing!" I shoved the brass tube back into my pack and tied it securely, slinging it on my back as I retreated.

"I don't know what you're hiding, but I do know I hate, hate, hate subterfuge and dishonesty, and I don't like being tricked." I spat at their feet.

Walking backwards, I slowly retreated to the door we had come in.

Az struggled harder.

The djinn looked at me.

I was suddenly furious at myself for falling for all of their friendliness. *All they'd wanted was the map. I should have known.*

"Jim, come on. We're getting out of here."

The djinn released the alchemist and put a finger to his lips, then retreated to where we were all standing next to the door.

"Wait," Az said.

"Why should we?" I fumed.

"Please, I do want to help you."

"Somehow, I very much doubt that." I turned to open the door.

"Our people are dying out," said Az, desperately. "Please."

I glanced back, hand still on the doorknob. "And that is my problem, how?"

"If your people are dying, there's little a scrap of parchment can do," said Khepri.

Kym and Christianne were whispering next to me, worried looks on their faces. They turned to me, whispering, "Charlotte, we have to get out of here. NOW."

Az started talking rapidly, trying to keep my attention, but I was having none of that. I wrenched open the door and slipped through, saying quietly, "Come on, troupe." I walked rapidly into the outer room, the room where we'd seen the others in discussion. As we all gathered here, I glanced and counted, making sure we were all out of that room, then calmly began to walk out. *No need to alarm these scientists. Safer to act natural.*

"Grab them!" yelled Az, coming out of the far room in pursuit.

There were at least a half dozen alchemists at study in the large room, with several young children whose job seemed to be remaining at their sides, at their beck and call. They held books open for the healers to study, and also had bags slung over their shoulders.

When Az called out, we knew the jig was up, and we started running. As we approached the far door, I reached out at random and grabbed the tunic of the smallest of the children, hastily saying, "Come with me, you."

We made a run for it, out the door, me dragging the little boy, and out onto the sidewalk.

The raft was gone.

"Where?! Which way?"

"Pick a direction!"

"Come on!"

"This way!" Khepri ran to the right, where the sidewalk went slightly downhill; it was darker down that way. The shadows were longer, the street was narrower.

Where was the raft?

The djinn scooped up the small boy and ran after Khepri, and I followed, grabbing Kym and Christianne. Caroline was ahead of us, on Khepri's heels. We ran as if our life depended on it. I wasn't sure why, but the foreboding in my gut had gradually grown into full-blown dread.

We raced down the sidewalk. I noticed the street was pretty much dry, which meant the raft had been taken away, and the water had been drained, pretty much right after we'd gone indoors. They'd planned on us not returning.

"Here!" Tupu had spied an alleyway. "Come on!"

We turned right and raced down the long narrow pathway, brushing aside several trash barrels next to small looking locked doors.

We heard a siren behind us. They had set off an alarm. Now everyone would be after us, drawn to our hurried run.

"Wait, let's slow down. Find someplace to hide."

"Okay but let's get a little farther first."

"Down this way!"

We zigzagged through alleyways, left, right, then left again, winding our way deeper into the city.

It was dark and shadowing when we finally stopped. This area wasn't illuminated like the broader streets where the populace did their shopping.

No, this was the dregs of the city. Like was darker here, doorways were poorer. We saw a few rat-like creatures scuttling away from us.

"We're making too much noise, shhh!"

"Okay, come on!"

"Wait, here's a good place to hide."

I dropped down to a stairwell that led from the street, down to a dark doorway. The stairs and walls of cobblestone were covered in a grime and the door was locked. But there was room for all of us.

We crouched on the stairs, and heard people running down the main streets, probably looking for us. I closed my eyes. *What is happening?* I heard whispers behind me and turned back to see the djinn and the boy speaking in hushed tones, their heads together.

Suddenly, some footsteps ran past our hiding place.

I ducked, reaching out my arm and covered Kym's and Christianne's heads. I put my finger against my lips and made eye contact with Caroline and the djinn and boy.

The footsteps passed us, and I let out a silent breath of air.

After about an hour, things died down; although I could hear running and calling out every now and then, the sounds came from far away.

I shifted and sat down in a more comfortable position.

"Charlotte," whispered the djinn after another hour of hiding, "This is Er, he is seven."

The boy looked at me with brilliant yellow eyes.

"Hi, Er. I'm sorry I pulled you along, but we may need your help. After that you can go, okay?"

"Okay," said Er in a small voice.

We hunkered down to wait out the search parties.

After another hour, I was feeling very cramped. I stepped up to the street level and looked around. I heard a far-off whistle but nothing else.

Sitting back down, I whispered, "I think we should stay hidden for longer before we try to get farther away."

"Charlotte, do you remember the way back to the surface?"

"I'm not sure, but it would stand to reason that if we keep heading up the sloping streets, we'll find ourselves closer to the surface, and if we keep heading downhill, we'll be going farther away."

"Of course, there are dangerous plants up on the surface, remember."

"We got the best of the most dangerous one. I didn't see much else to worry about up there."

"I think I'd feel better going back up, but I'm not sure if we're done down here."

"Yeah, I'm still wondering what that old writing along the bottom means."

"I didn't even realize it was writing at all."

"I know, me neither."

Well, maybe Er here can help us figure it out," I said. "But I'd rather get to a safe place before we take out the map and start examining it."

I looked over at the djinn, still holding Er, and he nodded. I took a deep breath and looked Er over. He looked like his clothes were too big for him. With a start I realized he was extremely thin. Almost starving. Er's bones stood out sharply against his tunic. I looked away, deep in thought. The alleyway stairwell was cold.

We huddled there until nightfall.

Chapter Thirty-Five
The Mills

I might have dozed off, but I jerked awake with a start, the pain in my neck a sharp reminder of the full day of sitting on the cobblestone steps of underground doorway in the dank alley.

"Shhhh."

"Don't push my legs."

"I'm sorry, I'm just trying ..."

"Stop. Wait."

"I'm just trying to get comfortable."

"There's no way in existence to get comfortable here, we're sitting on stones."

"Well, try."

"I can't."

"Shift around, try lying on your other side."

"It won't work, I just moved from that side."

"This sucks."

"Okay, listen, I know it sucks, but we have to hide."

"I haven't heard the search parties in hours."

"You dozed off."

"Oh my god. My rear hurts so much! Listen, I have to move."

"Please just shhhhh."

"Move where you need to but shhhhhhh."

"We do not want to be discovered."

"Maybe we should have run farther before hiding."

"Ugh, there's water soaked into my boots."

"Okay, this is intolerable."

"Do you think Po and Az are still looking for us?"

"What do you think they want with us?"

"I have no idea."

"Do you think we're ever going to get out of here?"

"Back to the surface, you mean? Soon, I hope."

"I miss the sun."

"Ugh," I whispered, reaching my hand around and rubbing the nape of my neck. I stretched my back and looked at Khepri.

"Shhhh, she's waking up."

"It's okay. I'm already awake. How long have we been here? Is it nightfall yet?"

It was hard to tell night from day in the underground city.

"I think it's night," Khepri said.

"Miss, it's nearly midnight. Maybe it's time to move?"

I crept out of the stairwell and listened. It was utterly quiet – as silent as a grave.

I turned and motioned for the others to follow me, and we stepped out onto the alley cobblestones.

Steam rose from an underground duct, and a faint light shone from the main street, perhaps a hundred feet away.

Looking right and left, I saw there was a way out if we kept going away from the main thoroughfare, so we slowly made our way down the lane.

The djinn walked behind me, Er's small hand firmly in the large blue-purple djinn's. He didn't look scared anymore, I thought. *What??*

My stomach let out a loud growl. Er's face turned to the sound, and I heard his stomach growl as well. *Oh, he's hungry.*

Where were we going to get food?

We walked rapidly down quite a few side lanes, until we had left the city behind. After an hour, we found ourselves crouching behind a derelict wooden building on the side of a broken-down cobblestone street. There was a drain at the bottom, and I figured this was one of the many places the water that ran down the streets to push the rafts ended up.

"We need food." I looked around. "Anyone have any ideas?"

No one did.

Looking around, we saw packed dirt, heard wet dripping sounds, and spied stone walls in the distance. Faint lights shone through the windows of a few old houses, and I idly wondered if any of them had food inside, but something in me rebelled at the thought of stealing from starving people.

I had realized the People here in this underground city lived very differently, depending on which caste they belonged to. Up near the surface, Po had shown us a lavish, well-fed world, and tried to show us some remarkable science labs and alchemists. But the workers, the younger ones, they lived differently. Er was so skinny it was scary. The djinn had carried him much of the way. He was weak and emaciated.

Strangely enough, Er had not been too frightened, and seemed to take to the adventure of fleeing from the authorities to heart. He helped us by pointing the way down the lanes that went the farthest, avoiding the shorter alleys and dead-end lanes.

"Er, do you live nearby?" I heard Christianne ask our new friend.

"Over there," Er pointed down the far side of a dark hill. We were in a large cavern; it smelled like water and dirt. He led the way to a small house among the rocks. The path to it was worn and old. We crouched, hidden behind a boulder on the side of the hill.

"Do you think it's safe?"

"No. In fact, this is the first place I'd check if I were them."

"You're right."

We sat in a dark crevice, where no one could see us from the road.

"Er, come here," I said, pulling the parchment map from my pack.

"Here, Charlotte," Khepri handed me a torch she'd lit.

I held the torch close to the map and pointed at the bottom words.

"Er, can you read that writing?"

The small boy bent and studied the scrawled scratched-looking words that none of us had realized were words at all.

He struggled with them. Then, he spoke.

"The ... People ... should take the ... earthlings ... and sort them ... into ... the mills."

He looked up at me.

"What does it mean?"

"Er, what are the mills?"

"Maybe it doesn't translate well?"

"Shhh, let him speak."

Er looked down, then up again at us. There were tears in his eyes. I took his arms, rubbing them. He was so, so thin.

"Er, it's okay, we just want to understand. What does it mean?"

The boy started crying, sobbing even. His stomach grumbled loudly.

"Do we have any food? Look in your packs, we've got to eat, anyway."

Christianne had a few pouches of crushed berries and dried rabbit meat. Kym and Khepri did, too. Caroline had some ship rations, even. Saved from before we passed the mermaids.

"Er, here, eat this." I looked up, "Does anyone have any water?" Someone handed me a waterskin.

Er hesitantly took the offered rabbit meat in his hand and tasted it. He must've found it palatable because he started chewing slowly, then faster. He wolfed down the whole sack of dried rabbit meat, then washed it down with water.

"Okay, then," I smiled at the small boy, patting his shoulder. "Feel better?"

He nodded, smiling.

I took a deep breath.

I had a worried feeling in the pit of my stomach. That sentence, about mills ... I wasn't sure what it meant, but I worried it was nothing good.

"Er, can you read the bottom again?"

Caroline held the scroll out again, and Khepri's torch shone on the whole expanse. Er looked again.

"It's a command. It says, 'The People should take the earthlings and sort them into the mills. Take the youngest and put them in the farms.' I don't know what the last part means," Er looked up at us.

"Okay, let's start." I took a deep breath. "Er," he looked at me. "What are the farms?"

Er thought for a minute, then shook his head. "I don't know."

"Do you have farms here under the ground?" asked Khepri.

"No, not for a long time, they teach us in school," Er said.

Okay, well, hmmm...

I tried again, taking a different tack. "What did the farms have, long ago when they existed?"

"Animals," said Er. "They would breed them before taking them to the mills."

Oh, no.

"What are the mills?" I asked.

I felt fear creep slowly up my spine and into my brain, making my ears ring.

"That's where they put the lichen and mushrooms to be processed."

Chapter Thirty-Six

Er

"Are you kidding me?" Christianne's voice was so high pitched it sounded incredulous, and who could blame her?

"I think ..." I stopped, unable to find anything useful to contribute.

"Charlotte, we need to find shelter," Jim said as he shimmered and transformed into his human form. He had Er by the arm, holding on while he changed, and the boy laughed because it apparently tickled.

"No, wait. Wait."

"What?"

"Seriously?"

"This can't be. The boy's made an error."

"Why would they want to ..."

"Ohhh ..."

"Listen, listen," I raised my hand to silence the troupe. "Jim is correct: We need to find shelter. I think we should avoid Er's home and travel farther, but swing around instead of going deeper into the ground. Our goal should be getting to the surface. Agreed?

"Agreed," said Christianne.

"Now, listen. Let's get going in ten minutes. For now, eat and drink what you have with you, rest up, because the next few hours are going to be hard running," I sighed and fished in my bag for my water-skin.

"Charlotte, should we let Er go?" asked Jim.

"Well," I took a drink of water, "I guess so." I knelt down and looked Er in the eye. "Do you want to go back home, sweetie?"

Er nodded. I looked up at Jim. "Wait until we're on our way, then release him."

Jim nodded.

We rested and ate a few provisions, and Khepri examined Er, then gave him some food to eat.

"He's malnourished. Nothing I can really help right now. I'm amazed they stay underground, to tell you the truth."

"I know," I said, agreeing with her. "I understand it's dangerous up top, but if your people are starving ..."

"They don't care," a small voice said. I turned around to see Er behind me, looking solemn.

I knelt down again, and took his hand. Looking him in the eye for a minute, I finally said, "Er, even one person may change the world. Work to change yours."

We were ready to begin hiking again, our bags were packed up and strapped back on our backs. Jim was murmuring to Er, giving him instructions.

"And don't tell them about us. If they ask, tell them we released you and you ran and hid, then made your way home."

The boy nodded; his face serious.

Jim gave him one last hug and then turned him and gave him a push down the hill. "Go on, then."

I took a deep breath as Jim rose to stand next to me. "Ready?" I asked him.

He nodded firmly.

We turned in the other direction Er had gone and began hiking across the edge of the embankment.

We skirted the edge of the outer town, trying to circle back up to the cave opening we'd come through. It was slow going in the dark. Lichen on the walls and roof of the cavern shone with their own bioluminescence, and this provided a glow that helped us to see well enough so we didn't stumble, but the farther reaches remained in shadow. Several times we had to skirt large rock outcroppings we could have gone around if only we'd seen it at a distance.

We talked as we walked, keeping our voices low, trying to wrap our minds around the words Er had read out loud for us.

"You know, to tell you the truth, I'm not sure I quite believe those words," said Khepri.

"What do you mean?" I asked.

"Well, the wording was not the same as the other words on the map, and it was in a different language."

"Ah, yes, I saw that. The Arabic words we could read were in a more archaic manner of speech."

"The words Er read out loud were more modern."

"And they were worded as if speaking directly to someone, instead of as a general warning."

"I wondered about that."

"I'm not sure they were original to the map at all."

"Could someone have gotten hold of the map in the last few days and added them?"

"I don't know. I didn't think so, as I had it in my pack the whole time, but now I'm not so sure."

"Charlotte, remember that one night when we first got here, they gave us food and drink?"

"Yes," I said, growing uneasy.

"I think some of that food or drink may have been spiked with some drug to make us sleep very soundly," said

Khepri. "I suspected it before, and now that I think about it, it seems logical."

"You think they marked the words on the bottom when we were asleep?" I stopped, suddenly remembering. "They did. Oh my god, that's exactly what they did. I remember now."

Jim and Tupu came and steadied me, as I swayed in shock.

"That morning after we arrived, I'd woken up, and my bag was not where I left it; it's like it had been moved! I remember thinking it was weird, but I felt happy and euphoric and so shrugged it off." I turned to Khepri and grabbed her arm. "And they gave us that drink, that ... tal! It was called tal! I bet it was drugged to make us slumber more deeply, so they could go through our things and alter the map!"

"And they took us to see the alchemist next. They likely wrote it so the alchemist would read it and think the words were original to the map!" Caroline said, gasping.

"You know, I really hate those people." Kym spat to the side. "I'd like to bite them. To scratch them with my talons. I'd like to destroy them." She glowered darkly.

"Okay, now that we know, I think it would be best to get the hell out of here." I braced my shoulders and started walking again. "Come on, troupe."

We hiked all night. Finally found ourselves near the back of the city, where the rock rose the highest. A small cliff overhang provided some shelter for us.

"Okay, troupe, looks like the city is about an hour that way," I said, pointing over the rocky ridge separating us from the outskirts of the city. "Let's sleep a few hours so we'll be refreshed and ready for anything." I dropped my pack and tried to find a comfy spot in the dirt and rock.

"Princess, here's the last of my food from the centaurs," Caroline handed me a small pouch.

"Thank you, Carrie. Let's share?"

"Okay."

We settled down to eat.

"Princess, do you think we'll ever get back home?" Caroline asked as she ate.

"Do you mean back to Earth? Or back to Swerighe?"

"Both, but mainly back to Earth."

Christianne came up and settled next to us to listen. She chewed on a piece of dried rabbit. "I'd like to know, too."

"Well," I said quietly, "The important thing is not to lose hope. Remember: the people who made the map probably also opened those portals that transported us to this world. We have to find where they were leading us."

"Does the map show any part of this world, Charlotte?" asked Christianne.

I pulled the parchment out of my pack to examine it again. I felt I'd looked at it dozens of times, but found something new every time.

Caroline lit a small candle and held it near the map so I could see.

I studied it, looking for any hint of hope.

"Look here, this is where the path brought us to the island," Christianne pointed.

"And look, this shows the two islands," I indicated with my finger. "Here is the first one, and here is the second."

"Does it show a close up of the second island?"

"Yes, just here."

"And the path to the volcano?"

"It doesn't show that."

"Wait, what's this?" I pulled out a magnifying glass I'd brought from *Pride of the Sea*. Holding it close to the map, I noticed a double line, and another line leading to the corner.

"I think this shows the second island and the volcano," I murmured while following the faint drawing.

"Oh my gosh," I mumbled, then turned the map over. There were very faint drawings on the back corner. The parchment had weathered to a dark brown color from hundreds of years of being handled. The sketch had all but disappeared into the background.

Khepri and Tupu brought more lit candles to the edge.

"The dimmer light helps illuminate the background more. We need to get this into the sunlight," I said. "I'm sure I saw something on the back, and it may be more of the map, drawn to lead us to the book here on this planet."

"Okay, let's sleep for a while and then start again," Khepri suggested.

"Agreed," I rolled up the map and replaced it carefully in my bag.

I thought it would be hard to fall asleep, but I was more exhausted than I thought. I dropped out like a light.

Jim remained on first watch, then woke me to take second watch after four hours.

When he tapped me on the shoulder to switch with me, he wordlessly pointed to the side of the rock wall we'd curled up to sleep against. I saw six slumbering bodies.

Huh?

I tiptoed over to check and yep, it was Er, curled up against Khepri.

Chapter Thirty-Seven

The Element of Surprise

"Everyone up," I whispered. "It's time to go."

We were up and ready within minutes.

"I cannot wait to see the sun again."

"I swear I miss that hedge, haha."

"Do you need any more packed dirt or rocks? No? Me neither."

"Okay, okay, let's just get on our way, okay?"

"Let's go."

No one said a thing about the fact that Er was there. Tagging along behind us all, he stayed back about ten feet; I guessed he was hoping he'd stay an afterthought, and it worked, too, for the first half hour. Then we came to a crack in the rock and a small spring, the water ran down into the city. It was about four feet wide where we had to cross it. We all hopped it, running and jumping over it without getting wet. When it came to Tupu and Jim, they just wordlessly beckoned Er with one hand; then, when he shyly came forward, each grabbed one of his arms, and they hopped it together, swinging the skinny boy between them. Still, not a word was said.

The unspoken agreement was that he could tag along. We'd told him to go home, he'd left for a few hours, and then he'd returned. We could only guess what had gone down at his home when he'd gotten there, and what might have made him leave again, but I think we realized what might have made him decide to come back to us. We'd all had our weird moments with our parents; whether we had grown up poor or rich, we could identify with Er, on some level.

An hour later, we were up high on the rocky hill overlooking the city. Off to our left we could see the cave opening we had to walk through to get back to the surface. Everything seemed deserted. We hid and watched the city for a while.

"I don't trust it," I whispered, finally.

"Charlotte, I have an idea," said Caroline. We gathered in together, our heads nearly touching. "I noticed the spring coming out of the crack in the wall that we passed was cracking further. I think if I can break it more, a rush of new water might come out that will cause a diversion in the city."

"I can help with that," said Jim.

"Sounds good." I nodded. "Go."

They left and we waited.

And waited.

"Do you think they got caught?" asked Kym.

"Oh, my gods, Kym don't even suggest that."

"Well ..."

"Maybe they're having trouble breaking the crack?"

As if on cue, a loud noise rang out over the rock surface, echoing down the hill toward the city. We could hear an answering cry down below as the water crashed through the small barriers they had erected to hold back the smaller flow.

I could picture the flooding streets in my mind and the rush to block the water from jumping the curbs and flooding the stores and businesses.

Too bad.

Jim and Er ran up, gave us high fives without stopping, and continued running up the rocky hill, and we followed them. We scrambled past the edges of the cave opening, the craggy cliff overhangs silently watching us as we hurried around and through and out. All in all, it took us less than a half hour, although to be fair, we were rushing eagerly. I think we'd all had enough of the underground.

We all stopped just outside the cave opening and put up our hands to shield our eyes. The sun was incredibly bright. As I slowly got used to it again over the course of a few minutes, I stared at the grass and the sky, the trees and the hills.

The colors were brilliant. The bright blue of the grass seemed welcoming. The trees shone a brilliant green. The sky was a rich red, with puffy white clouds floating in it. We could hear a breeze blow through the trees, and it beckoned us forward.

Er had his arm over his eyes; he was not growing more accustomed to the light. I realized he and his people probably never saw the outside. *But what about the woman and her child, the first of the People we'd seen?*

"Jim, tie a cloth around his face," said Khepri. "He'll take longer to acclimate."

A long piece of fabric was pulled from a bag, and soon the boy was ready for his outing. Jim and Tupu held his hand as we walked.

"Let's put some distance between us and this place," I suggested, then I started running down the side of the valley. The others followed, laughing. I guess we had no need for secrecy anymore.

We hiked up to the top of the hill where we'd first found ourselves, and decided to take a short break and plan.

We sat there, and I swear it was the exact same spot I'd sat in when I'd first found myself in this world, Caroline running up to me.

"You know what's different?" Tupu, next to me, said while munching on a piece of blackroot.

I turned to her, smiling. "What?"

"The sky," she said. "When we first got here, it was cloudless."

"That's it? But you know that clouds come and go in the sky."

"Well, yes. I just thought it might be worth mentioning."

"So," Caroline said. "What's the plan?"

I lifted out the map and brought out my magnifier. "Look here: There's definitely more on the back." I handed over the glass and the map so they could see.

"As far as I can tell, we proceed over these two ridges, then supposedly there's a settlement and the ocean. Remember Po describing the hot air balloons?"

"He called them 'air pillows'," Tupu laughed. "Sorry, I can't help it." She kept laughing. I guess we were all stressed from our foray underground. Tupu got the giggles and lay down in the blue grass and laughed for a long time.

I chuckled.

"Oh, hey, Charlotte! Look!" Kym pointed excitedly.

It was the hedge maze. It slowly crawled over the lower rise, roots digging in and out of the soil.

"Oh my god, there it is."

"Can you believe it?"

"I'm going after it," Tupu said, brandishing her scimitar.

"No! No, no, no. Tupu you stay put, it's over a half mile away," I said, pulling on her arm.

"If anyone is going to go, it should be me," said Kym, standing up and glowering at the bush maze.

As it turned out, there was no need.

It advanced another fifteen feet or so, but then it seemed to sense our presence. The movement of the plant stopped. It rose up to twice it's normal height and seemed to shudder; then it began to move away, more rapidly than it had been coming.

"Well, I guess it wants no part of us any longer."

"Nope."

"At least it has a good memory."

"Yeah! We beat you, and now you sad!"

"Oops, yike, yike, yike!"

"Ha HA! HA!"

I shook my head, smiling.

In the end, we decided to start hiking to the ocean settlement. I didn't understand how those People could live out of the underground if that's what they were so used to, for generations, but I figured I would find out.

Er walked next to Khepri, holding her hand. After a day, she was able to untie the cloth around his eyes and replace it with a fine gauze bandage, which served to filter the sun's glare and still permit him to see where he was going.

"There, that'll work." She patted his shoulder. "I bet you'll be fully used to the sun in no time."

Er smiled cheerfully. He seemed very happy traveling with us, and he was probably getting more to eat than he ever had before.

We harvested food as we went, to augment what we had in our packs.

"I really don't care if the plants bite when I pick them," Khepri said, laughing. She yanked up the leafy greens as we walked, stuffing them into the food packs.

It took us two days to walk to the ocean; the route turned out to be mostly rugged hills and sharp peaks. But we eventually made it, and were greeted by the sight of an expanse of blue sea.

"Well, except it looks a bit greyish," said Kym.

"Is the water blue, like at home, or grey, Charlotte?" Christianne asked.

"I'm not sure," I said, studying the sight before us.

We had arrived at the top of the last peak around mid-day and stopped there to look at the scene before us. The land made a point there at the water's edge, and it was surrounded by rocks, from the top of the low mountain, down to the ocean's edge. It was at the overlooking height that the People had made the hot air balloon camp, the "air pillow" camp, as they probably called it.

We were at the peak above, looking down on the whole scene.

"I think we're about five hundred feet up from it," Tupu said.

"Look, I count at least five of the People down there. We've got to get past them," I said.

"Well, at least they've got two balloons up," Khepri noted.

The camp was a collection of buildings made of stone, and the 'air pillows' they were blowing up looked huge, at least ten times the size of any back home.

"We've got to steal one of those," Jim murmured unnecessarily.

"Let's make a plan," I said. "Kym, you could transform into the extra-large form of the chimera, then you could jump down and block the entrance they're using."

"No idea which hut has the opening," Jim pointed out.

"Okay, new plan. Kym, you transform and smash the guys tending to the 'air pillows'..."

"I think she might run into trouble, Charlotte," said Jim.

I sighed. "Okay, well, what do you think we should do?" I turned to the djinn.

"I think we should all walk up, Kym in chimera form, I in my djinn form, and tell them we're taking the 'air pillow' and that they're going to let us, or bad things will happen." He smiled at me.

I raised my eyebrows.

"Well, it could work," Khepri said, shading her eyes and watching the camp below us, "We do outnumber them, after all."

"True."

"But, no element of surprise at all?"

"Okay, but what if they have weapons?"

"Let's sneak down and scout first."

"Okay, I'm going down."

"Wait," I said, but Kym had already taken off.

I really needed to train the troupe on tactics.

We watched as Kym snuck down and scouted out the small camp. All five of the people were hard at work with the two 'air pillows' and there was no one on guard duty at all. *This camp has never been attacked.* Within a few minutes of scouting down at the camp, Kym turned to face us and waved her hand, then proceeded to transform.

Oh my god, what is she doing?

Chapter thirty-Eight
The Air Pillow

As we'd approached the small camp, the people had scattered. All except one. This fine fellow had actually been on board the cup, restocking the provisions. It seems the camp had been preparing for another journey. The larder had been filled to capacity by the man, who hadn't heard us approach. We'd caught him in the saucer itself.

"What do you want?" he said sullenly. It turned out he wasn't too thrilled at being forced on the journey with us, but I'd figured we might need someone with knowledge of how to operate the thing. I'd assured him he'd be let free once we were done with the air pillow, but he'd still been unhappy.

"What is your name, fine sir?" I asked.

He didn't answer.

Okayyy.

"You *will* operate the air pillow safely and take us to the island of the quamernats, correct?"

He sighed.

I raised my eyebrows.

"Yes, yes, I told you before, yes. I will operate the air pillow and deliver you safely to the island. There is no need to worry. I have a massive stake in this, as I am on board as well."

"Why are you so grim, my good man?" asked Jim, laughing. We were all in high spirits.

"If you must know, I left my mate this morning back home in the city, and we are expecting the birth of our baby any day now. It's something I'd rather not miss."

"Well, I am sorry if you miss this grand event," I said. "But we have a pressing need to get to the quamernats, a pressing need that cannot wait any longer."

"We ourselves were delayed in that infernal city for many days, while one of your fellow People made plans to 'mill' us and eat us. EAT US? If you can believe it. And after we told him we'd defeated the hedge maze!"

"I know, right?" Christianne said. "Did he think we'd go down without a fight?"

"Wellllll, to be honest it was more of a fleeing than a fight," laughed Caroline.

"Huff!" the pilot turned from us then, tired of the mockery.

The hot air balloon they called an air pillow was huge – easily as big as one of the smaller mountains we'd climbed in this new land. The thing was crafted of some unknown material, it looked like spun web of some sort, although I'd hate to have met a spider that could spin so much silk.

"It's woven out of the soft stuff that comes from a plant," said Er.

Ahh.

"He is correct, the plant fibers are very light and airy; they practically float when we pick them," the man operating the air pillow said. He seemed to have a small interest in us after all.

The saucer under the air pillow in which we found ourselves spanned at least thirty feet in diameter. It was indeed cupped in shape, and had a rim on the edge that measured nearly five feet tall – to avoid falls, no doubt.

In the center of this saucer was a massive fire that never went out. It was designed to keep the air pillow aloft. There were also soft jets embedded in the bottom of the saucer. These were controlled by the operator of the fire, who could use them to point the air balloon in any direction they wanted.

The man was gifted, we felt no jarring as we took off, and the saucer travelled swiftly. Khepri estimated we were traveling faster than a galloping horse.

When she said this, I instantly missed Shêtân, who I'd left on board the ship when we'd dropped anchor off the coast of the first island.

Akim had promised to exercise him, and I knew he'd take good care of him, but I still missed my horsey companion. I promised myself I would brush him and feed him treats from my hand when we got back.

If we ever got back.

I shook my head, unhappy at the thought. *I must remember: Hope is the key to success. Attitude is everything. We WILL get back.*

I turned back to the pilot. "Please tell us your name."

The man pressed his lips together in obstinate refusal, stubborn as ever.

"Fine. Sir, I will give you a name!" I thought for a moment, then, "Aha!" I pointed at his chest. "Your name is now 'Pilot'! We shall call you Pilot and you shall respond to our queries, for that is the way to get out of a fix alive and well, and you certainly want to do that, don't you Pilot? This is the way to get back to Mrs. Pilot in once piece, isn't it?"

The man turned away, holding his hand to his mouth to hide his smile, and busied himself with the operation of the ship.

"I say, Princess, that was a grand speech," Caroline laughed as she came up to me with a bowl of stew. Er trailed behind her with his own stew bowl.

I took it gratefully and tasted it. "Oh! Yum, Carrie, this is delicious. Well done!"

We had been in the air pillow for a few hours when Khepri declared she wanted to make us a meal using the central fire that held the pillow aloft, and, in fact, Pilot had instructed her exactly how to do this. It was a common usage of the central fire, he told us, because the air pillows had been regularly used for long journeys, some as long as a month. Our journey was expected to take just a few days, he told us, certainly no more than a week. Pilot had explained how it was a good craft, well made and well operated, but, all the same, we were at the whims of the wind.

We passed over the ocean for days. From most places on the craft, we couldn't see the water below us, as the air saucer held us in such a way as to obstruct the view of whatever was underneath us. But a few glass windows near the central fire afforded us a glimpse of what was below. Not that there was much to see: I watched the ocean pass under us for a while before realizing it was as boring as watching grass grow.

Caroline came with a bowl of stew and handed it to Pilot, who took it and began to eat it with relish. I was beginning to understand that Pilot wasn't a bad sort, he was just exceedingly grumpy. I tried to talk to him as we ate.

"Your wife is expecting a baby any day now, you say?" I said politely.

"My what?" said Pilot.

"Your wife. The baby," I prodded.

He blinked. "No, it is my partner, he is expecting a baby, any day now." He took another bite of food.

"Your partner is a male?"

"Yes," He licked his spoon.

"How is it he can have a baby?" I asked.

"He just can. What do you mean?" Pilot said.

Khepri came near with her own bowl of stew, to listen in.

"Pilot, are you male?" I inquired.

"Well of course I'm a male." He sounded grouchy.

Khepri spoke then, "I think what Charlotte is wondering is, how will your male partner have this baby?"

Pilot blinked at us for a minute. "With his body, out of his uterus. How are babies born where *you* come from?"

Khepri smiled. "Babies are born from a female's uterus, a female's womb."

"Well, it's the same here," Pilot said, then took another bite.

"But where we come from, only females have uteruses," said Khepri.

"What? Why?" Pilot seemed stunned.

"They just are," Khepri said.

"I ... I don't know what to say to that," Pilot said.

"Now this is interesting," murmured Khepri.

I asked, "Pilot, when we went into your city, underground, we saw females. So, your society has females, correct?"

"Yes, of course we have females. I don't understand your point," said Pilot.

I stared at him. I could not think of anything to say.

Pilot finished his bowl of stew and went for a refill.

I turned to Khepri, "this is a strange land, isn't it?"

"Not that strange," she replied. "I know of men who would like to be able to have a baby."

"Really?"

"Oh, yes."

Pilot returned; his bowl full again.

"Charlotte, this stew is the best thing I have ever tasted," he said.

"Tell that to Caroline, she's the chef this time." I laughed.

"Oh, I did, I did. She's quite talented," said Pilot.

"Okay," I finished my bowl, and licked the spoon. "I have to ask, Pilot: in your world, you are male and your partner is male, correct?"

"Correct."

"And males have uteruses here?"

"Some do."

"Which ones?"

"The ones who are males with uteruses."

"But you also have females?"

"Yes."

"And do the females have uteruses?"

"Some do," said Pilot.

"Some?" I asked.

"Yes, some." He looked exasperated.

"Which ones," I pressed.

Pilot blinked at me.

"The females with uteruses are the ones born with uteruses."

"I'm so confused."

"I think I understand," said Khepri. She turned to Pilot. "You have males and females here."

He nodded.

"And some males have uteruses and some females have uteruses."

He nodded again.

Khepri asked, "Are the males with uteruses males that were born female and changed to males?"

"No, what on earth is that?"

"I give up."

Kym started giggling.

"What?"

She came over, giggling harder than ever. By the time she reached us she was having a hard time walking she was laughing so hard.

"Ch ... Charlotte ... ha ha ha! No ..." She gasped for air. I waited; eyebrows raised.

She tried again. "Charlotte, some are born with both male and female parts. Both genders are sometimes born with both types of reproductive organs." She collapsed into laughter.

I scowled.

"I guess that's what we get for assuming these people are like humans," Khepri smiled, looking down at Kym, who was rolling on the floor, laughing and holding her stomach.

Pilot looked at me, smiling. "She's actually correct, for the most part. Also, humans are weird." He laughed.

I rolled my eyes.

Chapter Thirty-Nine
On Names and Heritage

It took us five days to get to the island of the quamernats.
On the morning of the sixth day, the sun rose over the edge
of the saucer, and in the distance was something other than
a massive expanse of water.

Er was having a great time, running back and forth,
watching the island appear in the distance.

As the air pillow approached, the island grew from a
small sliver of land on the horizon, to a larger, irregularly
shaped island of approximately two thousand acres. Not
very large, but large enough.

"It's actually about two thousand and twelve hundred
acres, and the quamernats are concentrated in the northern
reaches." Pilot pointed out the island as he explained.
"There are the steepest mountains in the south, as you can
see."

The mountains didn't look that large from so far away, but as we approached, they started to appear larger and more foreboding.

"I'm setting her down right at the far edge, where they've made a flat spot for us," Pilot gestured. "Now, when you go down, be careful. The quamernats are not exactly happy to see strangers. And I'm putting it mildly." He busied himself with the rigging and lowered the main fire to a steady flame. The saucer glided gently down as we moved forward, and I once again marveled at how smoothly Pilot guided the air pillow.

We all lined up on the far edge to watch our descent. The people on the island definitely looked like centaurs, at least like distant cousins of Iilcendorr and his people. There were obvious signs they had spotted the descending air pillow, the people down there were still the size of ants, but their movements became more rapid.

"Looks like they saw us," said Jim, peering down through the glass.

"They look a little upset." I straightened and turned to Pilot, "Hey, why do they look upset?"

Pilot just shrugged.

"When was the last time anyone was here?" asked Khepri.

"I'm the only runner who comes out here." Pilot fumbled with the ropes on the sides of the fire spout.

"Well, when were you last out, and what happened?" Khepri asked, staring at him.

He shrugged and mumbled something.

"What?"

"Two years."

"Two years ago?" I waited for a response. This was driving me crazy. "Pilot, did you say you were last here two years ago?"

He nodded, still working on the fire system.

I looked at Khepri and Jim. It seemed like he was concentrating a little too hard on his task. I shook my head, then nodded to Jim, who transformed into the huge, muscled djinn and grabbed Pilot, yanked him up, and held him.

I walked up to the man. The ridges on his forehead and ears grew red. His eyes would not meet mine.

"Friend, I would like to know exactly when you last came to their island here." I gestured at the people racing in panic below. "I would like to know exactly, precisely what you and anyone with you were doing, did, or planned to do here."

"I could stop landing the craft," he said quietly. "I could not help you anymore."

"And I could have the djinn toss you overboard." I smiled evilly. "You'd fall almost a mile before you went splat." I looked him up and down. "Considering your body type, you'd break into a hundred pieces upon landing. Now wouldn't that be a shame for your poor partner, who you said is about to have your baby." I stared him down.

He just looked at me.

I kept staring at him; I didn't blink.

Finally, he spoke. "It was two years and three months ago. The leaders from the city come about every three years. We rounded up at least a dozen." He closed his eyes.

"A dozen people?"

"Yeah. About that many. Maybe fourteen."

"You just took them?"

"Yeah."

"You kidnapped them? Took them against their will?"

"You could say that."

"For what purpose?" I felt a chilling foreboding creep up my spine.

He didn't answer.

"Throw him overboard," I turned from them and walked away. I made it maybe four steps, then heard Pilot's voice."

"Wait. You said if I told you, you wouldn't toss me off."

I turned back to him. "You didn't tell me everything." I stood there ten feet away, my hands on my hips, waiting.

He took a deep breath. "They took them for the leaders. They took them to the mills to be processed." He looked down.

Just as I thought.

Well no wonder they're running about and trying to flee or defend themselves. I spat and nodded at the djinn.

353

"Release him, let him do his work, but watch him like a hawk."

The djinn nodded.

Pilot was released. He rubbed his arms, glanced at us, then bent down to his work again.

I felt disgusted.

I walked down a way, wanting fresh air. Air that wasn't tainted by this person didn't think twice about stealing people to kill and eat later. It was no big deal. Nah, no reason to tell us about it. Huh, maybe we wouldn't've asked, yeah, he was a rat. No doubt about it.

I spat again.

Caroline came up behind me, put her hand in mine and squeezed my palm.

"The people of this world are harsh, Princess."

Harsh. That's putting it mildly.

I didn't say anything, just walked. After a while she let go of my hand and let me go walking on my own.

I strode to an area far from everyone, and found myself at one of the glass portholes. I studied these people as we descended. They had lived on this island, and had not joined the others on the mainland. Pilot had said they could live here without fear because the vegetation on the island had not evolved with the mainland vegetation. Here on the island the plants were not sentient. They could not move; they were not deadly. He'd explained the people were mostly fishermen, and had lived a quiet life creating art, content to be apart from the others on this world.

The island was more than a thousand miles from any continent or other land. They were quite alone here.

Legend had it that this was where the book originated. This was where much of the artwork and magic on this world came from. These were the people to talk to in our quest for *The Book of Mysteries*.

I watched as we approached the far edge of the island, the flat expanse Pilot has said he would aim for.

The touchdown was smooth and uneventful. I went and gathered my things, having packed my bag earlier that morning.

The djinn was holding Pilot again, as per our earlier discussion. The troupe had wanted to ensure we were not stranded here in this remote location.

Pilot was not thrilled, to say the least. As I passed him, I shot him a humorless grimace, and went to confer with Caroline and Khepri.

We were ready. The ramp was lowered, and we walked, single file, down the steep incline, I in the lead, then Khepri, Kym, Christianne, Caroline, Tupu, and then the djinn with Pilot in the rear. Jim held the man easily in his djinn form, his strength and iron grasp as important as his imposing muscle-covered figure and coloring were. Pilot did not struggle now. Before we even walked off the saucer he'd wiggled fiercely, testing the boundaries of the djinn's strength and fortitude, and had been rewarded with an unmovable jailor and a hard fist-pound atop his head that made him see stars, which he had made sure to complain to us about.

We all walked from the ramp to the center of the grassy expanse. I noted that the turf was a darker color blue than on the mainland. It seemed softer as well.

The people of the island were gathered at the far end of the meadow, waiting for some sign from us. We obligated them by walking slowly forward, then waving to them, and calling out.

"Hello!" Tupu waved her long, slender arm slowly back and forth, and smiled. We were all smiling, careful not to appear aggressive in any way.

They came forward slowly, and we could see them clearly now for the first time. They were indeed centaurs, like Iilcendorr and Rhalofetorr and Glynbelarr and the rest. Except the adult centaurs we'd left behind on the island back home had been huge – their equine shoulders rising at least five feet high, and their human heads nearly eight feet from the ground. These quamernats, by contrast were smaller. Much smaller.

They carried spears tipped with wicked-looking barbed slate points. They looked extremely fierce in expression and in mannerism. This was likely needed because the human head of the tallest quamernats came to just below my own chin.

"Hello, hello," I called out gently, smiling and extending my hand. "We have traveled over a great distance on a quest. We were told you might be able to help us."

Tupu came forward, carrying a book from the small collection she had brought from the ship. It was a leather-bound, color-plated edition of fables from Alkebulan, a prized possession in our own land, and priceless here on this world. She stood next to me, the book resting on the extended palms of her hands. The bright smile on her face in the sunshine was a happy sight, we were hoping.

It was a tense few minutes as the two people considered each other.

I saw the quamernats glancing behind us and seeing Pilot held in captivity, and I hoped that would ease some of their fears. We were definitely not the same as those People from the underground city.

They took us in, looking at everything, then withdrew a few dozen yards to confer with one another for a few minutes. Soon enough, though, they came forward again, and one of them – the leader, I surmised – approached us.

I walked forward with Tupu.

"Hello, we are the dwellers of this island." They bowed low, their faces touching their extended forelegs. *Just like Iilcendorr & Co. had.*

We all bowed, then rose again. "Greetings. We come from a very faraway land, on a quest."

Tupu came forward and gave them the book she'd brought, and smiled as she bowed and retreated.

The quamernats took the book, and three of them examined it, murmuring among themselves as they flipped through the ornate pages. The leader looked up at us again, then took another step in our direction.

"My name is Jhdavhid," said the leader. I had sounded a bit garbled in my ear. It sounded like he'd said ... *what?*

Tupu came forward smiling and extended her hand, "I'm sorry, what did you say your name was, sir?"

"My name," the quamernat said a little louder, although I could tell these were a soft-spoken people. "... is David."

I felt my jaw drop open.

Chapter Forty

The Old Librarian Grady

I hoped Iilcendorr would forgive me, but these island quamernats here in this two-sunned world were fantastic and easily way cooler than the centaurs we had left behind.

After the introductions and after we'd picked our dropped jaws up off the floor, we were very surprised when we were taken into their town, which had been well hidden by huge trees from above. The entire island was protected by a high stone wall, reinforced by wood and spikes; it stretched from the cliffs we'd seen to the south, all the way around, and to the other side.

They had only excluded the meadow where the saucer had landed; in fact, you could not see the wall from the saucer nor from the air, and this was by design.

These people knew they were hunted by the mainlanders.

"Their names," I whispered to Caroline. "They are so similar to the names we have back home, especially in Swerighe."

"I know! I wonder if these people have had contact with our world back home?" said Caroline.

"It has to be more than a coincidence," Khepri remarked as we walked.

We found ourselves in the town center, which was covered by the thick branches of the trees, which reached hundreds of feet into the air.

None of the plants moved or seemed aggressive in any way, which was an extreme relief. Even Er was amazed, stooping down to examine several different types of foliage as we walked past.

The quamernats were all artists. They had paintings, artwork, sculptures, beadwork, carvings, and every type of created beauty we could think of, all on display in every house and building in the town. Many murals covered the walls around town, and these were all large and amazing. They also had small pieces of art, in places where we least expected to see it. There was a line of wall that met another bit of wall, and the small two-inch space where they met was decorated in an intricate painting of exquisite beauty. I stopped walking and just stood there, marveling at it, until Christianne took me by the hand and urged me forward.

Musicians played a lilting tune near the town square, and many quamernats sat in the dark blue grass, listening intently. The music sounded as if it had been composed by faeries and mermaids, and I found I was mesmerized by it. Christianne continued to pull me along, until we both became lulled into a visual paradise by a large scene painted along the wall of a building, and Kym had to come get us both.

We were welcomed with opened arms, and embraced as friends. The djinn placed Pilot in a neck hold so he could grip him with just one arm and enjoy the samples of wine and fruit offered to us with the other hand. Er stayed by the djinn's side and stared up at Pilot from time to time, awed.

"Tell us," David said, "of your quest, the quest that brought you across space and time to us here."

Another quamernats galloped up to us just then, and came to sit next to David.

"Ah, this is my younger brother, who I am grooming to take my place when I retire from public office." David smiled fondly at the other quamernat. "Jamie, say hello to these newcomers."

"Hello," the smaller quamernat said, grinning from ear to ear. He was obviously very curious. They all seemed to share that curiosity. Their grins were infectious, and I found myself smiling broadly as I spoke.

"Well, we come from a world with just one sun and one moon, and we came to your land on a quest for a certain book."

"We love books, we have created many different types of books," said David. "Tell me about this book you seek, I may be able to help you on your quest."

"We seek *The Book of Mysteries*. It is said to hold all the knowledge of our world's antiquity. It contains the wisdom given to humans, from cures to all cancers, to the secrets of navigating the stars and heavens. The book is said to have come to our world from beyond the stars – where we seem to be now," I finished, laughing. I felt so excited and hopeful.

David look intrigued and turned to Jamie, "Brother, fetch me old Grady. I think he will know something of this." He turned back to us. "We have heard of this book you seek. We just might know more about it."

Er jumped up and down, then Caroline and Christianne both let out small shrieks of happiness and promptly fell off the bench where they were seated.

Laughing, Khepri helped them both up, with Tupu's help.

"Oh, my gods, David, your words have filled me with so much hope. We have been through some incredible travails in our journey, and we've come in search of the book, following clues that have led us all the way here, and I think, no, I am sure, that this," I waved my hand, indicating their entire world, "is a different world from earth." I nodded toward the two glowing orbs burning brightly in the sky.

Kym squealed in happiness. "You've got TWO SUNS, so this is a very far-away place!" she exclaimed in a high-pitched voice.

"Truly, sir, we would be eternally grateful for your help," said Khepri.

The quamernat smiled. "I feel excited for you! A quest! And you've come so far. How incredible is that?"

Within minutes Jamie was running back, dragging the hand of an old quamernat. He had grey in his dark hair, his skin was black as Tupu's, and he was laughing.

"Grady!" David turned to me. "Please tell our historian everything you told me earlier."

"*Senior* historian," Jamie said, his finger in the air.

I repeated the description I had outlined to David. Grady listened intently, nodding at every point I made.

I finally stopped to take a deep breath, my eyes on the elder statesman.

Grady looked solemn, then nodded deeply. "Yes, I think I have heard of this book. It is a thick book with all manner of encyclopedic knowledge in it."

I held my breath.

"You see," he leaned forward. "Now, what was your name again, young lady?"

I grinned. "My name is Charlotte."

"Charlotte, well," he patted my hand, then sat back, "our ancestors – and by 'ancestor' I mean my grandfather's grandfather's grandfather – they lived a long time ago, it is true, but they did not live life as dangerously as we do here." Grady spread his arms out to encompass their entire planet.

"Our ancestors had knowledge of magic that has now been lost to us, well, at least some of it. They traveled the stars, you see."

I nearly fell out of my chair.

I watched Grady's face, trying not to blink, wanting not to miss a word.

Grady continued.

"They lived at a time when our planet was not so hostile, a time when there was food in abundance. In fact, it is said they were much larger than we are, here today," his hand waved to include all the quamernats on the island.

"They traveled through portals and visited many worlds, spreading our seed and knowledge wherever they could. They had a strong belief in sharing the seeds of each world with the others." He put his fingertips together and tapped his chest with them.

"Wait, I know what to do. Let me think." And the old quamernat put his hands together and closed his eyes, and was silent for a minute.

"I think I remember," he motioned behind his shoulder. "Simon, where is Simon?"

A young quamernat came forward from the back of the small, gathering crowd. "Here I am, grandfather."

Simon carried several books under his arm and had a small pair of spectacles perched on his nose.

I turned to Khepri and whispered, "I cannot believe how similar these people are to us on earth!" She nodded.

It was incredible and odd, surely much stronger than any coincidence. The names they all had were names plucked out of the northlands and Alkebulan on earth. They were Earth names! Or were Earth names brought from this island? I couldn't be sure.

But Grady was speaking again.

"Simon, do you remember that heavy old book in the antiquities section?" Grady asked, his hand on Simon's arm.

"Yes, sir. Was it on the green shelf or the brown shelf?" Simon asked.

"I think it was the brown, on the bottom, on the far left side, second from the end. It has the tree on its spine?"

"I know the one, sir. Would you like me to fetch it?"

"Well, that book is very large and heavy, I think it would be good for us all to go down to see the library. Together." Grady struggled to rise. "These old bones don't move very fast these days," he chuckled.

David showed the book Tupu had brought for them to Grady. "Sir, look. They brought us a gift." He placed the book in Grady's hands.

Grady stopped in his tracks. "Oh, my goodness," He held the book reverently, his hands caressing it and lifting it high so he could examine it from every angle. "My goodness. My goodness." He looked up at us. "You have brought us such an exquisite gift, my new friends. I honor you." He bowed his head, then stood upright, holding Tupu's gift to his chest. "Come, let us go to the libraries." He beckoned us all. He walked slowly, and held the Tupu's gift as if it were a precious, living thing.

Chapter Forty-One
The Library

We walked through the village, which had a latticework of branches woven overhead, about twenty or thirty feet off the ground. The trees and vines were thick, and I could see how the view of what existed on the ground would be completely obscured from view.

David had other quamernats come and retrieve Pilot and lead him away, assuring us they would hold him in a secure location and not allow him to leave while we continued.

Grady led the way, stopping here and there to pluck fruit from nearby vines and offer it to us.

At one point, we passed under a plant similar to our earth's own grapevines, except the fruit hanging from the high, woven vines was in many different colors. Light green, rich red, dark blue and purple, the clusters of grapes were each a different color, and the effect was that of a stained-glass window with the sun shining through.

Grady plucked a cluster of fat light purple grapes and handed it to us, and also indicated we should help ourselves. I accepted the fruit and found it warmed from the twin suns' rays, and very sweet and juicy.

The fruit was out of reach for Kym and Er, and I plucked a few more multicolored clusters and handed them down to my companions.

We ate as we strolled down the center of the town, and the sunshine filtered down to us, gentle on our heads. A light ocean breeze caressed our faces and refreshed us. Multicolored butterflies flew in and around all the vines, a fascinating sight, since we'd seen no sign of insect life on the mainland.

We mentioned as much to our hosts.

"The island has its own ecosystem, different from the mainland. We are far enough away that the spores from the carnivorous plants there cannot reach us," David said as we walked.

"We also noticed no animal life on the mainland. There are no birds, no small flying animals," Caroline said.

"No, those are all gone, I believe, for the most part," said Grady.

"It was not always so," said Jamie. "A few generations ago, there were still snakes and lizards, but the mainlanders hunted them to extinction."

"There's nothing to eat from the outside, just things from under the ground," said Er in a small voice. He held a cluster of grapes in each hand, and juice ran down his chin as he took another bite.

"Was the mainland always like this?" I asked. "Always so dangerous?"

"We were attacked by a massive labyrinth hedge and had to fight fiercely for our lives," said Tupu.

"That sounds perilous," said David, his tone concerned.

"Those living under the ground seemed to be in fear of it," I said. "They were amazed we had fought it and survived."

"I imagine they would be. I believe they fled underground several generations ago," David said.

Er spoke up. "We are taught in school that the overworld became too hostile when the plants became aggressive." I looked at the little boy as we walked. "The plants attacked everything and destroyed it."

"Insects, too?" Christianne asked.

"Everything."

"This world, at least on the mainland, seems extremely hostile to even indigenous life," Khepri said.

"Oh," David said, "the people on the mainland are not indigenous to this planet."

What??

Grady glanced at me and saw my face. "Oh, yes, it is true."

"How? Why ...?"

David nodded grimly. "They were brought here because their own worlds were hostile to them; they had almost died out."

"Almost died out?" Khepri asked. "You mean on their own planets?"

"Yes, our ancestors, back when they were space travelers, before the knowledge was lost to us, brought them back from their own planets." Grady stopped to take a breath. He sat on a nearby bench to rest and we gathered around him to listen.

"Back about a thousand years ago, my ancestors encountered them, and brought them here to live. About the same time, or maybe just afterward, our ecosystem began to change. I think it might have been an error for our grandfathers' grandfathers to introduced a non-indigenous life form to our world. It had an adverse impact. Then there was a war. We had retreated to our island here, a few generations before, and thankfully were able to bring most of our collection of books and scrolls here with us."

"Tell me about the war, Grady," I prompted quietly.

Well, it was after the People had been brought here, rescued from their own dying worlds. They had depleted much of their own planetary resources, and polluted their atmosphere to the point that their plant life had all but vanished."

"They had lived here maybe two or three generations, and the plant life of our own world had begun to change." Grady waved his arm. "Thankfully it didn't affect our island here."

"How did the plant life change, again?" asked Tupu.

"The plants became more self-aware, and began to exhibit the ability to move faster than they had to. The war was between the new People and the plants."

I gasped.

Khepri looked troubled.

"The hedge maze you say you fought?" Grady continued. "There were many of them in those days. The war was for dominance over the land. The People were eating the plants, and the plants began to fight back. The People had also begun to create factories, taking minerals from the planet, processing them, doing much of the same things they had done on their home worlds that had brought about the collapse of their own ecosystem. But here, the plants evolved to fight back."

"It was not an evenly matched war. The People were driven underground. We quamernats had already moved to the island, maybe a hundred years before, to escape the pollution the People had begun to produce."

"So, the folks trying to survive underground now are having a much harder time. And we have heard from the travelers that they have built up a large mythology surrounding the plants. When it was their own changes that were the catalyst for the eventual evolution of the plant life." He sighed and looked toward Er, who was off playing on the side.

Er was having a delightful time; he explored as we walked, and tasted all the fruit he could.

"I am not sure what to make of this little one." Grady glanced over at him. "The boy is from the People underground? I noticed the difference in his forehead and ears." He indicated his own head area.

"Yes, I believe the boy is indeed from the underground mainland," David said.

"Hmmm, we will have to see about that," Grady said quietly.

"What do you mean?" Khepri asked, sounding worried.

"Well," said David, "The boy seems very young. For instance, he has not acted hostile to us at all, whereas the adults of the People usually do – or certainly act contentious, at the very least. This boy, what did you say his name was? He seems bright and happy."

I called out to Er, and he came running, a grin on his face. "Er, are you happy here? Or do these people upset you?"

"Happy!" he grinned.

I smiled at Grady. "I believe his name is 'Er' – at least that is what he told us."

"Errand," said Er.

I turned to him. "Your full name is 'Errand'? Really?"

"That is what I did in the apothecary. I ran errands," he said.

Oh, dear.

Grady leaned forward toward Er. "And do you like your name, Errand?"

"I like Er. Just Er," said Er.

"Then we shall call you Er, just Er," Grady laughed. He straightened. "If he stayed here with us, we could head off the stories and attitudes that would have filled the boy's head at an older age, and he could grow and learn with us. Maybe even grow into a new name. You never know."

I was amazed.

"Have you ever done such a thing before?" I asked.

"Oh, many times, mostly in the distant past. Our last adoption of this type was about fifty years ago, and she has been happy ever since," said Grady.

"Is she still around?" asked Caroline.

"Yes, she is definitely still around," Grady laughed, then took a deep breath and stood again, and we continued walking.

He finally came to a stop in front of a large stone building, which had moss and ivy growing in abundance at its base and up its sides. There were grapevines growing up a trellis against the building, and ornate engraved artwork all along its front edifice.

Grady stopped in front of the building's old carved wooden door.

"Welcome to the library."

Chapter Forty-Two
The Challenge

We entered the old building through its ornate doors, held open by Grady, his face beaming with pride. Clearly, this was his life's work, and he was very proud of the collection.

Once we were all gathered inside the foyer, we were approached by a senior library assistant, who greeted us and pointed out all the ornate artwork along the walls. Grady went to confer with David and Jamie while we were led, entranced, from art display to hanging tapestry, to ornate painting. The library was as much a museum as it was a receptacle for books.

Grady joined us as we descended to the lower floors.

"We keep the more valuable books down here, it's cooler and safer for them," he explained. He indicated the historic section of the library, and it was well guarded.

Grady led the way, followed by David and Jamie, and then our troupe. The hallways were winding and intricate, and I lost all sense of direction early on. I said as much to Caroline.

"I think that's by design, Miss," Caroline whispered back.

"Do you think they're trying to get people lost down here, Carrie?"

"No, I think they like winding tunnels and they love books, so they've married the two," she smiled at me.

If they have, this design born of love has also resulted in a confusing and mysterious place.

"Now, please take a seat anywhere you'd like," David said as we entered a new room.

This room was lined with floor-to-ceiling bookcases, all filled with heavy, leather bound tomes. The ceilings reach at least twenty feet high, and the walls not covered by bookcases were adorned with numerous tapestries, all depicting a fertile, verdant land filled with every color of quamernat imaginable. We even saw tapestries depicting stained-glass windows, tapestries depicting the exploration of space, and smaller wall hangings that showed the arrival of the People. These smaller scenes showed the aliens disembarking from large space-flying ships, and walking out onto the planet they had been transplanted upon.

David saw me studying these particular scenes. "Not all of them were happy at leaving their home world."

I glanced at him in surprise.

"Oh, we didn't force any of them to leave," he said conversationally. "They left grudgingly, but it was their situation that compelled them to do so. Their planets were crumbling around them. They were experiencing a mass extinction, you understand. They had little choice if they wanted to survive."

"To leave all you've known, your whole life, your history, where your ancestors are buried, for a new land, knowing you can never return, must have been hard," Khepri said.

"It was indeed hard. Some of them did not survive the trip. It took over twenty years to complete," David said.

My god.

"Did any of them stay behind?" asked Christianne.

"Oh, most of them stayed behind. Our ancestors spent more than a year explaining the situation, showing them scientific proof, offering different solutions. In the end, transportation and transplantation onto our home planet was a choice made by fewer than seven hundred thousand of them. Out of a planetary population of three billion."

Christianne's jaw dropped open. "And the rest, the ones that remained?"

"There were dozens of different escape plans used during that time. But yes, more than two thirds of their population elected to remain behind," said David.

"Even though they were doomed," I said sadly.

Tupu thought for a moment, her hand to her chin, then spoke. "What happened to those who remained on their home worlds?"

"Our ancestors kept monitoring their situation. In one case, it took fifty more years, but every last one of them died. On that planet, they had been rendered sterile by the chemicals polluting their planet's atmosphere and soil and water. A group of scientists stayed behind, working to reverse the process: stubborn individuals who insisted it wasn't as bad as all the evidence indicated. They perished along with the others," David said solemnly. "The last indigenous life forms on that planet larger than bacteria died out nearly a thousand years ago. The last of the People were left in a village, very sick, with no one to care for them. They died very painfully of radiation poisoning."

We all fell silent, deep in thought.

We rested there among the books and tapestries, investigating all the treasures the quamernats had in glass display cases, but soon we were ready to go on.

"Grady, you've shown us some incredible treasures, and we've seen many wonderful books, but ..." I said, trailing off.

Grady laughed. "You are wondering about the specific book you are seeking? *The Book of Mysteries?*"

"Yes."

"That book is part of a collection held on the lowest level of the library. Follow me." He set off again, and we followed.

To get to the lowest floor, the builders had carved ramps made from the rock, and they curled around the inner walls of the building, descending lower and lower into the catacombs of the island's bedrock.

"We must be below sea level at this point, surely," whispered Khepri.

"I think we must," I replied, hurrying after Grady.

Grady half turned as he walked. "We are indeed below sea level; in fact, we are about fifty feet below the shore. But don't worry, we are entirely surrounded by rock, and quite safe here." He hummed as he turned another corner.

We finally arrived at an ornate gate made of very old metal. We could see beyond to the small room that held a table, several lamps, and one enormous bookcase. Grady opened the gate, which was not locked, and led us in.

The room was cold, and I felt goosebumps rise on my arm. The light emanating from the lamps was steady but low, and the edges of the room resided in near total darkness, especially at the far end.

The gate we passed through was maybe twenty-five feet from the bookcase, and as we came through the threshold into the room, I thought I saw something on the lower bookcase glow. Then, suddenly, Grady stopped us with a nervous jump.

"There is something I must explain first," he said. "This particular book you seek is the last of the books my ancestors made from their galactic journeys to different planets. It is very, very old. It is surrounded by a very strong magic." He glanced back at the bookcase, then to us again.

"I have been able to study this book, and well as my assistants, such as Simon. It is very heavy, but to us, it is not dangerous."

"However," he continued, "there is a legend surrounding it. It is a legend that surrounded all of the books created by the ancestors from their cosmic journeys."

He sat down in a nearby chair.

"You see, you are not the first to come searching for a book."

My eyes widened in surprise.

"Others have come to our island on quests over the last hundred years. It has been our policy to give aid to these seekers whenever we can. If you look at the bookcase behind me, you might see spaces here and there, as they have come in search of books, and the books have gone with them."

We looked, and sure enough, there was quite a bit of space left empty in the bookcase.

"As I said, I and my assistants have studied the book you seek; we've studied all the books in our possession. We can feel the magic in each tome, but in the book you seek, there had been no adverse reaction to our handling of it."

He looked at us seriously.

"That will not be the case with you."

"I don't understand," Caroline said.

"The book's magic will react to you because you are from the planet it was created for. The book will in fact, test you, your worthiness, your origins. It will test the most important quality of your species. We've all seen it."

"What do you mean, you've seen it?" Khepri asked.

"In every case, the book has surrounded the people seeking it, and encased them in a ball of magic and light, and tasked them. We on the outside," Grady waved him hand around the room, to include himself, David, Jamie, Simon, and the few other librarians who'd followed us down, "can see the events as they unfold in the ball, but the people inside cannot perceive us, nor much else."

David came forward then. "You should know that you do not have to touch it. You do not have to enter into the challenge the magic demands."

"What happens if we don't?" Jim asked.

"You may stay here on the island, you may depart, you may do anything you wish."

"But we'll be trapped here in your world?" I asked.

"We do not know how to return you." David looked sad.

"It was the magic of the map that brought you through to us on this quest, to our world. We have no idea how the magic of our ancestors works," Grady said.

"Okay, well, what happens if we complete the magic's challenge? We go back home with the book, right?" Tupu asked.

"That is what the book says, yes."

Wait a minute.

"And what," I swallowed down a growing feeling of fear creeping up my neck. "What happens if we fail?"

"We do not know," Grady said simply. "Every time people have come to seek a book and have entered into the challenge; they have simply disappeared. We can see them in the globe of light, but after a while, the globe disappears. We have no idea where they go or even if they've completed the book's challenge."

"Well, what does the book say happens if the quest seekers fail the challenge?" asked Jim.

"The books do not mention failure. They simply say what happens when the challenge is completed."

"You could enter into the challenge and never figure it out, never triumph. You could be locked in for a very long time as you attempt and fail and attempt again and again."

Oh, great.

Chapter Forty-Three

Going In

We decided to confer with each other, apart from the others, the quamernats and Er.

"What do you think we should do?" I asked.

"I don't know."

"Will we be stuck here forever if we don't try?"

"Will we be trapped forever trying if we *do* try?"

"Is there any danger?"

"I don't think they know."

"Is it a battle?"

"No, he said it was a test of 'the most important qualities of our species', whatever that is."

"What are earthlings' most important qualities?"

"Not sure, but should we be experts at being earthlings?"

"No one else would do it better, right?"

"I don't want to be stuck here forever."

"We don't even know where 'here' is, and this planet is hostile."

"Very hostile."

"There are cannibals here; that's pretty hostile."

"Not to mention the plants that want to kill you."

"The island's not so bad."

"Okay, people, concentrate. We came on a quest for the book, right?"

"I'd rather my baby is born on earth," Tupu said. "I'm rather fond of my planet."

"Me, too."

"Jim, have you ever been off planet? Do you have any way to travel between solar systems?"

"No."

"I don't know, but I think we need to try this challenge."

"Even if we're locked in and can't escape?"

"You don't know if that's the case, not for sure."

"If we go in, we can't take Er with us; they said that book only works on earthlings."

"I know."

"Let's make a decision."

"I think we should face it."

"Face what?"

"Any danger that presents itself."

"The reward is the book, right?"

"Yes."

"Well then, let's go for it."

"I need a show of hands."

"All in favor of going in, raise your hand yes."

...

"Okay then. Let's do this."

"Bring it on."

"I'm going to miss Er, if I'm honest," said Jim.

I thought I heard him sniffle.

"You okay?" I asked the djinn discretely. He nodded and then blew his nose on a handkerchief he pulled from thin air.

I put my arm around him, then beckoned Er over from where he stood near the assistant, Simon.

Er walked over and looked up into my face.

"This is your world, Er. You must stay here. It will be safest if you stay with the quamernats on this island. Do you understand?" I asked.

The boy nodded solemnly.

Jim knelt down.

"Remember what I told you?" said the djinn.

"Yes," Er replied in a small voice.

Jim put his enormous arms around the slight figure. "I'm going to miss you so much, Er." He pulled back to look into the boy's face. "Remember, you are bigger than your job was; you are much more important than those People ever gave you credit for."

I knelt down, too. "Er, never forget: you have the ability to change your world. Never stop trying. Never give up."

Caroline sat on the floor next to us, patting Er's hand. "Child, if you can, create something beautiful each day that was not there the day before."

That was beautiful.

I felt tears rise in me and choked them back. Giving Er one last hug, I took a step back so the others could have their turn. Jim stayed with him the longest.

But finally, we were ready.

We turned around and faced the bookcase.

Goodbyes had been said, and Er stood back, safely in the arms of Simon, the library assistant.

We were ready.

"As you approach the book, it will begin to glow with recognition. It will be bright. Pick it up anyway, and open it and begin reading it. Stay together. Be strong," Grady said. "It has been a privilege knowing you this short time, quest-seekers."

"Good luck," said David.

I turned to the others. "Ready?"

Each of them nodded in turn.

I took a step toward the bookcase. There were books on four shelves. The book on the bottom shelf, on the far left side, the second book from the end, was glowing.

That's our book. The Book of Mysteries. It's right there. All you have to do is pick it up and open it.

I realized there was no use hesitating. We'd made a decision.

I strode forward. By the time my fingers reached for the book, the light coming from it was blinding. My left arm came up in front of my eyes, and my right hand reached out for it. As soon as I touched the book, grasping its massive edge and pulling on it, the light vanished. The thing was massive. I needed two hands just to lift it. But I grabbed it, and finally had it in my arms.

Since it was so large and heavy, it was unwieldy. I struggled a minute but finally had the thing balanced on my left arm, and steadied against myself. I reached for the cover with my right hand, took hold of the hard leather, and pulled it open.

* * *

Greetings, earthling.
* * *

I blinked.

Everything around me had vanished. The books, the bookcase, the walls, the table, the people. Everything was gone.

* * *

We have pulled you out of time to test your worthiness. Do you wish to possess this book and all its knowledge?

* * *

"Uhh," my voice sounded small in my own ears. I cleared my throat and swallowed my fears. In a strong voice I said, "Yes."

I sensed amusement and satisfaction.

* * *

You are an earthling. The denizens of your planet are known for their courage, their tenacity, and their joy.

* * *

Our 'joy'?

But the voice was speaking again.

* * *

You are a human. Your species is known for its capacity to endure, for its capacity to be stubborn, and for its capacity to sacrifice.

* * *

Uhhh. I guess this is accurate. I felt a surge of pride, but also a growing sense of misgiving. *Where is this heading?*

* * *

Are you ready to begin?
* * *

I took a deep breath. This was it.
"Yes, I'm ready."

* * *

Who do you love the most?
* * *

What?
There was an evil sounding chuckle.
Then.
The world went black.

Chapter Forty-Four
Oblivion

I blinked from the sudden change in light and opened my eyes to the dock, the dock where Caroline, Christianne and I had first been brought after the slavers had stolen us and put us in chains aboard their ship.

"Miss, hold my hand; I'll help you walk," Caroline put her hand in mine and grasped it tightly.

The sun was bright in our eyes. We were being led off the gangplank from the ship, down to the crowded dock where sailors and merchants alike were busy and loud and hard at work, doing whatever it was they did.

Wait a minute. I know this.

I was back at the same place where Caroline, Christianne and I had been brought into the town and to the slave market. *But, didn't that happen at night? I could've sworn …*

"Be careful. It's slippery!" a sailor cautioned.

I blinked from the sudden sunlight in my eyes; my foot slipped, and I stumbled.

"MISS, CAREFUL!" Caroline grabbed at my hand as I pitched sideways.

I grabbed at the gangplank too late, and fell heavily across it on my stomach.

"Oof!" I felt my breath get knocked out of me. My legs pinwheeled in the air, trying to find purchase where there was none.

"Careful, there, the ship is shifting ..." said a sailor.

I felt the ramp move, and tip as the ship bobbed upward in an ocean swell.

"Hurry!"

"GRAB HER, TAM!"

I heard a cry and a splash.

"NO!"

"She's between the pilings. Grab her!"

"CAROLINE!" I heard Christianne cry out.

Another scream. Then, "The ship! Pull the rope, PULL THE ROPE!"

"IT'S GOT HER!"

I felt a deep panic rise in my chest. Looking down, my line of sight was obscured from view of whatever or whoever was in the water.

Are they in the water?

I grabbed the edge of the ramp and swung my leg over, gripping the side and pulling myself up to a sitting position.

"Come here, girly," a rough voice grabbed at my arm. I shook it off, thrusting my hands down and getting to my feet by myself.

Where was Caroline?

I heard another scream. *That sounded like Christianne.*

"Charlotte, CHARLOTTE! CAROLINE IS IN THE WATER!"

I whirled around and looked to the side. I couldn't see anything, just dirty seawater, trash and an oily scum floating in the bay ... WAIT.

"CAROLINE!" I screamed. I ran down the gangplank and to the dock, and then back up to the top of the pilings.

Caroline had fallen in the water, from twenty-five feet up. She'd been pushed against the pilings the huge ship was tethered to.

"CAROLINE!" I screamed.

What is happening?

"Someone throw her a rope!"

"She can't grab it, she's holding on to the piling."

"HELP HER!"

I dropped down to the lower deck of the pier. Rats scuttled away from me as I swung down to stand on the horizontal brace holding the heavy jetty.

"Leave her, she's a lost cause."

"No way, that's valuable property, fish her out."

"She's already half dead."

"I don't care!" This was the first mate's voice. Tam, wasn't he called?

"Get her OUT NOW!"

"Hey, HEY!"

"GET BACK HERE!"

I felt hands grabbing at me, and I shook them off. My eyes hurriedly looked for another foothold.

Aha!

I grabbed another brace and swung down again.

I was now within seven or eight feet of the piling Caroline was clinging to for dear life. It was one of the outer supports, the ones thrust out next to the ships, designed to hold them at bay while the gangplanks were lowered, and as the water swelled up and down, the edge of the ship was thrust closer and closer. She would be crushed ...

"CARRIE!"

My voice cut through all the noise, and she turned her head around to face me.

Her face. Oh, god, her face.

Her face was cut, a huge gash running from the right top of her temple, down to her lower left chin. The ship moving with the ocean swells had crushed her against the piling and her face had taken the brunt of the impact. She was frantically grabbing on to the pier, but she kept slipping off. The cut on her face was deep. Her lower jaw was dangling in the water, and there was a growing blood stain floating away from her. I could see bone through the gore.

She closed her eyes and screamed, an ungodly scream that sounded above all the other noises on the dock and ship. It resounded in my ears until it penetrated my brain.

I dropped down farther and tried to reach out for her. We were maybe ten feet apart. I shifted my foothold and reached again, a few feet closer. But still ...

I felt my feet slipping ...

"Here! Take the rope, TAKE THE ROPE!" Someone had lowered a length of rope to us, and it dangled just out of reach.

I lunged for it and grabbed it, but in doing do, I lost my foothold and slipped off the piling; suddenly I was hanging on to the rope and banging against the piling I had just slipped from.

Caroline was right in front of me. If I could only ...

The water shifted again, and the ship rose on a swell and moved against the dock.

It hit Caroline.

I heard her groan as she hung on. It was a groan of misery. A groan of death.

I put my feet against the ship and tried to push it off of her, but the massive weight would not budge.

"Caroline!" I cried out.

The water swirled her around and against the ship. She was rotating toward me, and I could see blood coming out of her mouth. Her eyes were open and frantic, staring at me, unseeing.

The water shifted again. The tide was coming in.

Oh, God, the tide is coming in...

The ship shifted again, crushing her.

I heard her groan again and realized her breath was being forcibly expelled.

The large ship was flat against her now, rubbing up and down, crushing her slowly but surely.

She turned to me again, her arms still grasping at the piling. Her eyes lifted to meet mine again.

I saw blood running from her ears.

"CAROLINE!" I screamed, trying in vain to push the massive ship away.

It just kept pushing.

The water splashed against us, and I was blinded for a moment. Then I shook my head, rubbed my face and looked again.

I saw blood running from her eyes. The ship was up against the piling, and as the piling was designed to do, it was holding the ship there, up against the jetty, wood against wood, unyielding, unyielding.

A sudden shift allowed her to open her mouth, and she gasped for breath and screamed again, a gurgling, dying scream of intense pain.

I jumped.

I grabbed at Caroline, one fist grasping a handful of her hair, another clutching a bit of her tunic, I let my weight fall, holding on to her, the water full of blood ...

The ocean tide shifted again, grinding us against the piling, and I felt my bones being crushed.

But as the water momentarily receded, it pulled the ship away far enough that it let us go.

Caroline's grip on the piling loosened.

I glanced at her face. There was blood everywhere. Her eyes were staring straight ahead, bloodshot, unseeing. Her mouth was open, blood pouring from it in a stream out into the water. Her arms let go of the piling.

I tried to grab for the rope with my teeth as it dangled enticingly against my shoulder, but I was unwilling to let go of her.

The water swelled.

We sank.

I kept hold of her. I refused to let her go.

We sank together into oblivion.

Chapter Forty-Five

My Heart's Best Beloved

I opened my eyes to a dim light and the figure of a centaur sitting next to me. No, not a centaur, a quamernat. He was small, as small as Grady had been.

Wait.

It was Grady, but younger, much younger.

* * *

Hello, Charlotte.

* * *

The voice was in my mind, but coming from the young Grady.

I stared at him. Then ...

"WHERE IS CAROLINE?" I demanded.

* * *

Be calmed, Caroline is fine.
* * *

I took a deep breath.

"Can you just talk to me? I mean, you're sitting right here."

* * *

I am appearing to you this way, but my voice comes through your mind. I cannot alter this.
* * *

Okay.

"What just happened? Caroline is okay? You're sure?"

Everything was in shadows, the only sights were the young Grady and myself. I looked around us, hoping for a glimpse of my friend.

* * *

She's more than your friend. I think I see that now.
* * *

"Caroline is my family. She is my ... Caroline." I could not explain it better.

* * *

I understand.

* * *

I took a deep breath, willing myself to calm down. "So, what now?"

* * *

Now? Now you go home with the book.

* * *

"But I want my friends to come home with me, too."

* * *

They will.

Charlotte, you have passed the challenge. You have been tested and have passed.

* * *

I felt a growing annoyance. "Wait a minute. I need an explanation. What was all this? Why did I have to complete your challenge? Why do this to us?"

I felt more amusement coming from the young Grady in front of me.

* * *

We needed to know that you were worthy of the book. You accepted the challenge.

* * *

"And the challenge was to kill me and Caroline?" It had felt real. The pain and anguish were fresh in my head, my heart still pounded with what I had gone through. *What Caroline had gone through was much, much worse.*

* * *

Caroline did not go through anything, just you. You represented your world in this challenge.

* * *

"Why would you put me through that? It was awful ..." I felt a tear run down my cheek, and impatiently brushed it away, unaware I had begun to cry.

The young Grady regarded me silently, waiting.

I screwed up my eyes and muffled a scream. "Do you know how horrible that was?"

* * *

We know.

* * *

"If you know, then why on earth ..."

* * *

The challenge was to make sure you were deserving. Make sure your heart was pure and worthy.

* * *

"And if I had failed?"

* * *

We would have kept trying.

* * *

Oh, god ...

I felt a shudder go through me.

Calm down, Charlotte. You passed. You did it. You got the book. You bought your way home: You and your friends are going to be all right.

I was feeling so many things ...

Wait.

"And are you the being in charge of all this? In charge of the challenge?"

* * *

We are in charge, yes. We are the last of the ancestors.

* * *

"What, you're just trapped in each book, waiting to torture people?" I felt anger in my chest, and closed my eyes, trying again to calm down.

* * *

Not trapped in each book, but waiting in the planet. We are a part of this world.
* * *

I took another deep breath, and stood. "Okay, well, thank you for ... whatever that was, and I'll just be on my way, I guess." I turned from the young Grady, then stopped and turned back. "Just curious ..."

* * *

Yes?
* * *

"Exactly how did I pass? How would I have failed that challenge?"

* * *

The challenge was a test of your heart. You would have failed had you chosen not to sink into oblivion with your heart's best beloved. If you had let her die alone. If you had chosen to save yourself, instead, all would have been lost.

* * *

I took a shuddering breath and felt a new course of hot tears flow down my face.

I crumpled to the unseen ground.

Chapter Forty-Six

The Pirate Queen

"I was telling her, 'You would not believe how well these centaurs are taking to life on the southern island,' " Tam laughed, smiling easily in the sunshine.

Caroline stood beside me, watching me silently. They were all there. Tupu, Khepri, Jim, Kym, and Christianne. They were watching me.

"Yeah, well, I knew it wouldn't be any trouble." I scuffed the sand with the toe of my boot.

Shading my eyes, I looked inland at the centaurs. They were busy.

Iilcendorr was up on the roof of a new building, calling down to Rhalofetorr for a hammer. Glynbelarr was beside him, holding palm fronds in place, as he reached down, grabbed the offered hammer, and got to work setting the roof into place.

He caught me looking at him and smiled. "The rains are coming soon. We've got to make sure this island's medical bay is ready for anything."

"The school goes up next." The young centaur next to me smiled, and I recognized with a start the young colt who'd been injured in the fall from the waterfall. I looked down at his leg and saw it was completely healed. "I'm feeling much better, thanks to your healer, Khepri," he grinned. He had Chowder in his arms, and he was petting the little rock demon, who was purring.

Exactly how long had we been away?

"Well, it's all good, I did wonder what had happened, you know, but when they came through the cave and explained where you'd gone, well, I knew you might be a while," Tam laughed easily.

"And we had Akim to help, of course," he ruffled the boy's hair as he went by, and Akim turned and grinned at Tam.

"Everything's going well. The mermaids were very happy to see the centaurs. Apparently, their mythology spoke of centaurs on the northern island, but they had never seen them. They threw a party when the first centaurs arrived." Tam laughed.

"Charlotte." Christianne ran up to me. She held out a small white cage, and I looked inside. It was empty. I looked up at her, my eyebrows raised in a question.

"I let the butterfly go into a field of flowers when we got back to the islands." She grinned happily. I smiled at her fondly.

"Hey, Charlotte, the centaurs have asked to speak to you, in the ceremony tonight. You're in charge, so I thought ..." Tam trailed off, raising his eyebrows.

"What?" I asked, smiling.

"Well, they want to ... I mean, they feel incredibly grateful to you." Tam ducked his head in embarrassment.

"What the young sailor is too flustered to tell you, Charlotte," said Iilcendorr, coming up to us, wiping his hands on a rag, then extending a handshake, "is that we would like to honor you in a ceremony tonight." He finished, shaking my hand gently.

"Another ceremony?" I chuckled.

"Well, you should know by now that we love gatherings." Glynbelarr winked. "It's a great excuse for a feast!"

"Don't let that scoundrel tease you, Charlotte, we have something real and huge to celebrate tonight," Kiphaentren said seriously, coming up to us.

Iilcendorr looked at me solemnly. "Charlotte, we want to make you our queen."

"What? No, no, not me," I said, embarrassed.

"You cannot refuse; it would be bad manners," smiled Kiphaentren.

"Do not worry, Charlotte, it is a purely ceremonial title, there are no real responsibilities that come with it," said Iilcendorr softly, grinning from ear to ear.

"It's just that, after all you went through to get the book, bring it out of the volcano ..."

The volcano. I glanced at Caroline and Khepri, smiling.

"And freeing us. Now we are colonizing this southern island, and we even found a new fruit to cultivate!"

I dropped my hand to my side, resting it on the leather bag hanging from a thick strap on my shoulder. The Book of Mysteries lay nestled inside, wrapped in a cloth, safe and sound. I patted the heavy weight, a fleeting sense of amazement going through me at everything we'd been through to retrieve it.

"Well, Charlotte, I hope you'll accept. It would mean the world to us..."

"One last celebration before you push off on *Pride of the Sea,* on to your next adventure ..."

A small centaur filly trotted up to me then, holding out a flower wreath. "Princess Charlotte, I wove this just for you!"

I had no words, and I felt tears welling in my eyes again. *Oh, lordie ...*

The girl was waiting there, in front of me, holding out the flower wreath.

I bent over wordlessly, and she promptly placed it carefully on my head. I grinned.

"How does it look?" I tilted my head sideways, striking a pose.

"You look like a queen," smiled Tam.

The centaurs all chuckled and patted my arm, happier than I'd ever seen them.

I looked over at my troupe. At Caroline, Khepri, Christianne, Jim, Tupu, and Kym. They caught my eye and smiled at me, and I had a feeling they knew everything that had transpired during the challenge.

Caroline came and gave me a hug, whispering, "Thank you, Princess."

"Anytime," I answered.

"Charlotte!" I whipped my head around at the call. It was one of the sailors, waving at me and running toward us.

Tam ran to meet the man, then both came running.

"Charlotte, the mermaids have found something in the water, about two miles away. They brought it to just outside the lagoon, and we fished it out." The sailor looked alarmed.

I hurried with them to the edge of the atoll. Seagulls circled overhead, squawking.

"Oh, yuck." Christianne and the others had run with us, and we all stood over the figure in the blanket, dragged up on the rocks by the crew.

"What could do this?" I asked.

"No idea. These are fierce creatures, not easily bested in battle," Jim said.

I looked grimly down, worried.

What could do this? Would it threaten the ship and crew?

Iilcendorr trotted up to us, looked down, and recoiled.

The sight of a dead siren, her guts ripped out, would do that to anybody.

Dear reader-

I'm so glad you read The Pirate Queen and I hope you loved it. I do hope you'll consider leaving a review. It means so very much to hear what you think.

Here ends The Pirate Queen, the second book of The Paladin Princess series. The third book will be called The Lost Treasure.

ABOUT THE AUTHOR

Samaire Wynne grew up in a lot of different places, and now happily resides on the East Coast, laboring away at writing stories every day. She is an animal lover with far too many pets, yet she still muses how she'd like to add even more. A lover of all things night and gothic, she also loves to read and reread her favorite books. Owned by a cat named Tyrion, she can be found haunting the shadows and mists that hang low over the hills of southern Virginia.

www.ingramcontent.com/pod-product-compliance
Lightning Source LLC
Chambersburg PA
CBHW020634020726
47494CB00001B/194